RIVER
MUSIC

Mary Soderstrom

RIVER
MUSIC

PAPL
DISCARDED

A novel

Cormorant Books

Copyright © 2015 Mary Soderstrom
This edition copyright © 2015 Cormorant Books Inc.

No part of this publication may be reproduced, stored in a retrieval system or transmitted,
in any form or by any means, without the prior written consent of the publisher or a
licence from The Canadian Copyright Licensing Agency (Access Copyright). For an Access
Copyright licence, visit www.accesscopyright.ca or call toll free 1.800.893.5777.

  Canada Council for the Arts **Conseil des Arts du Canada**  ONTARIO ARTS COUNCIL
CONSEIL DES ARTS DE L'ONTARIO
an Ontario government agency
un organisme du gouvernement de l'Ontario

 Canadian Patrimoine
Heritage canadien **Canada**

The publisher gratefully acknowledges the support of the Canada Council for the Arts
and the Ontario Arts Council for its publishing program. We acknowledge the
financial support of the Government of Canada through the Canada Book Fund (CBF)
for our publishing activities, and the Government of Ontario through the
Ontario Media Development Corporation, an agency of the Ontario Ministry of Culture,
and the Ontario Book Publishing Tax Credit Program.

LIBRARY AND ARCHIVES CANADA CATALOGUING IN PUBLICATION

Soderstrom, Mary, 1942–, author
River music / Mary Soderstrom.

Issued in print and electronic formats.
ISBN 978-1-77086-415-3 (pbk.). — ISBN 978-1-77086-417-7 (html)

1. Title.

PS8587.O415R58 2015   C813'.54   C2014-905130-1
C2014-905131-X

Cover photo and design: angeljohnguerra.com
Interior text design: Tannice Goddard, Soul Oasis Networking
Printer: Friesens

Printed and bound in Canada.

The interior of this book is printed on 100% post-consumer waste recycled paper.

CORMORANT BOOKS INC.
10 ST. MARY STREET, SUITE 615, TORONTO, ONTARIO, M4Y 1P9
www.cormorantbooks.com

For Jeanne Nivon, Thomas Soderstrom,
Kirk and Oliva Grimble,
and the rest of the next generation

Without music, life would be an error.

—— FRIEDRICH NIETZSCHE

OVERTURE

THIS PART OF THE STORY Gloria told her granddaughter Julie several times, but even though she told Frances too, her daughter never listened.

The piano, when it came, arrived before Gloria's father, on the second Saturday morning in early April when the snow was just about gone, revealing the streets dirty with trash accumulated during the winter. When Gloria woke up, her mother was already in the kitchen, which was unusual for a weekend. On weekdays, her mother made Gloria oatmeal and saw that her face was washed and her school uniform was neat; on weekends her mother slept in.

"That's the big problem with my job," she told Mrs. Meade. "The schedule is so different from what a kid needs." This morning she was up and dressed. She had on a skirt and blouse, stockings, and low-heeled shoes, which also surprised Gloria because her mother rarely looked so plain. Gloria liked the way she looked when she went to work, in a neat little black dress with a colourful scarf topped with a scarlet jacket. "Working clothes," her mother said. Mrs. Meade would often make some remark about how she ought to be careful not to be too flamboyant or some people might think she was another kind of working girl.

Her mother didn't reply to comments like these, and Gloria was given to think there was something wrong about them. But she was particularly pleased to see her mother dressed so nicely this morning, as if she were a teacher or the secretary in the church office.

"Look out the window in front," her mother said after Gloria had eaten her porridge. "Tell me what you see."

The two windows in the front room, which doubled as a sitting room and bedroom for Gloria's mother, looked down from the second storey directly onto the street. Gloria ran out of the kitchen, down the hall past the doors to the bathroom and her room, and across her mother's room to the windows. She pushed aside the curtains and looked down.

Their building was flush with the sidewalk, only a stoop and a low, brick wall separating it from passersby — not that there were many. The houses along this street had been built when the first factories and warehouses had gone in along the railroad line thirty years before; few people besides those who lived here had reason to use the street. On Saturday the foot traffic headed toward the shops on St. Lawrence or St. Denis, depending on whether the shoppers were English or French or immigrants. Gloria's mother and Mrs. Meade always headed west, to St. Lawrence. Through the window, Gloria saw a truck, which was a rare occurrence on the street. It was painted white with big black letters: *George Smith and Sons, Carters.* Two men, both of them dressed in checked, woollen shirts, with black caps on their heads, stood, appearing to wait for a taxi, which pulled up. A tall, thin man in a grey overcoat, wearing a fedora, emerged. The brim of the hat obscured his face, but the way he walked over to the men and began gesturing seemed familiar.

The men listened, their hands on their hips. One of them said something and then all three laughed. The man in the fedora stepped out of the way and the other two opened the back doors of the truck.

Gloria's mother had walked up behind her, and was now holding back the curtain farther. "What do you think they're doing?" she asked.

Gloria looked up at her. The smell of lavender was very strong. She was puzzled at the excitement in her mother's voice. "I don't know," she said. "Somebody's moving?"

Her mother didn't reply. "Look, there, they've got something very big," she said.

And there it was: an upright piano. The man in the fedora looked up to the window. He saw Gloria and her mother and waved. By then her mother was struggling with the window frame, stuck with the winter grime. Eventually, she threw it open and pushed open the outside double pane. "Arthur," she called. "Shall I open the door?"

Arthur Foster was Gloria's uncle, her father's brother, who lived in the West End in a big house he and her grandparents had all to themselves.

Arthur tipped his hat. "By all means," he answered. "Is the little princess there too?"

Gloria pushed herself in front of her mother and waved out the window. "Is that for me?"

"Yes," her mother said at the same time Uncle Arthur nodded agreement.

"For me?" she repeated. "For me!" She tried to hoist herself up on the windowsill so she could see better what the men were doing, but her mother pushed her aside.

"Walk downstairs and open the front door," she said. "Put your coat on first. You can watch while I finish clearing a space for it."

Mrs. Meade opened her door as Gloria ran down the stairs. "It's arrived, has it?" Uncle Arthur picked her up and twirled her around, even though she was too old for this childish play. "So, what do you think?" he asked. "Your Daddy sent it."

Gloria shut her eyes and buried her face in his shoulder, which smelled of tobacco and wool and something that reminded her of the stuff her father used to splash on his face after he shaved. "I am too, too happy," she said.

But of course, it wasn't as easy as that. The men were not experienced piano movers. They had trouble manoeuvring the instrument through the narrow front door. Gloria danced around on the sidewalk while they struggled. She hung on her Uncle Arthur's hand as he gave advice. She waved to her mother, who was still upstairs in the open window.

The men put the piano down on the sidewalk, and turned their backs to Arthur. They busied themselves with screwdrivers and other tools until they'd taken the back off. From where she stood, Gloria could see a great, gold-coloured something set in the wood frame. The men set the wood panel on a piece of canvas they spread on the sidewalk. She started to move closer to get a better look, but her uncle pulled her back.

"Stay out of their way," he said. "They don't know what they're doing as it is." She thought he might be going to say something more, but he shouted instead. "Watch the hell what you're doing."

The men had the piano wrapped up in slings. The first one made it through the front door and started up the stairs. But there was a loud thump when the man behind dropped his end.

"Whoa," he yelled. "What's going on?"

Her uncle dragged Gloria down the street, away from the

doorway so she couldn't see. "Stay there," he said. "I don't know what might happen."

Her mother was leaning out the window again, waving at her. "Get away," she was saying, her voice shrill with anxiety. Mrs. Meade was at her window too. So were many people in other buildings on the street. What was happening had begun to become clear to Gloria. This piano was for her, a gift from her father; it was the answer to her birthday wishes, the Sunday school prayers she had made for the last two years. But these men were not going to get it up the stairs and into the house.

THE PIANO NEVER worked properly. It wouldn't stay in tune; there was something wrong with its frame and soundboard that no amount of tuning could fix. Gloria knew that from the beginning, but who was paying attention to her at that point? They'd all done something wonderful for her — her mother, her father, and Uncle Arthur. If they disputed just who deserved the most credit — Arthur, who had arranged everything, her father, who had sent the money, her mother, who found a way to pay for lessons — Gloria paid no attention. She forgot herself when she practised. She loved her piano.

Gloria's friend's aunt gave her lessons once a week, on Saturday mornings. She got up on her own and made breakfast so her mother could sleep in. She picked up the two quarters her mother left for her and carefully put them in the pocket of her skirt and went out into the early morning. She skipped when she got to the street, running sometimes when the weather was particularly nice. She rang the buzzer for the janitor in her teacher's apartment building — she couldn't reach the button for the teacher herself — and waited outside until he waddled to the front door to let her in. Then she'd climb the two flights to the teacher's floor and wait in the hall, sitting on the bench outside her door. The sound of the boy before her floated through the door, and she marked out the rhythm with her right hand on her lap. He played long pieces, although frequently he had to start over two or three times before he managed to play it to the teacher's satisfaction. When the piano became silent, Gloria would stand, waiting excitedly for the sound of footsteps inside the door and muffled words as the boy said his goodbye.

When the door opened, he would rush by her, as if to escape into the rest of his Saturday, where things more exciting awaited him. Gloria could not imagine, however, anything that she'd rather do than take a lesson.

Her teacher had started her off by showing her where middle C was, where the other Cs were, talking about how the notes had names, and how going to the right on the piano meant going higher, while going left meant going lower. Gloria was tempted to say, *Isn't that obvious?*, but she didn't. She listened and moved her fingers as the teacher demonstrated. She was enchanted by the clear sound of a good piano. She very carefully carried the little exercise book the teacher had given her, along with a note for her mother.

"Very good," the teacher said. "I can see you're an eager little girl who may do very well. I think you'll need another book very quickly. Ask your mother to send the money for it when you come next week."

Her mother was up when she returned home; the apartment smelled of coffee and cigarettes. She rushed over to her mother and flung her arms around her, breathing in the smell of tobacco and lavender hand cream that clung to her. "It was wonderful," she said. "Truly wonderful."

The money for the extra books must have come from her

Uncle Arthur and her grandmother, because there were telephone calls back and forth during the week, and a pained look on her mother's face when Gloria mentioned the new songs her teacher said she'd learn soon. But, on the next Saturday, there were two dollar bills waiting for her in the kitchen at breakfast. "This is something you really, really want?" her mother asked.

"More than anything else," Gloria said, drinking her milk as fast as she could.

"Mrs. Meade told me when I came home that she heard you practising after you were supposed to be in bed."

"Only last night," Gloria said. "Oh, Momma, I just had to get it right. I went to bed at the right time, honest, but then I remembered that there was something funny in the scale, so I wanted to make sure I could do it and so I got up and practised and then I wanted to play the next song in the book and it was so lovely that I played it again ..."

Her mother laughed. "And you didn't get cold sitting there in your nightdress?"

"No," she said. "Not at first. I was moving. You stay warm that way. Besides, it was music."

It was music, and having pieces and scales and exercises to do every night was very good. When she was alone, after her mother had left for work, she would sit down at the piano and play the compositions she was supposed to play for the week. Afterwards she would sometimes make up her own tunes, or try to play along with the radio.

Week by week, she earned gold stars. She went through workbooks quickly. She carried notes back and forth between her teacher and her mother. "You are very talented and hardworking," her mother read one out to her. "You should be encouraged." Her mother looked up to no one in particular.

"Christ, isn't that what I'm doing?" She looked at Gloria. "It's not easy, you can be sure." Then she gave Gloria a hug. "You tell your teacher that I know just how special you are." She didn't have the money for the next workbook: the note she gave Gloria to take with the money for the lesson said so. By then Gloria had realized that she ought to know what was being said about her, so she taught herself to decipher grown-up handwriting.

GLORIA'S FATHER CAME back to Montreal two autumns after that, but it was only to say goodbye again. By then Gloria was almost eleven. She practised playing a Chopin étude as well as a ragtime piece her mother said he'd like. She had written to him, care of the mine where he was working. She asked him what his favourite song was, but he didn't write back. He wasn't much for writing, they all knew that, Gloria's grandmother included — until the week before he was scheduled to arrive. "The Skye Boat Song" or "Twinkle, Twinkle, Little Star," he wrote, and Gloria was offended that he picked such easy things. But she had Mrs. Meade sing the first for her until she got it in her head, and learned to play it out straight. Her teacher helped her figure out some ornamentation. "Twinkle, Twinkle" was something she'd learned right at the beginning of her lessons. She practised both songs; she wanted to be sure she played the best concert for her father.

In her head this was the way she expected things to happen: her father would arrive in Uncle Arthur's car. He would be taller than his brother. She thought she remembered him as being a big, big man. He'd wear a dark grey suit. He'd have a suitcase with him, shiny leather with brass fastenings like the one in the window in the luggage shop on St. Lawrence. He would step out of the car and look up at their window. He'd see her and her mother leaning out, and his smile would be as wide as the sky. Somehow they'd all be upstairs sitting around the kitchen table eating roast chicken with potatoes and carrots, and there would be chocolate cake for dessert. But before they started dessert, her father would insist she play for him. So they would go to the front room and she would play. Her father would applaud and he would pick her up even though she was such a big girl now. They would all be very happy.

Her father's return did not happen that way. She was beginning to realize that things rarely happened the way she dreamed they would, but she would never, as she was happy to say to her children thirty years later, stop dreaming so vividly. Her dreams were her reality.

Her father arrived late at night, when her mother was at work and she was asleep. Mrs. Meade opened the door for him. Because Gloria was not allowed to open the door when she was alone, her mother must have told him to get Mrs. Meade to let him in. Mrs. Meade showed him into the front room, but didn't come to tell Gloria what was happening. After lying in bed listening to him walk around the apartment for several minutes, she got up and tiptoed to the door to peek out and see what he was doing.

He was in the kitchen with his back to her. His light brown hair stood out from his head almost like a halo and his shoulders were broad in the checked shirt he was wearing. He appeared to be fussing with the stove, getting ready to boil water for tea. He leaned toward the gas flame, then stood up and turned around, a cigarette in his mouth. His face was so much older than the picture she had on her dresser. Narrow and tanned, with white lines where the sun didn't reach when he scrunched up his eyes.

Before he saw her, they both heard her mother's key in the lock, the door open, her little shout when she saw his suitcase by the door and realized he was home. Gloria hesitated just a moment, not sure whether she should run to her mother or to her father. Just a moment, but it was too long. Her father, strode down the hall and took her mother in his arms. He said something Gloria didn't understand. Her mother replied. Then they walked quickly into the front room, the room where the piano was and where her mother slept.

For a moment longer, Gloria stood, listening and wondering what would happen if she joined them, if she sat down at the piano and played for him. But there were noises coming from the front room that she didn't have a name for, but which she recognized as grown-up sounds. The creak of the bed being pulled out, the thunk of boots on the floor, whispers. Frances would say hearing that explained a lot about her mother, but Frances did not know. There was more, but Gloria shut her door and crept back to her own bed where she sang "The Skye Boat Song" over and over until she fell asleep.

In the morning her mother woke her up. They'd overslept, and it was a regular school day, she had to dress, eat breakfast, and rush.

"But Daddy?" she asked

"Daddy?" her mother said. "You know he was here?" She didn't wait for Gloria to answer. "He'll be here when you get back. He's tired now."

"But I need to practise this morning." She always practised for fifteen minutes before school and half an hour after her mother left for work in the evening.

"Not this morning. Practising can wait. Now hurry up."

She didn't hurry to school, but was one of the first out at lunchtime. She ran most of the way home, ready to rush up the stairs and ask a thousand questions; but before she'd got half way to the top, Mrs. Meade met her. "Come eat at my place," she said. "They've gone off to do some things."

"What things?" Gloria asked when she had sat down at Mrs. Meade's kitchen table in front of a cold, fried-egg sandwich. The bread was soggy with grease from the egg. The apple set out for her had a big brown spot. Only the milk looked all right, but she took a sip from it carefully nevertheless. It tasted funny, but she knew that if she gagged there would be trouble.

"Things," Mrs. Meade said. "Your father has been away a long time."

Gloria did not disagree, and because she was sure she'd get no better answer from Mrs. Meade, she quickly ate the greasy sandwich. "I've got to go back to school right away," she lied. "I have to help someone."

Mrs. Meade nodded. "Don't forget to drink your milk," she said, standing up. "I have to get away too."

Gloria held her breath and swallowed, gulping down what was left in the glass.

She was pulling on her coat and heading out the door before Mrs. Meade realized she hadn't eaten the apple. Gloria heard the old woman calling after her as she slammed the door at the bottom of the stairs. She didn't stop until she crossed the street and could look up at the windows of her apartment. The blinds were drawn, but the window was open. Her mother never left it that way when she went out.

Her father met her just outside the schoolyard when school was over. She saw him before he saw her, and she felt the greasy sandwich from lunch jolt in her stomach. Quick, she told herself, go to the bathroom before he sees you. You don't want to be sick in front of him. They weren't supposed to go back into the building once they'd left, but she slipped in when some younger girls came out, and ran to the girls' room where she thought she might throw up. She didn't. She splashed some water on her face when she was sure she would be all right and looked at herself in the mirror.

The grade six teacher stuck her head in the door, making the rounds to see that the building was empty. "What are you doing here? Don't you know you're supposed to be outside?"

Of course she did. She didn't know what to say. She allowed herself to be ushered out to the girls' playground where a few grade fours were jumping rope. The parents who had been waiting for the little kids had all left, and she hoped her father had too. But there he was, in his heavy jacket and his boots, wearing a white shirt and a tie that showed because he hadn't fastened the jacket up in the warmish afternoon.

"Princess," he called when he saw her. He hurried over to meet her at the edge of the playground. "I'd almost given up on you," he said, leaning over to look directly in her eyes.

"How's my sweetheart?" he asked, putting his hands on her shoulders and pulling her to him. "You can't imagine how glad I am to see you."

She wanted to ask him if that was the case why he hadn't come in to see her the night before? Why he wasn't there at lunch? Then she thought to ask him if he'd made his fortune. Mrs. Meade had said that's what he'd gone off to do. But she couldn't speak: the words were all there, but they tumbled around, fighting with each other. She couldn't decide which way to begin.

"I can play 'The Skye Boat Song,'" she said. "Let me play it for you when we get home."

"Of course," he said. He turned around, because the barber was coming out of his shop, and shouted, "Gerry, is that you?"

There were handshakes and laughter. Another man came

out of the barbershop, a man crossed the street to join in the conversation.

"Signing up," her father was saying. "Came back to say goodbye before I go off."

The barber nodded. "Lotta young folks doing that. Money's not too bad."

"Twenty-five bucks a month and a widow's benefit," the man from across the street said. "Lotta women are keen on that."

There was laughter, and Gloria was afraid she was losing him. "Daddy, you said I could play for you."

"Of course, Princess," he said. "Gentlemen, you'll have to excuse me. The little lady is going to give me a recital." He took Gloria's hand. "We'll talk again later."

But of course, they didn't. She played for him as soon as they got home and he smiled and gave her a hug and told her he was proud of her. Her mother listened from the doorway. She was making something good for dinner, she said; she was taking this night off, and to hell with what her boss thought. They both were drinking rum and Coke, and let Gloria take a sip from each glass. As soon as dinner was over they hustled her off to bed. The next day was another school day, but she didn't see why she couldn't stay up later than usual.

GLORIA WOKE UP when her father came in to say goodbye very early in the morning, before the sun had come up. He didn't turn the light on in her room; she saw his silhouette over her bed in the light from the hall. "Princess," he said. "Are you awake? I have to go."

She sat up so quickly that she dumped the doll she slept with to the floor. "Go? Where?"

He didn't answer immediately, just stood there, looking down at her. Gloria could hear her mother moving around in the front room. "You know there's a war?" he asked.

She nodded. There had been a lot of talk about the Germans since the end of the summer. It was a little disappointing that he might think she didn't know, but she wasn't going to say so.

He leaned over, his face near hers. She smelled the sourness of tobacco and rum on his breath. "I think I should go and fight the bad guys." He pushed her hair back from her forehead, then kissed her just below her hairline. "Momma will tell you more about it."

"She knows?" That's not quite what she meant, what she really wanted to know was how he could leave, how her mother could let him leave, when he'd only been back a couple of days.

"Of course," he said. He paused as if he were going to say something else, but didn't. He straightened up. He patted her on the head.

"You'll write?" she asked. The question was much larger; it had to do with whether he would remember her, would come back.

"Of course," he said again. "Now go back to sleep, it's still very early." He turned to go out the door, but she was jumping out of bed, her bare feet on the cold linoleum. She reached out for his arm.

"Can I play something for you before you go?" she asked. "'The Skye Boat Song,' maybe?"

"It's so early, you'll wake everybody up," he said. He pulled his arm away from her hand.

"Just one song," she said. "Quietly."

"No," he said. He was at the door now, and she saw that he'd left his suitcase in the hall just outside. "I've got to go."

She knew it was a lost cause then, and started to cry. He didn't turn back. It was only later, when her sobs had quieted, that she heard her mother crying too.

THE LESSONS CONTINUED. "He'll pay for them, that's the least he can do," her mother said to Mrs. Meade. "I take that right off the top of the cheque. Even when I know my hours aren't going to be good."

Mrs. Meade nodded and looked carefully at the tablecloth she was crocheting from string she'd been collecting. "He's doing his duty," she said. She had begun knitting socks for soldiers but she said crocheting calmed her down the way knitting for the war effort didn't. She brought her crocheting when she had a glass with Gloria's mother. "You can be proud of him."

Gloria's mother didn't reply to that. She held up her glass in a little salute, and then drank it down. She shivered. "Terrible stuff. I'll have to see what I can get from the boss."

Gloria noticed that Mrs. Meade looked over her spectacles at Gloria's mother. "Be careful," she said.

Gloria, who had been playing scales, switched to "Onward Christian Soldiers."

"Listen," she said. "Do you hear the chords my teacher showed me?" She pounded away until her mother said she had a headache and had had enough.

The lessons continued and, after a while, her mother stopped worrying out loud about where the money was going to come from to pay for them.

I

THE REST OF THE STORY Gloria did not talk about, certainly not to her granddaughter, Julie. Frances had no idea, either. If she had, she might have understood her mother better since she had to fight for her dreams too.

The supper club where Gloria's mother worked was in one of the best hotels in Montreal. She had been lucky to get the job as hostess. Gloria's father had been out West for three months and, despite his promises, no money had arrived. She tried first for office jobs, but she had no training, and there was the problem of what to do about Gloria before and after school. When she saw the ad in *The Gazette* for a waitress in the hotel's coffee shop, she swallowed her pride and applied. The coffee shop manager took one look at her pale face, thin arms, and the dress she wore and told her he didn't think she would be strong enough for the job. She controlled herself until she left the restaurant; but, as soon as she was on the street, she burst into tears. She'd steeled herself to accept something she would not have considered had she not been desperate, but she was turned down!

She couldn't help herself. She stood outside the coffee shop where people were coming and going, where she might easily be seen by someone she knew, and cried. Two women stopped to ask her if she was all right, and she nodded and turned her face away from their sympathy. But then she heard a familiar voice ask how she was, and she looked up to see her husband's brother. They hadn't spoken since the brothers had quarrelled, and in other circumstances she would never have done more than nod politely to him. Certainly, she would never have told him what great problems faced her had she not been at her wit's end. Arthur knew the hotel manager, he was a regular in the dining room, and he had represented the hotel in several legal matters. He knew that a supper club was opening in a week. The young man they'd pegged for the maître d' job had turned out to be a drunk.

"So what I'll do is hand people their menus and show them to their tables," she told Mrs. Meade when she came home. "The hours will be better than a day job. It's a classy place. I'm supposed to look refined." She laughed. "Arthur said I should wear this dress, but I'll have to see what else I've got."

Gloria sat on her bed while her mother took her nice dresses out of the closet, dresses that dated from the time before their troubles began. Gloria liked the white dress with the floaty skirt and the blue flowers down the front, but her mother said that was far too *jeune fille* for the job.

With her first paycheque she bought a navy blue crepe dress with a plunging back, which Mrs. Meade sniffed at. "This is a respectable place, isn't it? You're somebody's wife," she said.

"Of course. And I'm a mother and a decent woman pushed into a corner who is doing the best she can," Gloria's mother said, putting her arm around Gloria and pulling her close.

"And don't you forget it," she added, so softly that only Gloria heard.

The white dress with the blue flowers hung in the closet for several years, getting pushed to the back as Gloria's mother acquired more snazzy things for work. But when it came time for Gloria's first recital — a real recital in the Tudor Hall in Ogilvy's, one organized by her teacher and a colleague for their best students — the dress was hauled out and looked at carefully. Skirts were shorter by then, but Gloria was now taller than her mother, so with a little adjustment at the waist, they both decided it would do. The skirt flared out when Gloria twirled. It was not a thing a pianist did often, but Gloria liked the way it looked and felt. She knew she would play very well when she wore it. She only wished her father could see her in it.

It was 1942 by then and he had been in England with the RCAF for a long time. Her mother made Gloria write, and she made certain he was still a presence in both their lives. Her temper unravelled more often now, and sometimes Gloria heard her arguing with Mrs. Meade on the landing late at night. There was no need for Mrs. Meade to look in on Gloria anymore, she was indeed a big girl. Nevertheless, the neighbour kept track of when Gloria's mother came home.

It was often late. Gloria didn't care.

What did Gloria care about? About the dismal state of the piano that refused to stay in tune. There was something wrong with the action going back to the time it was dropped. Her Uncle Arthur had bought it from a friend, and what did he know about pianos? Who was the friend who sold it to him? Gloria didn't ask, but she noted that her uncle didn't come to her recitals, even though his mother, her grandmother, made it to the first one at Tudor Hall the year before she died.

And her father? Her father she rarely mentioned. He was fighting the war, there was nothing to be ashamed of there. What else did she care about? Her music, of course, and her teachers. By the time she was fifteen she'd worked with three. The last — and, she knew, the best — was Lotte Gruber, whose arthritic hands could no longer bring music from the piano, but who sometimes was able to explain what Gloria needed to do to get the sound they both heard in their heads. Lotte talked about further study. McGill University had a conservatory and the province of Quebec was setting up one, but in Lotte's opinion a serious student of music could not expect to get a first-class musical education in Montreal, or to launch a career from there. New York was the place to go. For a musician with ambition, it was the place to study and perform.

"Look where the greatest musicians in the world are now: in New York or Los Angeles, or starving in some bombed-out city. I hate to say it but it's true," Lotte said. She mentioned Juilliard; she said there might be friends who could help Gloria, but Gloria's mother said for Gloria not to get her hopes up. She always added, though, that she was on the lookout for help also.

And when help came, it came through her. The hotel wanted someone to play the grand piano in the hotel lobby beginning the first week in December. It would be a touch of class in the difficult holiday season of 1943, an inducement for people to linger, particularly if the pianist were a lovely young woman. And who was lovelier, Gloria's mother told the hotel manager, than her daughter?

The question was, once again, what should she wear? Money was still short and there was the problem of rationing, so they went back to her mother's closet.

"Black," her mother said. "Black is best because that's what musicians always wear." She now had a half-dozen black dresses, two of which she hadn't worn in a couple of years because she didn't like the way they fell across her bust since she'd begun to put on a little weight. "With your lovely skin, black will look terrific. We'll let your hair curl around your face." She held the dress up. "Take off what you have on and we'll see how it looks."

Gloria obeyed. It had a neckline that dipped in front, and long sleeves, but it fit smoothly through the waist. The skirt, cut on the bias, fell in graceful scallops to just above her ankles. She pulled the neckline down, so more of her front showed, then raised her arms. "It's too tight through the shoulders," she said. "I'll never be able to play in it. I can't move my arms."

Her mother stepped back to look at her. "We'll take the sleeves off. And we'll tweak the neck a bit so it fits better. You've got a nice bust now." Gloria blushed.

Mrs. Meade altered the dress and the hairdresser in the hotel did her hair. It bounced around her shoulders, with the frizz tamed into curls. Gloria liked the way it felt, falling forward when she leaned into the piano. A little lipstick, some powder across her nose, a sprig of holly on her shoulder to look festive, and she was ready.

The first night was a Wednesday — the idea was that if things worked out she would play four nights a week from early evening until ten p.m. The fall term was nearly over, and even if she missed a couple of days of school because she was tired, it wouldn't make much difference. The exposure and the experience would be good for her. She would be paid far more than she got from playing for choir practices, which was her principal source of income.

The piano stood in the middle of the central hall of the hotel, which rose six stories to a big skylight that in daytime allowed the sun to pour into the lobby. Balconies ringed the hall, each screened with gilt fret work so that sometimes it looked as if the interior of the hotel glowed. But the sun had set two hours before Gloria sat down at the piano. A knot of people stood next to the registration desk, two men read newspapers in big chairs at opposite sides of the fireplace, where the cold floor was covered with inch-thick oriental carpets. No one waited on the three settees or the half-dozen other armchairs on the other side of the grand hall. Outside it was snowing.

Gloria interlaced her fingers and ran through a suite of quick exercises to warm up. Or maybe not entirely to warm up, but to put off for a moment the point when she knew she would cross a line. What lay on the other side she wasn't sure, but she knew she wanted to go there. Her heart pounded and she felt her hands grow damp with sweat.

For a second she thought of opening the folder and bringing out the music, but Lotte had said any pianist who was any good should play solo from memory. The music was just there like a good luck charm, nothing more. She took a breath and began Debussy's "Arabesque No. 1." The first few notes were hesitant, her fingers felt stiff, but then the music grabbed her and she floated free. She was swept along, the notes buoying her up, leading her somewhere she wanted to go, where she knew she was created to live.

It was a piece that Lotte sniffed at: even though she had left Germany just ahead of the Nazis, her admiration for German composers, especially for Bach, Beethoven, and Brahms, was enormous. No other musical tradition was so rich, she said. Nevertheless, it was she who chose the Debussy for this place and this hour. "Give them something like that and maybe they'll listen," she said. The other works she suggested were Liszt's Consolation No. 3 and the "Warsaw Piano Concerto." "Sometimes you play to the crowd," she said. The last piece had been featured in a movie about an injured pilot and made it to the top of the pop charts as "The World Outside Will Never Know."

"People can hum it," Lotte said. "The film's a patriotic love story and that doesn't hurt in these times."

When Gloria surfaced after she brought the arabesque to its close, she looked up to see two men in uniform watching her. Young men, smiling men. She blinked and then smiled back as they applauded. The sound of clapping came from the far side of the lobby, too, where the elderly gentlemen were sitting. She saw her mother looking around the door that led to the staff rooms, her face radiant. Then the door closed and Gloria realized that she was on her own, that the music had launched her toward some shore she could only dimly see.

That night she played her pieces three times each, taking a break between to walk carefully on her high-heeled shoes to the staff room, holding her music folder in front of her like a shield. The listeners changed as the evening progressed. She did not think anyone stayed longer than five or ten minutes, the time to meet their friends or to rest before dinner. But when she finished her last set at ten p.m., she saw that one of the first listeners, the younger of the men in uniform, had come back.

"Miss," he said, "I just wanted to tell you how lovely you and your music are." He put his hand out and rested it lightly on her arm. "If you were free, I would like you to join me ..."

The bell captain, whom her mother knew well, stepped forward. The young man looked over at him, and although he made no other move, the young man obviously reconsidered. "That is ..." he began.

She didn't know what to say, she had to go home, that was one of the things she and her mother had agreed. She wouldn't even wait until her mother finished: she was to take the street-car on Sherbrooke Street at 10:15 which connected with the streetcar up St. Lawrence that would get her home by 10:35. She looked at the young man and then turned abruptly from him. "I can't," she thought she said, but the memory of the words was lost in the flush of embarrassment she felt flood her face.

He watched her, she was pretty sure, and when she had collected her coat, scarf, and boots, she peeked out of the staff door to make sure he was no longer there. The bell captain smiled at her. "Next time, go out the service entrance," he said. "You won't be bothered that way."

The service entrance: her mother had said she never used it; she always made a point of going out through the lobby, as if she were a guest, not just someone who worked at the hotel. That was one of the things that her position required, she said: she was not an ordinary restaurant employee, she was a hostess; the hotel was an extension of her hospitality, it represented the largesse and graciousness that she would have had as her due in another life. The same applied to Gloria.

So Gloria simply nodded at the bell captain and lowered her eyes. She scurried across the lobby, nearly empty at this hour with the grand piano rolled over to the side. The doorman nodded to her and touched his hat as he opened the door for her, and she stepped out into the night where the snow continued to swirl.

The thought of the young man and his smile stayed with her the next day, even as she struggled to pay attention in class.

The next night he wasn't there when she began. The snow had stopped, but even though the sidewalk in front of the hotel was cleared, each time the main doors opened, the people entering stamped their feet to clear their boots of snow. Cold air swept in with them; outside the night was frigid, with the stars cold fire in the clear night sky. Gloria found herself looking up when the draft reached her: maybe a dress with long sleeves might be better for the dead of winter, no matter that it was easier to play with her arms free like this. She shivered and turned her thoughts back to the music. There was a tricky bit coming up a few bars ahead, and she couldn't let her attention wander, not if she wanted to play the way she knew she could.

Halfway through the first set, when she felt she could allow herself to relax for a moment, she looked up to see that the young man in uniform was standing off to her right. He wasn't so close as to be distracting, but it was clear that he was watching her attentively. He was alone this time, and he stood with his hands clasped behind his back, his feet apart, at parade rest.

She felt her face grow red. Her concentration flickered. She stumbled over the next phrase. She recovered quickly, but it was all she could do to keep the notes floating freely. She felt his eyes on her and despite the chill swirling in from outside, she felt herself growing warm and the sweat began to bead on her forehead. She played on; whatever grace she'd felt earlier vanished as she tried not to look over at him. But then when she finished, she felt compelled to look. Above him, at the centre of the great lobby, the enormous chandelier glowed so brightly that she couldn't see the expression on his face. The hundreds of small lights looked like a halo. In two steps he was by her side, unfolding a large, immaculate white handkerchief. "Might this be of help?" he asked.

"Thank you," she said, and took it because she did not know how to decline gracefully. She dabbed at her face, and then stood up even though she was supposed to play another ten minutes. She held out the handkerchief to him and tried to look composed.

"Keep it," he said. "You play very well," he added.

"Thank you," she said again. She rubbed the handkerchief on her hands. Then she wondered what she should do with it. If she had a pocket or sleeves she could just tuck it in, but that was impossible. She found herself standing there, twisting it between her fingers, wondering what she should do next. When he made no move to leave, she said, "I'm supposed to play for a while longer."

He nodded and smiled. "Then I'll just sit here and listen." Gloria glanced around to see if the bell captain was watching. "That would be nice," she said, and began to sit down, tucking the handkerchief under her skirt. When she looked up, she saw he had pulled one of the big chairs over so he could watch her more closely. She cast a half-alarmed look at him from the corner of her eye, but he seemed not to notice.

"What's next?" he asked.

She had been planning to play the "Warsaw Concerto," but its connection with the handsome, wounded pilot in the film made her hesitate. Since Lotte had given her the piece to play, she had seen the movie three times. Such a love story! Such a handsome man! But somehow it seemed like asking for bad luck to play the concerto for this man. Better to do something else. "Chopin," she said. "An étude."

She was pleasantly surprised when he asked, "Which one?"

"The 'Winter Wind,'" she said.

He laughed. "Ah yes. Opus 25, number 11. Very appropriate," he said. She was even more impressed.

"Do you play yourself?" she asked.

He paused, as if considering. "Once, in another life, I tried," he said, settling back to listen.

She could feel his eyes on her as she played the short theme through twice, slowly, almost mournfully. Then the storm hit full blast, and notes rushed from her fingers over and over, up and up, the tension mounting until the final resolution. It was a showboat piece, one that it was a pleasure to play, and — he was right — perfect for a December evening.

When she finished, she looked at him and smiled. He was standing up, applauding again, as were another half-dozen men in uniform. "Marvellous," he said, coming over to take her hand and make a show of kissing it.

"Thank you," he said again. "I look forward to hearing more."

Yet when she came back from her break, he wasn't there, and she had to tell herself that she was silly to expect that he would be. That was the kind of thing she supposed she should expect. Her mother had talked to her about how she should be cool and professional. Lotte had also dropped hints about the need to be polite but nothing more when men became enthralled by her music. She picked up her music folder at the end of her last set, smiled at the old couple who applauded. The bell captain smiled at her when she passed him on her way to get her things so she could go home. "You sounded lovely," he said. "Good night."

There was no question that she leave through the service entrance. Her mother was right: she was not an ordinary employee, she should go in and out the front door like someone whose grandmother lived in a nice house, whose uncle was a lawyer, whose father was fighting for the King.

And there the young officer was, by the door, holding his

great coat over his arm, waiting for her with an invitation for supper or a drink.

She knew her smile for him was too inviting, and she stumbled saying "no," that she had to go home.

"Then I'll see you there," he said. He put an arm around her and called to the doorman. "Taxi, please."

"So," he said once they were settled in the cab, "you turn into a pumpkin if you don't get home on time? You have a strict father? A jealous boyfriend?" He was sitting quite close to her. She could smell some kind of stringent soap, tobacco, and a faint scent of alcohol. His voice was light, as if he were joking, but she thought he really wanted to know more about her.

"No," she said.

He shifted closer to her and put his arm along the back of the seat. "Very good," he said. "Very good indeed. But why must you go home so early?"

She took a deep breath. She had to say it, he would find out anyway if he asked the bell captain. "I have to go to school tomorrow," she said.

"School?" he asked. "McGill?"

"No," she said. "Commercial High. I'm fifteen."

He took his arm away. He sat silent for a minute. "In that case, tell the driver the quickest way to get you home."

GLORIA PLAYED ALL through the Christmas and New Year's holidays. School was out the Thursday before Christmas, but by then she'd just about given up on it anyway. There had been exams, and she'd slept through two of them. When her mother found out she would not be pleased, but for the moment Gloria decided she would pretend that everything was all right. Certainly she wasn't going to give up playing; she had a feeling that she was making progress here, that the steady performances would result eventually in a door opening onto the next stage of her life.

She had no lessons during the month of December. Lotte was ill; her arthritis had settled in her back, she said, and there were mornings when she couldn't get out of bed. That was just as well. Gloria continued to practise, but she was tired; there was too much going on. She found herself restless as she had never been before. Her mother was busy also; the holiday season always meant more work for her. There were more tips too, and sometimes private parties that she was invited to, which meant that she didn't come back at all. Mrs. Meade, who would otherwise have commented on her absences, didn't. She wanted them to come for Christmas dinner — she said she'd been able to find a big hen and she was going to cook it the way her mother did and she would be all alone if it weren't for them, and she wanted to give back a little of what they'd given her, and it would mean so much if they were together, and now that Gloria was working nights she never saw either of them.

She said that on the landing, as Gloria's mother was heading off to work. Gloria was still in the front room practising — even though the lessons were languishing she worked at two new pieces that Lotte had given her because she was getting tired of playing the same things over and over at night — so she heard quite clearly what was said. Her mother didn't reply immediately. Gloria could imagine what she was doing, standing there, checking to make sure she had her gloves and cigarettes, her makeup, and her carfare in her little black leather bag. Gloria could see her mother click the purse shut, hang it jauntily from her shoulder, and pause just a moment to look at Mrs. Meade's red face.

"My in-laws, Arthur and his wife, have asked us for dinner," she said. "We should go for Gloria's sake, I think."

"You never go there. You don't like them, after they treated you the way that they have, all these years. If he dies, they'll cut you out and try to capture the girl ..."

"Gloria is not to capture. Besides, Arthur has gone through all the money since the old lady died. He's as much a spend-thrift as his brother, just more clever at staying respectable," her mother said. "I know what I'm doing." She paused before taking a step down the stairs. "But we could come by for brunch before. Why don't we do that? I'll bring some eggnog."

There was the sound of Mrs. Meade blowing her nose. "Oh, yes, that would be fine. That would be really wonderful."

"We will go by Lotte's too," her mother said to Gloria when they spoke about Christmas the next morning. "And then we'll spend two hours at your uncle's. And then we can do what we want."

Do what they want. Gloria did not know quite what she wanted yet, but she could feel it coming on.

In retrospect, Gloria realized that she should not have been surprised to meet her admirer at her uncle's house. It was wartime: people were encouraged to be hospitable to service-men, and of course her piano-playing officer qualified as an object of patriotic charity. He was, it turned out, the son of someone who had been in Arthur's class at Osgoode Hall, a man who was called to the Ontario Bar the same year that Arthur was. They'd not had much contact since Arthur came back to qualify in civil law so he could practise in Quebec, but James's father had contacted his old crony when James was affected to the command in Montreal.

"This girl has great talent," James told Gloria's uncle. "She could have a grand career in front of her, if all goes well."

"Oh," Arthur said, handing round whisky to the men and sherry to the ladies before dinner. "We intend to help her all the ways we can."

Gloria's mother overheard that. She smiled. "She does play nicely, doesn't she?" She took a sip and looked over the edge of her glass. "She is hardly more than a girl, but she is turning into a lovely young woman."

James said later that he was a bit surprised at her mother's tone, but by then Gloria knew what was going on, and had decided to have none of it.

That was the winter her father was invalided home. He'd fought in the invasion of Sicily, but no one heard his war stories, because he wouldn't or couldn't say what had happened to him. Gloria went to visit him at the veterans' hospital; she told him about what she was doing, and once she played the piano for him and his ward mates at the request of a nurse. But he remained less of a presence in her life than he had been before the war, when she could count on the fingers of her hand the times she had seen him, but at least she had had her dreams about what he might be, might do.

There was no question of him moving back with them. Not until he was much better, until he got used to the artificial leg, until he didn't cry and hide whenever an airplane flew over the city. There were telephone calls between Gloria's mother and Arthur. "We must wait and see." He probably was a hero — he was mentioned in dispatches — but how could anyone expect them to take him back into the small apartment where Gloria and her mother remained.

There was talk of divorce. Mrs. Meade was shocked by it, and Gloria's mother only laughed. When Gloria asked, her mother said it wasn't likely, that divorce was so complicated, you had to have an Act of Parliament, you had to have grounds, and how could she prove anything when her husband was not much more than a shell? "I should have done something about it before, when he was waltzing around the world. Something might have been arranged then, but I wasn't smart enough."

There was an edge to her voice that Gloria didn't like. But she had her own life to lead. Lotte had plans for her, even though she herself had put teaching behind her by the spring of 1946 when she had a stroke.

Juilliard, she wrote in large, clumsy letters when Gloria came to see her at the nursing home. *Money from uncle, boyfriend*. She couldn't speak — the whole right side of her body was affected — but her mind was still sharp and with much effort she had recovered enough movement on the left side to communicate by notes.

Lessons with her had ceased definitively six months before, when she'd handed Gloria off to one of her friends. The man was a Pole who'd had a career in France but who ended up in a refugee camp some place before making his way to Montreal after the war. The lessons were not going well, but Gloria didn't have the money needed for a better teacher.

"My uncle? Not much chance, they don't have as much as it seems. And boyfriend? What boyfriend?" Gloria said. The room was small and hot. Lotte shared it with another woman who spent most of her time snoring in her chair. The whole facility smelled of urine when it didn't smell of disinfectant, and Gloria hated visiting nearly as much as she disliked going to see her father. "Boyfriend?" she repeated. She had no boyfriend. She had steadfastly avoided all hints from her mother about who might be appropriate. When she went out it was with a crowd, singers from the choirs she accompanied or with a group of young men and women who had discovered classical music during the war.

Lotte shook her head, and her right eye began to water. She wiped the tears away — tears? or just the rheum that collected in old people's eyes, Gloria didn't know. With her good left hand, Lotte reached for her tablet again. It took great concentration for her to find the right angle so that she could hold the page steady with her right elbow and still be able to write. Her lips moved but no sound escaped except a sort of animal grunting. *Soldier*, she finally wrote, and she shoved the tablet toward Gloria.

Soldier? James? Hardly. James was nice, but she had made clear to him she was not interested in anything more than being pals. Gloria shook her head. "He's not my boyfriend," she said. And laughed and ran her fingers through her curls because it was a habit she'd adopted once she'd noticed how men looked at her when she did.

Lotte reached for the tablet, leaned forward, and pressed heavily on the pencil as if to make the message stronger by the effort she put into writing. *Vater*, she wrote. *Money*.

"You mean ask James's father for help?" Yes, of course, Gloria knew that's exactly what she meant. There was no question that she could go to Juilliard or anywhere else without a sponsor.

Lotte nodded her head vigorously. "Ja," Lotte said. "You ..." There was a long pause as she worked her mouth to get the words into position ... "need ... money."

"Don't I know it," Gloria said, looking down at her hands. She'd begun to wear polish on the nails, even though she had to keep them short so they wouldn't interfere with her playing. She rubbed the nails of her right hand lightly on her skirt, and then looked up at Lotte. The old woman was watching her.

"You never had to ask for money," she said. It wasn't a question, it was an assertion born of a certainty that Lotte had been the darling of a father who had shoe factories and who was delighted at the idea of a beautiful daughter who played piano like an angel. Like *ein engel*, as the clippings in the scrapbook Lotte had shown Gloria put it.

But Lotte shook her head and the side of her face that moved frowned. "No," she said, the word exploding from her mouth in a cloud of spit. She moved her good hand to point to herself. "Ask," she said. "Often." Her mouth worked to find the words again. "Concerts." Another pause as she struggled. "Come Canada."

"But how," Gloria asked. "How do you ask?"

Lotte leaned forward and with her good hand she pushed up her old, saggy breast. She manoeuvred her face into a parody of a smile. She made a little kiss with her lips.

Gloria watched, repulsed and puzzled. "Sex?" she asked, after a long moment. The clippings showed a young woman with a cloud of dark curly hair dressed in gowns with plunging necklines. Lotte had been lovely once. But was she seriously suggesting what Gloria thought?

She was. She nodded, and her eyelids fluttered once before her shoulders relaxed, and she let her hands drop into her lap. She still watched Gloria, but the intensity was gone, as if she had put all her energy into getting her message across, and now was exhausted.

Gloria stayed long enough to see that there would be no more communication today; Lotte had retreated into her frozen body to recuperate. As she walked out to the winter afternoon, Gloria began to laugh. "Sex," she said aloud. "Is it as easy as that?"

JAMES WANTED TO meet her for a drink that night. Since he'd been demobbed, he'd resisted doing what his father wanted, which was to return to Toronto and the slot waiting for him in a good law firm. Maybe he ought to stay in Montreal, he said several times in Gloria's presence. "There's more excitement here."

Gloria had a lesson with Lotte's friend that afternoon. One of the reasons she'd gone to see her that day was so she could assure Lotte she was still working with him. But she'd forgotten to say that because he was easy to forget. James said that he'd had a brilliant career in the 1930s in Europe and one of his buddies had heard him play during the war in London. But when the Pole tried to explain what he wanted from Gloria, she had no idea what he was talking about. It was only when he sat down and demonstrated that she began to understand. The tempo. A little faster. Slightly lighter in the adagio. But was that enough in a teacher? Most definitely not.

She hated his room as well. It was in one of the houses that had been changed into hotels near Atwater and Saint Catherine. The best thing about it was the bay window, which let in sunshine on winter afternoons — if he opened the curtains. But most often he didn't and his place — someone's sitting room, transformed into a lodging smaller than the place she and her mother shared — smelled of dust and sausages cooked on the little gas ring in the corner, or, worse, his own breath that cried out for a dentist to take a look at his mouth. She hated it when he stood too close to her. It had been much better in the fall, when he opened the window. She decided to walk after her lesson, before she met James, to chase away any foul emanations that might cling to her after an afternoon in the company of talent that would never be heard again, that would probably never get the credit it deserved.

James was sitting at the bar in Chez Pauzé when she came in. He'd been looking for her, and got up from his stool immediately to come over and take her coat. He did not try to kiss her cheek; she'd been rather mean about that. No kisses, she had told him, not in public, not in private. If you want my company you'll have to put up with my caprices.

Caprices: a lovely word, a musical term, of course, and she liked to use it in tight situations. To let James think that he could kiss her anytime was not what she was planning for their relationship. He was nice, no question about that. But she felt absolutely nothing when he touched her, except when his hands were cold, and then it was a shiver of displeasure. She smiled at him, though. She owed him that.

Two of his friends were sitting at the bar. Mike Caplan and Robert Murray. She smiled at them: they both seemed to like to hear her play as much as James did.

"Tell her," Mike said. "Tell her before I have to go meet my better half."

Mike had married on leave, just before he was shipped out. Gloria gathered that what he found when he came home was not what he had hoped. But that was another story; he had two children now and a wife who wanted to buy a house.

Robert stepped forward. "No, I get to. I made the arrangements, after all." He'd been drinking already, she could tell from the thick smell of Scotch on his breath. "We're going to be impresarios," he said. "We're going to bring music to the philistines."

James frowned. "That's overstating it …," he began.

"No, I think that's what we agreed among ourselves, and certainly we have to include this lovely lady as one of our inner circle, don't you think?" Robert moved toward Gloria, reaching to put his arm around her, but she stepped aside enough to make it difficult for him to complete the gesture, particularly given the way he was a little unsteady on his feet. "Such a lovely little lady," he repeated.

"Come on," Mike said. He looked at his watch. "I told my wife ..."

"You tell your wife far too much, my friend," Robert said. "But to continue. We have arranged a concert series with some of the best musicians in Montreal. Five recitals this spring at Tudor Hall, beginning in February, one a month until the summer, beautiful music to lift the spirit and instruct the soul. What this benighted city needs ..."

"Come on," Mike repeated, cutting Robert off. "When we were in Italy we met these young string players. You remember, we told you about them," he went on. "They were really terrific and now they've formed this group, and they're going to tour, and they'd love to come to Montreal."

"And so, we'll kill two birds with one stone. Launch their North American career by contributing to their travel fund with the proceeds from our concerts, and give terrific musicians who live here a new series to play for," James said.

She looked from one to the other, their faces flushed from the heat of the bar and the drinks they'd already consumed. "A concert series," she said. "With who?"

"You, of course, darling girl," Robert said. "And that curious Frenchified Pole who is your teacher now. We were thinking you could play a couple of duets with him, and then each of you could show your stuff. And the string quartet that those new players that Defauw brought to the symphony have formed. And a singer, or singers, only we don't know who yet."

"In Tudor Hall?" she asked. The symphony played there

sometimes, the CBC used it for broadcasts. It was a lovely oak-panelled room, with a good, warm sound. It held three hundred. Enough to make a good crowd, but not so big that the music was lost.

Robert nodded and took a long pull on his drink. "You really must have something to toast this with, my sweet." He turned back to the bar, and waved his hand at the bartender. "A sherry for the lady? That's just the ticket. A concert ticket," and he laughed.

"What do you think?" James asked as Robert handed her the sherry. "Don't you think it's a terrific idea?"

Of course it was, and she was sure Lotte would like the idea of her playing with first-rank musicians too. But she knew enough to wonder how it was all going to be financed. Maybe they had an angel, and if so, maybe the angel could help her. She took the glass and smiled up at Robert. "Terrific," she said. She reached out with her free hand and touched James's elbow. She smiled up at him. "So, you've got the hall for the dates, and started planning and sponsors and everything?"

"We've got the hall, that's no problem," James said. "And sponsors, well, that's next on our list. We thought maybe you could help us with that."

"Me?" she asked. "Me? I don't know anybody. Not anybody with money, anyway." She laughed, listening to herself burble, remembering Lotte pushing up her old and sagging bosom. "That's part of my problem."

Mike interrupted. "You fill her in, all right? I've got to go." He reached around to put his glass back on the bar. "It'll be great, really something," he said. "I can't wait."

"Nor can your wife," Robert said. "Hurry along home."

Mike socked him gently on the arm. "I'll tell her you send

her love." For a moment the three watched him make his way to the coat check.

"And that is the reason I stay away from all eligible women," Robert said. "Present company excepted," he added when he noticed the way Gloria's face wrinkled in annoyance. He reached for her and this time succeeded in putting his arm around her, pulling her close. "You are, of course, extremely eligible, my dear. Extremely desirable, I might add."

She wriggled away from him as gracefully as she could. "What's this about me helping you out? I'd be very pleased to play in the series, but what else can I do?" she asked.

"We'll talk about it over dinner," James said. He looked at his watch. "And don't you have someone waiting for you too?" he asked Robert. "I thought you said you were meeting your father for dinner at the club."

Robert looked at his own watch, bringing it close to his good eye, the one that had not been injured in the war. "Oh yes," he said. "A working supper. How I love working suppers, particularly at the Mount Stephen. They put you away in one of the little rooms and shut the door and it gets unbearably hot and even when you ring it takes a long time for the waiter to come and ..."

"Go," James said. "We know what a difficult life you lead."

The restaurant had filled up as they talked, and once they were seated at a table in the corner the noise made it necessary for James and Gloria to lean close to each other. Or maybe it was just an excuse on James's part. He took her hand and held it on top of the table after the waiter had come to take their order.

"Yes?" she asked. She was hungry, and the sherry had made her tired. Going from Lotte's to her lesson had meant five different streetcar trips.

James sipped the fresh drink he'd carried from the bar, then put it down so he could turn her hand over and look at her palm. He ran his right index finger along her lifeline. "You're going to live a long time," he said.

"So I'm told," she said. Mrs. Meade had often remarked on the way the line arced across her palm to curl around under the joint of her thumb. Nonsense, Gloria's mother had always said: don't give the girl ideas.

He took her left hand and folded it so it made a fist, then looked at the creases her skin made as her fingers bent. "Those are supposed to be union lines," he said, touching the little marks between the large fold at the base of her little finger, and the fold made by the end of a line on her palm. "How many love affairs or marriages."

She pulled her hand away so she could see. There were three, she counted, with one much deeper than the others. "You don't believe any of that, do you? All that is just old wives' tales." She looked at her other hand. The same folds and creases were there too. "Married three times! Perish the thought!"

"I didn't say 'married.' Love affairs count too, I'm told." He took another sip from his drink and lit a cigarette. He didn't try to capture her hand again, but began to fiddle with his lighter and cigarette case.

She put her hands down on the table and folded them together. "And who told you?" From the way he was fidgeting she was sure he was about to confess something. She hoped it wasn't some sort of a declaration.

"A woman I knew in Italy," he said, cutting through her thoughts. "A pianist with hands even bigger than yours."

She spread her hands out in front of her. They were big, she was proud they were so big. Big and strong. Once Lotte had said she'd always wanted to have hands like Gloria's, that even before she heard Gloria play she hoped she'd be able to help those hands make music.

"And? Is she one of the musicians you want to bring over?" she asked. That might explain the project in part.

"No," he said. "She's dead."

For a long moment she watched him watching the smoke rise from his cigarette. Then he waved it away with his hand. "But I don't want to talk about that. There are more interesting things we have in front of us."

The plan was so simple, he explained as they ate. Robert had served with Aird Nesbitt, owner of Ogilvy's department store, and now that everyone was back home, it was a simple matter for him to go talk to Aird as one former military man to another. Nesbitt liked challenges — after his father bought the store when he was in his twenties, he'd made it into the place for the elite to shop in Montreal. He knew what his friends liked, and what pleased them he knew would please others who aspired to Montreal's upper crust. During the war the store had done reasonably well — anything they could get their hands on sold, of course — but now Nesbitt was back at the helm full time, and he was charting a course for new heights in a world that was full of postwar optimism.

"Aird likes the idea a lot," James said. "But he'll need a little nudging to give his full support. That's where you come in."

"You mean you'll need more money to get the series off the ground," she said.

"Money, and clerical help, and a word here and a word there," James said. He lit another cigarette. "Aird has a soft spot for young musicians," he went on. "He is particularly fond of young lady musicians. We would like you to come with us the next time we meet with him so he can see the calibre of the talent we want to promote."

"James," Gloria said. The word came out louder than she expected, with the emphasis on the sibilant at the end. "What are you suggesting?"

"Nothing bad," he assured her. "It's just a matter of putting our best foot forward. You are, you know, the best advertisement for what's happening in music these days. Young, bright, beautiful — and an angel at the keyboard." He smiled at her. "We all love you, you know." And, before she could respond, he added, "Some of us more than others."

She felt her blood rush to her face. "I'm the bait, eh?" she said. She started to look for her purse in preparation for leaving even though she had only eaten a few mouthfuls and she was still hungry. There wasn't much at home.

"No," he said emphatically, reaching out again to capture her hand so she could not proceed with collecting her things. "No, most definitely no. I wouldn't let anything bad happen to you. I told you about the woman in Italy. I've never mentioned her to anyone in Montreal. I want you to know that I loved her as much as I am learning to love you. I wouldn't want to lose you like I did her, or have you harmed or ..."

"Nevertheless, you want to use me ..."

"I want — we all want — to help you, you silly girl."

She pulled her hand away, knocking over his drink. "No, thank you," she said, standing up. "I don't need your help." She felt his eyes on her as she walked across the dining room. She half expected him to catch up with her before she collected her coat and boots and headed out the door. But he didn't.

In the morning she tried to make music on the piano at home. Her mother was asleep and she would have to work again tonight, so Gloria closed the door to her room, where the piano was now. She played the scales her teacher had given her — a question of working on the left ring finger that wasn't keeping up with the increasing strength and precision of her other fingers for some reason — and then she went on to the Bach Partita No. 2 that he wanted her to work on. It was a piece of music that she didn't like very much — he wanted her to play it gaily, but she didn't see it that way at all. But she knew he had an idea of where he wanted her to go. She wasn't sure she agreed, but for the moment she had no better advice.

Her left ring finger did not seem to be any more obedient than it had been. It dragged and the rhythm wasn't precise, a bad thing anytime but particularly bad in Bach. What about push-ups for fingers? Would that help? Or would repeating the phrase again and again help?

The phone rang. She stopped. It would be for her mother, since Gloria's friends left notes for her with the doorman at the hotel, where she still played, or with the secretary at the church, where she accompanied the choir. The procedure meant that she sometimes missed messages but she would rather do that than have her mother know everything she was doing.

But Gloria owed it to her not to let the phone ring too long. She stood up and went into the next room to answer it. She was noting down the message when her mother came to the door of the front room and looked down the hall.

She still was a good looking woman, Gloria thought. She'd begun to put a bit too much henna in her hair, her fingers were yellow from cigarettes, but she was careful to make sure her teeth stayed white and her makeup was perfect. Her red silk dressing gown was wrapped around her waist, and her hair was tousled. She blinked a little at the light pouring down the hall: the sun was sufficiently low in the sky these days for it to penetrate deep into their apartment.

"Fashion show," Gloria said, answering the question her mother didn't pose. "He wants to know if you're interested. What's this about?"

"Branching out," she said, running a hand through her hair. "These late nights are getting to me. Maybe it's time to get involved in something else." She reached out for the slip of paper where Gloria had written the telephone number to call. "I'll get back to him as soon as I've had some coffee."

Gloria watched her turn and shuffle toward the kitchen in her backless slippers. For a second Gloria wondered if she should ask her mother if she knew Aird Nesbitt. But what did it matter if she did? Gloria was going to have to make her own decisions.

As she pounded her way through the Bach again, she began to see the life her mother had been leading for the last ten years or more: making a living not far from the edge of respectability. She'd done it for Gloria's sake, she'd told Mrs. Meade. But there must have been things she'd liked about it, too. The laughter and late nights might have been fun for a while, but perhaps now she was thinking that it was time for her to find something more *comme il faut*.

Fashion and department stores were more that way than hostessing in supper clubs, no matter how classy the hotel.

The thoughts went around in Gloria's mind as she struggled with the music. That five-note sequence. If she could only get it right, perhaps she would have the key to what was necessary. Over and over she played it, and just before she knew her fingers would rebel, the notes came effortlessly, seemingly unbidden, as if the wisdom of the music had finally been incorporated into her nerves and muscles.

"Give it a rest," her mother was saying. She was standing in the open door, a cigarette in one hand and a cup of coffee in the other. "You're beginning to sound like a broken record."

Ordinarily Gloria would have ignored that, but this time she smiled in triumph. "I've got it," she said. "I know what I'm going to do."

She called James the next day at his office. "Of course, I'll be pleased to go see Mr. Nesbitt with you," she said. "I want to talk to you about a project of my own too."

LOTTE WANTED TO hear her play before the concert, wanted to hear both Gloria and her teacher, their duet — Mozart's "Turkish March" — and their solo pieces — a Bach partita for her and something by Chopin for him. One side of Lotte's face smiled broadly. She wrote on her tablet in big letters: *I Coach U*. A good idea, Gloria knew. The hospital had a piano in the activity room, so she went to check it out. The action was loose and half a dozen keys were mute, but short of moving another piano to the hospital or transporting Lotte somewhere else, it would have to do. She persuaded her teacher to come along, warning him that Lotte had deteriorated a lot in the last couple of months. She knew he hadn't been to visit; he hid most of the time in his rooms — playing, practising, teaching a few students — but was withdrawn for reasons that Gloria knew she did not want to learn. He seemed alternately happy to have found a safe place, and depressed that the world no longer beckoned to him. He greeted Lotte by going over to where she was sitting in the day room, to bow and kiss her hand.

Half of Lotte's face broke into a radiant smile, and even the eyelid that drooped moved upward a fraction of an inch. "Play," she said. "*Spielen Sie.*"

"*Avec plaisir*," he said. Gloria and he stumbled through the program they'd chosen — the piano did not lend itself to the four-hand piece, they both had trouble with the action and pedals. Lotte made no comment until they finished. Then she took her tablet and pencil and prepared to write. Her good hand shook as she filled a half page, concentrating with her mouth pursed in a knot, the words slowly appearing. It took her ten minutes to finish. Then she pushed the tablet toward Gloria. There was sweat on her forehead and she smelled slightly of urine, as if she might have wet her pants in her efforts.

Gloria took the tablet, but could make no sense of the words. They might be German, she realized, so she nodded to Lotte and handed the tablet to the man. For several minutes he stared at the writing before he glanced over at Gloria. He put the tablet back down on the table next to Lotte. "*Sehr gut*," he said. "*Très bien*." Then he looked back at Gloria: "Of course, that's just what we'll do."

When they were outside, he told her he had no idea what the words meant. "She played like an angel, you know," he said. "We will have to summon her spirit if we want her to guide us."

So they practised in his rooms because his piano was the best they had access to. They had a run-through in Tudor Hall, just the two of them, the week before the concert. Then the boys — James, Robert, and Mike — wanted to check the details of the hall the evening before the concert. Her teacher could not be there for the time they fixed, so they insisted Gloria play an excerpt from her part of the program after they'd seen how the chairs would be set up and tested the way a voice carried into the corners of the hall.

It was the Chopin they wanted her to play, the Waltz No. 14 in E Minor. Lyric and lovely, but which few women could play with power, they said. "You've got the energy and strength, you ought to show it off," Robert said approvingly from the middle of the hall. James was sitting near the front; as soon as she finished, he rushed up to the stage. She stood up and turned around to meet his arms. This time he would not let her step aside; he wrapped his arms around her and rocked her back and forth. "You were terrific, my darling," he said in her ear. "Absolutely wonderful." She pulled away from him slightly and saw the tears in his eyes. She reached up to wipe them away, then turned her face up so he could kiss her.

"Thank you," she said. She smiled at him, an unforced, uncalculated smile. That he was pleased with her performance made her enormously happy, she discovered.

"She has to go to New York," Robert went on. "We owe it to the world to see she continues. She's terrific." He was beside her now, ready to embrace her too. "Stick with us, baby, we've got a long way to go," he said.

Mike stood where he'd been sitting, clapping wildly. "Encore, encore," he shouted.

Mr. Nesbitt who had been standing at the back, also applauded. "Perhaps we can arrange for her to audition at Juilliard," he said.

WITH THE PROMISE of an audition for Juilliard, Gloria played better than she ever had before. The young reviewer from *The Montreal Star* was impressed: *Where has this talent been hiding?* he asked in his review. She received a note from the interim director of the symphony, congratulating her. And her teacher was pleased enough to make the trek out to Lotte's place the morning after, to tell her of the triumph, and the promise of further study. When Gloria went herself later in the day, Lotte greeted her with tears and words that tried to flow from her mouth.

"*Ja, ja,*" she finally succeed in saying. "*Du bist schön.*"

"Go," James said. "We know what a difficult life you lead."

He was joking, but everyone knew that Robert had pressures that the others didn't. He'd done his *collège classique* with the Jesuits at Brébeuf and his civil and common law at McGill: his parents expected him to be the best of the best, *la crème de la crème*.

Gloria took the train to New York for the Juilliard audition, with James along for moral support. His firm needed work done there and they paid his way. As for Gloria, she took up an invitation from a cousin of Mike's wife to stay with her. James saw Gloria there before he checked into the small hotel his firm used. Mrs. Mike's cousin was short and dark and cheerful, and she gave Gloria a key to the apartment. "If I've left before you're up tomorrow morning, give them hell in the afternoon," she said before she went out.

Once the door was shut, Gloria looked for the piano Mike had promised she could practise on. It was in the kitchen, an upright wedged between the fridge and the door to the service stairs. She touched the keys — the sound wasn't bad. Then she checked the time. From the schedule she and James had figured out, she could practise forty-five minutes before she had to leave to meet him.

Her fingers felt shaky — too much coffee, too many new things — so she did the series of exercises that her teacher recommended for mastering hands that had lost their way "in the fog, *dans la brume.*" Then she pulled from her memory the most difficult passage from the concerto she planned as her *pièce de resistance* for the audition. The rhythm rarely went right, there was a quick change in tempo indicated in the notation that she rarely felt comfortable with, but this time the music rolled from her fingers almost as beautifully as the music she heard in her head when she studied the score.

"Good," she said aloud when she'd finished. "Oh yes, this might work after all." As she stood up to stretch, she noticed that the day was drawing to a close outside, and that the clock said she'd practised twice as long as she'd planned. She gathered up her coat, hat, and handbag and went out into the waiting city, half afraid and half exhilarated.

The Sunday before, James had bought a copy of *The New York Times*, and they'd picked out the best concert listed. He'd called to reserve tickets — a long distance call! They were so expensive. When she got off the subway at the stop he'd indicated, she felt herself pulled along by the life on the early evening street. The place was so huge — the people, the buildings, the traffic; everything was like Montreal at its most intense, but multiplied by ten or twenty. As she walked down the street, she could see James waiting on the corner of West 43rd and Broadway, where a crowd was already milling around the many doors of Town Hall. As she went up to him, she looked around for sign of the artists' entrance. Wouldn't it be terrific to play here? However, it would not do if she let that excitement show, so she forced herself to smile only slightly.

"You had no problem?" he asked. "I'd begun to worry that you'd gotten lost. We'd better go in." He took her elbow and began ushering her toward the entrance. "Did you get something to eat beforehand? If not, we should be able to find something around here afterwards; it's the theatre district after all."

To be honest, she really hadn't thought much about food — there had been too much in her head — but suddenly she was ravenous. "I practised and the time got away from me," she said. "They don't sell anything in the lobby do they?"

"Don't think so," he said. "This isn't a movie theatre." He leaned forward to nuzzle her. "This is quite a place, isn't it?"

She turned her head so his face touched hers. "Yes," she said. "Thank you so much." He slipped his arm around her and they moved inside as one.

Town Hall had been built right after the First World War by a group of women who thought New York needed a place to hold meetings, concerts, and educational events for ordinary people. The posters in the hall announced a meeting for the election campaign of Henry Wallace, the left-wing independent candidate for president in the next US election, as well as posters for a modern dance performance, and a presentation on the new United Nations headquarters, whose construction was supposed to start the next year. But the hall was also famous for the opportunity it offered young musicians: the mimeographed program had a list of a half-dozen concerts to be given over the next few weeks by people whose names were unknown to Gloria.

This night the featured performer was a Hungarian pianist; he was to play Bartok, Smetana, and Beethoven. "Wow," James said when he'd studied the program. "I've never heard those performed live before."

Gloria nodded, and looked around. Nearly all the seats near them were taken, although down near the front, where presumably tickets were more expensive, only half were filled. The four young men sitting in their row had scores open on their laps and pencils in their hands. She nudged James. "Look, I'm not the only aspiring pianist who wants to hear the music."

James looked over and nodded. "Maybe they're some of those Outstanding Young American Pianists," he whispered. "OYAPs. There was something about them in *Time* a month or so ago."

Gloria craned her neck to see if the young man next to her had all four scores, or if he was concentrating more closely on one piece. For the moment he was talking loudly to his friends. She could make out a few musical words — resonance, metronome, Steinway — above the restless sounds of the crowd. She leaned closer, but she still couldn't see what partition he held.

Then, as if he could feel her eyes on him, he turned toward her and with an involuntary gesture drew the score closer to him.

"Oh," she said, breathing out almost with a sigh, a little embarrassed at having been caught out. She was aware that the young man was studying her face in profile, weighing the import of James's presence, taking the measure of her big hands.

He asked, "Don't you have a score of your own?" And, then, more aggressively, "What are you doing there anyway? I thought this whole row was reserved for music students."

The fellow sitting on the other side of him looked over. "Now, don't give the little lady a bad time," he said. "She's not to blame because you aren't playing tonight and the Hungarian is."

"Yeah, give her a break," the third one chimed it. "Not everybody has your advantages."

"What advantages, you jerk," the first one began, laughing. But then the lights dimmed and the concert began. The fourth man hushed him.

Gloria wished she'd remembered to bring a notebook like the ones these men held along with their scores. This was music that she hadn't played before, and she knew that there was much she could learn. She glanced over at the fellow sitting next to her. He had closed his score and was scowling, but his friends were paying careful attention.

"He played like a pig," she heard him say to the others as the music stopped. "I hope you weren't impressed," he said to

James as he began to squeeze past them when the lights went up. "Do you play too?" he asked, when they were standing in the aisle.

"No, but Gloria does," James said. "She's here to audition at Juilliard."

The man looked her up and down. "Hmm," he said. "Very interesting." Then he walked up the aisle to the lobby with his friends.

Gloria shivered. She suddenly wasn't sure if she knew what she was getting into. The competition was going to be tough. She resolved that she would ask the men where they were studying when they came back; she would not be disturbed by their high-handed attitude. But they didn't come back, and she began to worry. Did they not appreciate this musician's fine phrasing or his touch, which she was sure would convey a deep understanding of the Beethoven that came next on the program.

Gloria remembered Lotte talking about the reasons why some music filled one's heart with sadness while other pieces made one's soul dance. Some reasons were technical — the progression of keys, the waiting for the sound which should come next but doesn't, the rapidity with which the notes rise and then spiral. To draw the most from the bare bones of the music, from the black marks on paper which transcribed the composer's thoughts and feelings required dexterity and mastery of the mechanics of striking the keys on the piano. But that was only the beginning, Lotte said. Any fool who worked hard enough could attain a level of competence. It might take eight hours of practice a day, but it was possible. She said she'd seen it in her fellow students decades before. But to take that expertise and make it real music transcended competence, a process that nearly always was beyond explanation. The pianist understood it, or didn't. Lotte had told Gloria that she did.

"Don't worry," James said when he put her into a taxi after they'd had an after-concert supper. "Don't spend all night going over your music."

She leaned forward so he could kiss her. "Don't you worry," she said. "I'll only do what I have to do."

WHAT SHE HAD to do, of course, was to sit down with the music once again and play it over in her head, trying to determine if anything of the marvellous playing she'd heard earlier that night might help. She didn't dare touch the piano itself — Mrs. Mike's cousin was nice, but she had to work the next day. By the time Gloria fell asleep she felt a wave of confidence roll over her. She would not play like a pig, she would do Lotte proud.

But it didn't matter. The people at Juilliard wouldn't listen to her play.

If they'd known they would have done it all differently of course, but in the end she wasn't the only one. Maureen Forrester ran into the same problem a couple of years later — Gloria wondered how Mo and her friends hadn't heard what happened to Gloria, but that just showed you the world of difference between singers and pianists. James blamed himself, because a letter or a phone call would have cleared up any ambiguity. What the problem boiled down was this: despite the letters of recommendation that paved the way to an audition date, no one had said that Juilliard did not accept anyone who had not graduated high school.

"You didn't finish high school?" James said, as they left after arguing with the associate director for half an hour. "But you used to have to get home right after playing because you had classes the next day."

Gloria stared straight ahead of her. Manhattan surrounded them, the traffic rushed by, the sun shone deep into the canyons between skyscrapers. She shifted her portfolio of music so she could hold it more tightly. A little breeze blew, ruffling the hair of women who had put aside their hats on this lovely, early spring, postwar day of prosperity and hope and ambitions waiting to be realized.

"But weren't you going to school?" he asked again, taking her elbow to steer her toward the intersection. "Weren't you?"

"Of course I was," she said as they waited for the light to change. "Back then. At the beginning. But it got too much for me. What was the point, anyway? I wanted to be a pianist. What did algebra matter?"

"A lot, it seems," he said. His silence weighed down the rest of the afternoon, which they'd left free for the audition. He saw her back to Mrs. Mike's cousin's place, and left her, saying that he'd be back the next day so they could do the sightseeing they'd planned. But she didn't stay any longer than it took to write a note of thanks to her hostess, and repack her suitcase. She was out the door, and on the subway, headed for Grand Central station and the afternoon train back to Montreal. She called the hotel where James was staying and left a message for him just before she got on the train.

Robert was at the station in Montreal to meet her when she arrived the next morning. "Silly, silly girl," he said, as he picked up her bag and tried to lead her out of the station. "I think you've ruined it for us all."

She didn't cry until she was home, until she'd made sure that her mother was out, that she'd taken the phone off the hook, that she wouldn't be disturbed as she wallowed in her sadness. What would Lotte say? What was going to happen now to the concert series? Because, Robert had told her, despite the good crowd they'd got for her performance they'd lost money on it since half the crowd was there on free tickets. They'd already paid for the passage of the Italian quartet, thank goodness, but they had hoped Mr. Nesbitt would step into the breach as he had with the mailing of invitations, with the printing costs, with the advertising for the series itself.

"Silly, silly girl," she heard Robert say again in her head as she lay in the darkened apartment and wondered what to do next. "Now Nesbitt can't be proud of you. You were supposed to be his protege, didn't you understand? He loved the idea of supporting a beautiful young woman studying in New York. But you didn't get to first base. And then you had to cut and run."

For three days she had the apartment to herself. When her mother didn't come home that night, she talked to Mrs. Meade to see if she should worry. The old woman wanted to know why Gloria was back so soon, but accepted a story about a mis-understanding about dates. Then she said that Gloria's mother was off visiting friends in the Townships. That was the first Gloria had heard about the invitation or the friends, but maybe that indicated just how little she'd been paying attention to her mother. Or maybe how much her mother had been protecting her from a parallel life she'd been leading. Gloria imagined her mother thinking that with Gloria gone for five days, what she didn't know wouldn't hurt her.

A picture of her mother sitting in front of a fireplace in some-one's country place in Sutton came to her, her mother drinking good single malt and laughing, being charming, having a good time.

Gloria had let her down too. All that effort to pay for the lessons and still keep one foot in the world of respectability while her father's family did stupid things like lose money during the war — who lost money then? Nobody she knew. The boys were always joking that they might have risked their lives, but nobody who stayed home came out any worse than when the war began, and now it was up to them to make up for lost time, and to capture back as much of the war plunder as they could.

The boys. She didn't want to think of them any more than she wanted to dwell on what she owed her mother and Lotte. At some point, she was going to have to see Lotte and explain. How was she going to do that? She caught herself wishing — just for a moment, just for a split second, she shouldn't feel guilty about a lapse that tiny — that Lotte would be worse; maybe Lotte wouldn't be able to understand what she had to say.

Or maybe Lotte would be so advanced in her decline that Gloria could lie, could say that it had all been wonderful, and explain that she wouldn't be able to come to visit anymore because she had to leave, had to go to New York immediately to start her studies. That the people at Juilliard had been so bowled over by her playing that they wanted her now, wanted to launch her career with — well, why not? if she were lying she might as well lie big — a concert at a small but elegant little hall that they engaged for the best and the brightest of their new students.

But she couldn't lie, not to Lotte. She couldn't face getting out of bed, except to rummage in the kitchen for crackers and cheese, and rum and Coke, which she drank until she felt sick. She spread out her arms to hold the bed down, she shut her eyes to see if that helped, she put one foot out of the bed, letting it hang down to touch the floor as if that would somehow ground her. The worst thing was that she knew she was acting like her father, who had dug so many holes for himself, one drink at a time, in binges that were never mentioned, she knew now.

But who cared at this point? No one. She woke up from a fitful sleep the late afternoon of the third day and stumbled to the bathroom. The floor was filthy with vomit and littered with the clothes she must have torn off. She was disgusted and hungry and aching all over, but she knew she had to make a choice. After she had washed her face and cleaned things up a little, she went into the kitchen, the cold floor feeling clean and unforgiving on her bare feet. She drew a glass of cold water from the tap, and then stood at the kitchen window, looking at the melting snow drip off the sheds along the lane. The late afternoon sunshine struck the top of the one tall elm that stood above the rooftops.

For a second, when the water reached her stomach, she thought she might be sick again, but she willed herself not to be. She leaned her forehead against the glass and breathed in the peculiar dusty smell of old windows with peeling paint. This was not the sort of place she wanted to live any longer. She was tired of being on the edge. In one sense she could understand Mrs. Mike's desire to live in a new, clean place with grass and sidewalks. She'd grown up a few blocks over. She had sniffed a little one of the times they'd met, when Gloria explained how her mother had never been able to move to a bigger place in a nicer neighbourhood. Mrs. Mike's parents had escaped as soon as they could, first to a triplex a little farther west and then beyond to the new apartments built on Van Horne just before the war. Now the house she and Mike had bought was even farther out — in Saint-Laurent. Even though it was at the end of the train line, Gloria could see it had advantages.

She had made a mess of things, but she wasn't going to spend the rest of her life in a crumby apartment, working crazy hours like her mother.

But what was she going to do? She hadn't finished high school, couldn't type, was bad at math, hated the idea of an office. She could get married to someone — there was no one besides James who was around at present — but she knew it wouldn't be hard to find someone; there were always men around, always souls looking for a body to find warmth in. That was what Mrs. Meade had been hinting at all along, what would be expected of her. Be like Mrs. Mike, latch on to somebody with a rising star.

But no, she wanted to be the rising star. She wanted to make music.

She turned away from the window and leaned against the sill, her hands spread out in front of her. Her big hands with the patchy nail polish, peeling off because she hadn't touched it up since she got back, just as she had done nothing but indulge herself, nothing but drink and whine, and crawl down the hole she had carelessly created for herself.

Her hands were the way out. Music would be what saved her.

When her mother arrived back late Monday evening, she had things cleaned up and was practising.

THE MUSIC SAVED her, the music sustained her. Even as she sat at her bad piano and tried to hold her hands the way her teachers had insisted, as her shoulders tightened above the keyboard, as the notes on the page in front of her swam in the dim light, she felt there was a current just beyond her reach, something that she might slip into if she only had the correct angle between fingers and wrist, if her elbows remained where they were supposed to, if she got the right tempo on that particular tricky part. She had been playing enough to know that the moments when she could slip into the river of music were rare, but that they were reward enough to keep going.

LOTTE UNDERSTOOD. SHE let her cry on that unusually warm spring afternoon when she had gathered up enough courage to explain what had happened. "I was out of my depth" she said. "I didn't understand what was going on. How can I do it? Am I mad to think of making music my life?"

Lotte, who was stroking Gloria's hand with her own good one, made a noise that could have been either a sob or a laugh. Gloria raised her eyes to see half the old woman's face crinkled into a big smile. "Mmmmmad," she said, pushing hard to get past the first sound. She nodded her head. "Mmmmmd."Then she gestured toward herself. "Mmmeee. Mmmmad." She swallowed, but a little spit began to run down her chin from the corner of her mouth. "You. Mmmmad." And then the chortle again — part gasp, part gargle. To be a musician you had to crazy, it seemed.

The glimpse of Juilliard made clear just what a long way Gloria had to go. If she couldn't study there she would have to find some other way to launch her career. Reading the brochures they'd given her suggested that. Concerts in Montreal were very well and good, but there had to be more. It was time perhaps to cultivate a few more friends. But she couldn't let her connection with the boys lapse; she was going to have to make apologies, somehow express both her gratitude and just how much she appreciated the difficult position she'd put them in, in the eyes of Nesbitt — who was, after all, their sugar daddy — and in the wider world of music insofar as anyone was paying attention to what was happening in Montreal.

She helped with the other concerts in the series, accompanied the young woman soprano who sang in the third recital, met the Italian quartet at the train station because none of the boys was free to see them to their hotel. She took tickets and called up the reviewers, joking around with the young critic at *The Montreal Star* who had given her concert such a good review. She made sure there were little flyers on the table by the cloak room in the hotel where she still played two nights a week. She saw that all the singers in all the choirs that she'd ever accompanied knew about the series.

In the end, by the time the Italians had come and gone to great reviews and a gala party given by the Italian wife of the head of Marconi Canada, the series had made enough so that with what the boys had pledged of their own money, the bills could be paid.

MONEY. SO, IF she couldn't go to Juilliard, what was next best? To take lessons from one of Lotte's colleagues in New York was a possibility. She could take the train down once a month and work all day. That was James's idea, and one Robert shot down immediately. "Once a month is not enough," he said. They were sitting on a bench in Dominion Square, waiting for the sun to sink behind the buildings and for a little coolness to descend upon the city. Summer heat had arrived in late May, a week of humidity and enervation. On the weekend, James proposed taking the train to Saint-Sauveur and lounging for a day at the hotel there, but Gloria couldn't; her summer schedule at St. James Church had yet to begin, and she was to play for choir practice on Saturday morning.

"Tell that old fart organist that he can play and direct the practice for once," Robert said. "It's not like he doesn't direct from the organ on Sunday."

There was no point in explaining that being a choir director and organist was quite different from being the person who played the piano for practice. Robert, for all his love of music, had never played or sung anything that Gloria was aware of besides an abortive attempt to learn the trumpet when he was ten. James, who had lived next door at the time, said that the dogs all howled when he did, which mortified his mother. She insisted he stop.

"Come on," Robert said. "At least let's get something nice and cold to drink. What would you say to frozen daiquiris? Or mint juleps? We can see if there is a breeze up on the terrace at the Windsor Hotel. Or come home with me, and see what has been left — no, that won't do, *chère* Maman said something about a dinner party *ce soir.*"

"Black tie?"

"Of course, if she planned it. Can you imagine, on a night like this?" Robert loosened his already loose tie. "What we need to do is take a cruise on the river. A nice breeze off the water, with the scenery slipping by. Can't think of anything nicer, particularly if we can get one of your daiquiris."

Gloria was aware that her sweat was making circles under the arms of her red checked cotton dress. A mistake: she had needed something light to wear and picked it off the rack at Morgan's without really looking at it carefully. It had a New Look skirt — long and full like what Dior was showing in Paris — but the seams were so small that any strain she put on them by moving was going to lead to rips shortly, she was sure. Not a dress for someone who had to move the way she did, and she was afraid that the dye was going to run as well. Cheap cloth for a cheap dress; her mother and Mrs. Meade both said they'd taught her better. At the mention of frozen daiquiris, she thought of how hot the apartment would be tonight, how the icebox would contain nothing but a pool of meltwater until the ice man came by in the morning, how she ought to practise another hour or two this evening, because she'd spent part of the day in Robert's office writing letters on his secretary's typewriter. Letters to follow up on her teacher's idea that maybe something could be arranged in France. Gloria hadn't mentioned the idea to Lotte, but what better plan was there at the moment?

"What do you say to that, my darling?" Robert said. "Daiquiris, they're a drink that even you would like. Maybe we should go down to the port and see if there are any cruise ships in. It's early in the season but that would be just the place to get away from the heat."

James stood up. "Cruise ships are just what we need, what Gloria needs."

Gloria stood up too, thinking that she would leave no matter what they wanted to do next. She felt her skirt stick to the back of her legs, she smelled not quite of sweat but something approaching it, better to go home and open the windows and practise with her feet in cold water than traipse around town.

Robert paid no attention to either of them. "Frozen daiquiris," he repeated. "Just what we need ..."

"Robert Murray," James said. "You could get your *oncle* Hector to hire Gloria this summer."

THE CRUISE SHIPS belonged to the railroad, and the railroad belonged to the Murrays. Descended from officers of the Wolfe's Highland Regiment who'd stayed behind after the Conquest, the Murrays had married local women and prospered, becoming one of the richest Francophone families in Quebec. For a couple of generations the luxury ships they owned had made the run from Montreal down the St. Lawrence and up the Saguenay River. Some of the villages, like Rivière-du-Loup and Métis-sur-Mer on the south shore, could dock private steam yachts belonging to wealthy Americans travelling up from Boston and New York. On the north shore, Americans also made up part of the summer people, but Canadians outnumbered them. By the turn of the twentieth century there was a railroad link and Robert's grandfather, then president of the railroad, had a spur line built that passed just below his estate about seventy-five miles downriver from Quebec City. During the war most of the cruise ships and the railroads were requisitioned and transported food, equipment, and men, but that summer the whole service was back to its prewar, even pre-Depression, standard. The publicity for the cruise ships was everywhere. The ships were cleaned and painted, their kitchens and other facilities updated. The steamship company obviously planned on cashing in on good times.

Gloria had to audition for the job as pianist on the largest, most fashionable ship, but Robert said it was a formality. "The organizers know what's good for them, and they've also heard just how good you are, so don't worry about it," he said. Since the disaster in New York, though, Gloria was careful not to take anything for granted.

"They really are going to hire someone?" she asked. "And I'm going to meet people who like my kind of music?"

"And people who may be able to come through for a travel fund," Robert assured her. "For example, my *oncle* Hector, he's my great uncle really, *mais peu importe*. We'll make sure you get to spend some time at his place. He's a real *mélomane*."

Gloria had heard that Sir Hector Murray — knighted during the brief period when the Canadian government encouraged such things between the two world wars — had a private concert hall on his *domaine*, and that most summer weekends he invited musicians to play.

James beamed when he heard that. "I'll come and pick you up when the ship docks in Murray Bay, and take you there the first long weekend," he said. "You'll see that we're invited?" he asked Robert.

"Of course, of course," he said. "I'll try to be there myself."

Mike, however, would not be included in the invitation, Gloria was told when she asked. "He's got to take his family up to some Jewish camp in the Laurentians," Robert said. "Besides my uncle would have a fit if he thought he were entertaining Jews."

Gloria let that sink in. "Even Jewish musicians? If he's such a great music lover, you mean he wouldn't jump at the chance to listen to Horowitz or Menuhin in the comfort of his own mansion?"

"Oh, maybe them, but they're not like Mike. And even with them, you never know what he might decide," Robert said. "He's a bit of a bigot, you might say."

Information to tuck away, and which Gloria had occasion to bring out more than once over the next little bit. It fell in the same category as the famous comment by Horowitz that there were only three sorts of pianists: Jewish ones, homosexual ones, and bad ones. If such were the case, where did she fit in?

Lotte had her doubts about the plan. When was she going to have time to work on her audition programs for wherever she might end up studying?

"But I'll have loads of time," Gloria said. "I'll have my mornings free and a good piano. That last is a promise, by the way. Robert said they'd make sure the piano was a good one."

Half of Lotte's face frowned. *No silly*, she managed to write.

Gloria took the tablet and tried to make sense of the crooked letters and their meaning. "Silly? You mean I shouldn't be silly?" she asked, looking at the old woman and trying not to see how her bad eye was red and weeping. "Don't worry about me. I know that this is a moment when I have to see what I can come up with. After the New York trip, I know what's riding on it."

Lotte nodded her head in agreement. Then a small smile turned up one corner of her mouth. "Sex," she said after a struggle. She brought her hand up to cup her old breast the way she had months before.

Gloria laughed. She understood better now.

James was waiting outside for her in the car he'd bought the week before. He'd helped win a big case for an aluminum company, and his firm had given him a bonus. The car was a sky-blue Mercury convertible, nearly as classy as one Robert had just bought. The new models were rolling off the assembly lines; both James and Robert said, half seriously, that it was their patriotic duty to buy. As James opened the door for her, he kissed her on the cheek.

She barely noticed. "Remind me not to get old," she said when he'd gone around to the driver's side and climbed in.

He took her hand and brought it to his lips so he could kiss it, but didn't say anything as he started the car. "Let us go out in a blaze of glory, with trumpets blaring and a pianist ready to perform Rachmaninoff," he said, after he'd neatly turned the car around in the parking lot and started down the nearly empty street.

For a moment, she watched the low buildings of the suburbs pass by. The top was down to the hot night air and the breeze felt good, but that did not lift her spirits. A nursing home on the edge of town was not where she wanted to end her days, particularly if she had never tasted real success. "I'm going to do it," she said.

"What?" James asked.

"Everything," she said.

At the moment, he didn't respond, partly because the traffic was clotting up and his attention was required as they drove back into town. But later that evening, when she had played one more gig at the hotel and he'd come back to take her home again, he reminded her of what she'd said.

"It's time, don't you think, to try some of that 'everything,'" he said when they were seated again in his car.

She didn't know what he was talking about at first, and then she realized that this was the moment she'd been dreading.

She looked at him. The heat had not begun to dissipate, even though it had been dark for several hours. She found herself perspiring so much that she could feel the sweat pooling under her hair and beginning to run down her neck. "After the air conditioning inside, I can't stand nights like this," she started to say. She opened her purse to look for a handkerchief, remembering the handkerchief he'd given her that first night when he listened to her play in the hotel. "I feel like I'm going to die. I can't wait until I'm on the river." The words came quickly while on another level she tried to figure out what to say next.

"We could find some other place that's air-conditioned," he said. He paused. "Look," he began again. "I don't want you to go off on the cruise ship without us talking about what's ahead. I love you, you know I love you, and I want you to know that I will support you in whatever you are going to do. I have had faith in you ever since I first heard you play and saw you sitting there, so sweet and demure. I knew that you were the woman I wanted to spend my life with."

She turned away from him. He'd pulled the car over to the side of the street that ran along the edge of Mount Royal Park. In the dark of the shadows under the trees, she could see a couple on a bench with their arms around each other.

Well, really, why didn't she say yes? Because of all those stories her mother and Mrs. Meade told about the fecklessness, utter uselessness of men? They had talked about their sad lives often when Gloria was young and not supposed to understand. The import of their words didn't sink in then. It was only later that she began to understand: a love story did not last.

Her hesitation was more than fear induced by cautionary tales, though. She had begun to wonder if there was something wrong with her because so far she had felt nothing when James kissed her or Robert flirted with her. It was all a game, and she pulled the strings, she kept her head even though she could see that sometimes they were ready to lose theirs. Too much time alone with music? Too much grand and glorious feeling when she was carried along by the river of music which flowed through her when she played? She didn't know, except that she was going to have to enter uncharted waters where she didn't have a score to follow.

"I can't get married until I have studied," she said finally. "You know that."

He sighed. "Yes, that's part of the deal. Your music is one of the things I love about you. But, like I said, we could have an understanding." His voice rose so that the statement was more like a question.

Now was the time for her to turn to him, to put her arms around his neck, to lean into his embrace. Why was this so hard? She took a deep breath and moved toward him. His mouth was smooth and dry and she felt his teeth underneath his lips. He tasted a little like whisky; he'd been drinking while she played. He didn't smoke anymore, though, so there wasn't the stale smell of tobacco on his breath that she remembered from hugs her father had given her. His tongue parted her lips and she allowed it to enter her mouth. A symbolic act, she thought, amazed that she felt so cool, that she could continue to analyze what was going on, that she seemed so removed from what was happening.

"Come back with me tonight," he whispered, pulling away slightly. "We'll find some place cool, we'll go swimming."

She leaned back toward him. "No," she said. "Not tonight. On the weekend ..." And she took his hand and cupped the palm around her breast. "I promise."

So there, it was done. All that remained was the rather unsatisfactory consummation in the guest house at his aunt's place in Senneville on the western end of the island of Montreal. That and the flag that James seemed to attach to her, the hand he put around her shoulder, the way he held the door for her. She suspected he had told Robert about what she'd agreed to, about what had happened, because she noticed that Robert did not call her "darling" as much, nor did he smile as archly in her direction. Mike appeared to be moving out of the picture. Mrs. Mike was pregnant again, he was getting more cases; he probably knew he was being cut out of part of the summer's activities.

Gloria did not react to any of it. She increased her practice time, leaving the house early in the morning to play on the piano that her teacher had discovered for her at the music school that was being organized at the Université de Montréal. The aim was to train musicians for the Catholic Church, but the priest in charge had broader horizons than that. As long as Gloria was in and out of the practice room in the convent by eleven a.m., no one would say anything. The walk there took twenty minutes along a tree-lined street.

AT THE BEGINNING of June the cruise season began.

She knew about the St. Lawrence — everyone who lives in Montreal does. It and its tributaries flow around the island; the city gets its water from it; it is always there in the background. But she never realized its force until she travelled it. The cruises began at the King Edward Pier and set off just beyond the wildness of the St. Mary's rapids, which had stopped ships from going higher on the river for centuries. Then the cruise ships entered the reaches where the river flowed several miles wide passing through flat, rich farmland. At Quebec — which means "where the river narrows" in Abnaki — it flowed underneath the heights of the city and around Île d'Orléans to widen out again. At Tadoussac, the cruise ships turned north to enter the fjord of the Saguenay. The St. Lawrence was nearly twenty miles wide there, even though it was still a couple of hundred miles from its rendezvous with the Atlantic.

Gloria liked to get up early and watch the sun rise on the river before she stole an hour of practice in the ship's recital hall. Several times she felt she floated on music, the way the ship floated on the St. Lawrence as it swept along, impersonal and powerful, transporting all in majesty, in glory.

Most of what she had to do was more mundane. She played light classical pieces during the dinner hour. She accompanied the would-be opera singers who gave concerts. Three nights she filled in — badly she knew, she had no feel for popular music — when the dance band's pianist sprained his hand in a drunken fall. And she spent three weekends at Sir Hector's estate in Charlevoix, on a hillside looking south toward the river.

Robert drove up from Montreal with James the first time, meeting Gloria in Murray Bay, which was where the cruise ship docked so the passengers could play golf at the railroad hotel. The other two weekends, James came by himself, speeding along the road which followed the coastline. The first weekend Robert and James had shared a room on the top floor of the rambling old house, a room assigned to James all alone on his second and third visits. The room, however, was not a place for Gloria and him to meet: Robert had told Madame Murray, his great aunt Thérèse, about their romance, and although his aunt clucked over them and left them alone when they were sitting on the veranda in the early evening, she — good chaperone that she was — saw to it that Gloria's room was on a different floor. Gloria didn't mind — she liked an interlude in his arms — but more than that still repulsed her. He had been so fast, so frantic the few times she had completely surrendered.

She was annoyed that Madame Murray sat them at different tables for the full dress dinner on Saturday night. All three times Gloria played in the afternoon in the music room. The concert on the last visit went particularly well. She began by accompanying Pierre Boisvert, a tenor from Saskatchewan, who also had a cruise ship gig and was a favourite of the Murrays. Then she finished the recital with Schumann, which was greeted with a storm of applause from the forty or so guests.

James beamed when he came up to her afterwards, hugging her, staking his claim. They stood chatting with the *mélomanes*, his arm around her shoulders, until it was clearly time to change for dinner. Encouraged by the warm reception of her playing and James's obvious pride, Gloria decided as they went out to wonder aloud why he didn't ask Robert's *Tatie*, Thérèse, to seat them together that night.

"I'm so lost," she said. "I feel so much better when you're beside me. I never know who I might be talking to."

"People who love music, that's who," he said, steering her carefully toward the central staircase, which led to the wing where her room was. "That's part of the reason you're invited, remember," James said. "You're supposed to charm these old duffers, so they'll chip into your study-abroad fund. Besides, couples are never placed next to each other at formal dinners. You should know that."

How many formal dinners have I been to? she wanted to ask, although when she thought about it she realized that she'd seen the same thing the few times she and her mother had dined at her grandmother's, back in the days before Arthur lost their money. But that didn't change the fact that Gloria found it difficult to talk about anything other than music.

"That's just it," James said. "They'll want to hear any little gems you tell them. They'd love to hear your story about the concert at Town Hall, about those idiots who were there to critique their colleague's playing. Remember the guy who said 'he plays like a pig'?"

"They'd like to hear that?" she asked. She couldn't believe those captains of industry and their well-dressed spouses would be interested in that sort of gossip.

"You forget the Murrays' friends are crazy about music and musicians. They like to hear the inside story. They want to feel part of something exciting yet refined," James said. "I ought to know. That's part of your charm for me."

He was joking, of course, and yet she found herself annoyed. There were times when she wondered if he understood what she really was, what hard work making music was. The guilt and worry and aching hands, the shoulders that cried out to relax, the sweat. The humiliation sometimes, too, when the notes would not come right.

"But you don't understand how hard it is for me to talk to people like that. If we sit next to each other, you can talk for both of us." After a moment, when he did not answer, she took his hand. "Besides, I want to be able to touch you now and then."

She expected those words to do the trick, but they didn't. "No," he said. "Couples don't sit next to each other at meals like this. I have to make conversation with my uncle's friends. You," — and here he turned his blue eyes toward her so intently that she thought his gaze would bore clear through her — "you should be talking to others. You want to make a good impression."

"A good impression?" She reached up with her other hand to touch his cheek. "Don't I always make a good impression?"

A shadow of a smile attempted to capture his face, but he looked away as he pushed her hand down. "Listen, my dear. Don't spoil it. Robert sent a note to his aunt, asking to make sure you had a chance to talk to McConnell, the newspaper publisher. Do I have to explain everything?"

"That old guy? He has 'lecher' written all over him."

"Just charm him. I'm here to protect you."

"Protect me?"

He said nothing.

"Protect me?" she repeated. And then many things that had been lying just beneath the surface clicked into place and she found herself saying things she didn't know she'd been thinking. What did he know about protection; she was the one who had to look out for herself; she'd been doing it for a long time. Just what had he done? Yes, just what had he done when she went to New York? He was the one who was supposed to be taking care of things, why hadn't he found out about the high school requirement? The boys had set her up, if you looked at it one way, set her up to be humiliated. She was aware that her voice echoed in the hallway, and that others could hear her, but she didn't care.

"You're making a scene," he said, and mumbled something about stupidity.

"Stupid? Are you calling me stupid?" She could hear just how shrill her voice had become, but she couldn't help herself.

He didn't answer and stalked away. After a moment she drew as much dignity as she could around her and went upstairs without daring to look to see who had been witness. Then when she was changing for dinner, the maid arrived with a note. James had left, he had things to do in the city that couldn't wait.

At dinner she and Pierre Boisvert, the other musician, were seated at the end of the room, alone, at a small separate table. He winked at her after Robert's great aunt indicated their places. "Where's your boyfriend?" he asked, whipping his napkin out so he could cover his trousers.

She didn't want to answer. "He had to go back."

"Beware of that guy," Pierre said, talking about the noise. "We're the hired help, and don't forget it."

She laughed. He didn't know anything about her and James. But he persisted. "I'm not kidding. He may have promised you the moon, but people like him feed off us. They pay us the way they pay for masses for their souls."

She didn't answer, she couldn't, so they sat in silence, eating, and looking around at the oak-panelled room with windows overlooking the hillside sloping down to the river. The waitresses brought the courses, the waiter filled their glasses, and when it was over, they all retired to the music room where Pierre sang Verdi, accompanied by Gloria, just as they did most evenings on the cruise ship where there was no pretense that they were anything but very talented pets.

The next morning, Sunday, Robert's great aunt was gracious, taking Gloria aside quietly to tell her that after the early afternoon concert their driver would take her and Pierre back to the ship. Then she smiled and said how much all the guests were looking forward to hearing them play.

Before then there was a short devotional concert in mid-morning, followed by lunch and then an hour or so of free time. It was Pierre who suggested they spend it by walking along the path behind the house toward a place where he said the view was truly magnificent.

The climb was so steep that Gloria was out of breath when they arrived at a bench at the edge of the wooded part of the slope. She wouldn't have said anything, but Pierre suggested they stop for a moment. The path continued into the shade, but at this point they were in the sun, looking down across the meadow and the St. Lawrence. The river was so wide here that the other side was barely visible. The air smelled of the hay cut by the farmers who leased three big fields from the Murrays.

Until then she had not paid much attention to Pierre. He was part of the decor, while she concentrated on her music, on her future, on what role James would play in it. But now she saw the way Pierre's shoulders moved under his navy blue jacket. His thick, light-brown hair touched his shirt collar as he bent forward to brush off the bench with his handkerchief, a blindingly white one.

She smoothed her skirt before she sat down. She was wearing her concert clothes: a long-sleeved black blouse and black skirt. They made her skin look pale and set off her hair, which, given the damp of the Charlevoix in summer, curled extravagantly — Pierre's word. Yes, extravagantly. She was so lovely, he said, that he could barely keep his mind on the music that morning.

His tone was light, but she knew there was truth in his words. She had felt his eyes on her while she played. Perhaps he had looked at her like that before, but she hadn't noticed.

"Come and sit," he said. She did, pretending not to worry that her black skirt might be dirtied by whatever remained on the bench. Cleaning concert clothes was a complicated matter. There was free laundry service on the ship, but she knew they could not expect the same care the paying customers were afforded as their due.

Pierre continued to stand, holding her hand and looking at her. He was tall. A picture of health too; ordinarily, she avoided singers because they were always worrying about their health, as if their bodies were as delicate as a Stradivarius or a concert grand. But Pierre seemed an exception; she had yet to hear him worry aloud about a draft and he walked quickly, as if he knew where he was going. No hesitation, little caution, much charisma.

SHE OPENED THE top button of her collar. The problem with black is that it absorbs the sun. She felt sweat begin to bead under her arms and across her back. She unbuttoned her blouse one more button.

Pierre said later that he loved the way her skin was creamy with just tint of pink underneath the pale surface. It meant blood rushing, heart beating, warmth.

She smiled at him. James wasn't there, so why shouldn't she?

"You didn't bring along anything to drink, did you?" she asked. She hadn't thought about the question in advance, but as soon as the words were out of her mouth, she knew she was also saying, *Take that, James. I don't want your frozen daiquiris and your sherry, I don't need you.*

She knew that Pierre, unlike James, didn't like polite drinks. He liked whisky, she'd seen him drinking with the dance band musicians on the ship. He'd invited her to join them the second evening out on the first cruise. She'd turned him down, because James was much on her mind and she knew what drink could do to people. But that was then; this afternoon she felt the need for something bracing.

"No ice, though," he said, sitting down and pulling the small flask from inside his jacket.

She laughed. "No matter," she said. "There is enough ice in this country during the winter. We should be glad it's summer."

He uncapped the flask and wiped the top off with his hand-kerchief. "No glasses either."

She reached out, and took a sip before replying, "Who cares?"

In the future, Gloria would remember this part of the afternoon and realize that whistles should have gone off. She could feel the way her cheeks flushed a little pinker almost immediately. She should have thought of her father. Pierre sat down beside her, and handed the flask to her again.

She took another sip, letting the liquid burn the inside of her mouth and her throat. She spluttered. He handed her his hand-kerchief, now mussed, and waited while she dabbed daintily at her mouth. When she'd finished, and held it out for him to take, he captured her hand and turned it over gently, palm side up, as James had. But, as she had already told herself, James was not here. It did not matter.

"With hands like this you can go a long way," Pierre said, rubbing his index finger lightly along the line where the hand joined the arm, where blood vessels showed blue beneath the skin. "It is the hand of an artist."

She shivered at his touch. He understood music the way James never would, and what she felt as Pierre lightly ran his finger over her skin, was a flutter that found an echo elsewhere in her body. Once or twice James made her feel a bit like that, but then they had always quarrelled because it was never satisfactory, never enough for her.

With Pierre, though, this was more than a meeting of finger and hand, flesh against flesh. She looked down, looked away from her hand and his hand as if what was going on there had no effect on her. "There is a chance that I could study in France, that the Murrays and their friends could help me," she began. "They helped you, didn't they?" She made her voice as matter-of-fact as possible. "Was it useful, to study abroad?"

"Anything that gives you experience, exposure, is useful," he said after considering a long moment, still stroking her hand. "Every little bit helps." He turned his head so he could smile at her. It was a beautiful smile, used in his publicity photos. "But it is a hard life, you know."

"But you love to sing still, don't you?" She was sure of his answer. She could not bear to think otherwise.

She watched his smile flicker a second, the way lights sometimes do during a storm. But then the smile came back. "Of course," he said. "Especially when you accompany me." He paused. "As much as I might love you."

James spoke of love, of her beauty, of her music. But there was something different here, the promise of a complicity that she would never find with James.

"There is a little gazebo in the woods I'd like to show you," Pierre said, standing and reaching out to her. She stood. When she took his hand, the electricity snapped between them. They had no idea of the future beyond the next half hour, but they hurried toward it.

THE ANSWERS HAD come back from Paris when she returned to Montreal: she had been accepted to work with the colleague of her teacher. Messiaen might agree to hear her too. She'd need money for passage and a small amount to cover her living expenses, but if that could be found, she should make arrangements to arrive by mid-September.

She called Robert to tell him. She didn't want to talk to James until he called her. Robert told her she was silly not to share the good news with him, that he'd been pining away since their fight. "And of course, we'll see about getting the money together. My aunt and uncle think you're lovely. They were disappointed when you and James quarrelled. They told him he was a fool to let you get away."

Perhaps. But there was now the problem of how Pierre would fit into the picture. Pierre had been explicit: this was an idyll on a lovely summer afternoon, nothing more. Neither of them could afford to become attached. "Your boyfriend will do you far more good than I," Pierre had said on the way back to the manor house.

When they were back on the cruise ship, it was business as usual. He joked with her, he slept with her twice, but he courted the women who sat in the front row when he sang.

What happened with Pierre was so much more than what had happened with James. James did not know what worked with a woman. Just as he only had a vague idea about what music was, even though he loved it, he assumed that because he was happy and fulfilled after their encounters, she was too. Nevertheless, here she was ready to go, and in need of James's help and that of his friends. She might have to pretend, pushing the memory of Pierre out of mind.

She found it relatively easy to avoid being alone with James. There was a lot to do as soon as her contract ended with the cruise ship. When she got back to Montreal she clung to him in public, but she had excuses when the possibility for intimacy presented itself. He did not press her, even the night before she sailed.

"I find I can't stop loving you," he said when he brought her home from the dinner Robert had arranged for them at Chez Pauzé. The night air was cool, so he had not put the top of the convertible down. He stopped the car on her street, but did not get out. She did not invite him in. She never had. He knew what kind of circumstances she and her mother lived in, but she did not want him to see for himself.

She looked at him, and waited.

"Is our understanding still in place?" he asked.

She thought of the help he had given her, the way that he — and Robert too, and Mike for a long while — had come to her aid. She could do nothing more than whisper "Yes." What would happen in France was in large part his doing and she should be grateful for it. "Thank you," she said, and she leaned over to embrace him. "You are so kind."

IN THE MORNING he was there, and so were her mother, Mrs. Meade, and her Polish piano teacher. The ocean liner was more impressive than the cruise ship, although she was glad she had a little seagoing experience. She was bowled over by the fruit basket sent by Lotte and the cards and notes of good wishes from the choirs she'd played for, and many of the musicians she'd accompanied. The Murrays sent flowers, and in her purse she had a money order that they and others had arranged. It was large enough — they thought — to cover her expenses for ten months. What would happen afterwards would depend. Her job was to study and play and write one letter a month, which would be circulated among the benefactors. James gave her a stack of forty postcards she was supposed to fill out and send each week. She cried when she saw them. She thought she had never been so excited or so happy.

AFTERWARDS SHE WONDERED if she should have suspected something when she became seasick before they'd passed the Saguenay. The truth didn't dawn on her until December. She didn't eat very well, which meant she was losing weight. That contributed to the delay. The money did not go as far as had been expected; she discovered that coffee and croissants could get her through the day, with a bowl of soup at a café for supper. There were shortages of this and that, but she didn't really notice because she was terribly afraid her money was going to run out. She walked forty-five minutes from the room she had on the top floor of a Haussmannian building on the northern edge of the Thirteenth District, where she could hear the railroad trains switching in the night and smell the dusty odour of the flour mills in the daytime, to her teacher's apartment near the Sorbonne. She saved car fare, and walking warmed her up enough so that she could move her fingers when it was time to practise. Thank goodness she had brought her Montreal winter coat, gloves, and boots; she felt for the young women who had to make do with clothes designed for warmer winters.

But by January the coat wouldn't button and she could no longer deny the evidence. The doctor at the clinic wasn't helpful. Her teacher studiously avoided noticing that anything might be amiss, unless it had to do with the progress she was making with Debussy and Ravel. There could be no appearance in a student recital at the end of the academic year. The baby would be born then. She poured herself into the music, practising and practising, reading scores, desperate to absorb as much as she could because she was sure there would never be a next time.

She'd sent weekly postcards back to James and wrote the letter full of news to the people who were paying for her studies. She dropped a note to her mother twice a month. She told the doctor at the clinic that she would be going back to Canada for the birth. He seemed relieved, told her she needed to eat more, and gave her a voucher to get vitamins from the *Mairie*.

In late February Mrs. Meade wrote that Gloria had to return home. Both her father and Lotte were not expected to live for longer than a few months, and Gloria owed it to them to come back. Gloria's mother hadn't wanted to say anything, but it wouldn't be right if Gloria didn't know. *Take the ticket they bought for you and change it for an earlier one,* she wrote. *You'll regret it if you don't.*

Gloria wrote back she would, that she'd be back by the middle of June, but not to tell her mother or James. She changed her ticket for the last week in March, and for a whole day allowed herself to think her problems were solved. As she walked home past the old buildings of the Pitié-Salpêtrière Hospital she started to cry. It wasn't until she stumbled on the curb — and a nursing sister caught her before she fell — that she saw with terrible clarity that she was going to have to find a place to have the baby. In Canada, near Montreal but not in it.

The sister wanted to know what her problem was, and so it was through her that letters were written and arrangements made for Gloria to give birth at the orphanage near Trois-Rivières, give the baby up, and then a few days later arrive in Montreal as if she'd taken a ship to Halifax and then continued on by train.

She only missed practising for ten days. She never saw her baby boy.

THE DEATHS FOLLOWED quickly; Gloria's father on May 10 and Lotte on May 12. For her father's funeral, they arrived at the cemetery about noon in three cars. The hearse came directly from the chapel at the veteran's hospital.

Gloria sat in front, next to James, who drove. Her mother and Mrs. Meade were in back.

"Too hot for black," her mother said as she opened the door and stepped out, not waiting for James to help her. She adjusted the veil on her small, black hat then smoothed her black gloves. "Too hot for May, in fact."

The memory of another hot afternoon when she wore black surged forward, but Gloria fought it back. As she stood in the sunshine, she felt perspiration run between her breasts. When she stepped forward the inside of her thighs stuck together above her stockings, held by the garters attached to the girdle she'd forced her flabby belly into. The waistband on the skirt stuck into her soft flesh and she began to feel cramps. She told herself she had no choice. If her mother saw how lax and stretched her body was, she would know immediately what had happened.

James touched Gloria's elbow and smiled at her. He might guess, which was one reason why Gloria knew she must be careful to avoid doing anything that he might take as an invitation. Since she arrived back, he been gentlemanly, apparently taking her coolness for evidence of just how deeply affected she was by the double sorrow. Fine, she thought; let him think that for as long as he can.

Gloria's Uncle Arthur drove the other car. In it were his wife and a cousin. The third car carried a man and a woman Gloria didn't know. There had been a half-dozen old men at the service, but none of them dared to leave the hospital. Perhaps they were concerned that a trip there would be merely a precursor of their own last one.

"He was gone too long and then he took too long to die," her mother said before the service began. Now she looked around, nodding to Arthur and his wife, but not saying anything to them. Gloria noticed that she turned quickly toward the sound of another car coming up the hill from the cemetery entrance. Then she frowned when it became clear that it would not turn toward the section dedicated to veterans.

As the men from the funeral home slid the coffin from the hearse and carried it to the waiting hole in the grass, she dabbed at her eyes underneath her veil. Gloria couldn't believe she was crying. "All my tears were spilled a long time ago," Gloria had heard her say to Mrs. Meade after the hospital called with the news that he had died. "Lots of tears, long ago."

James put his arm around Gloria's shoulders and Gloria knew he expected her to cry too, but she felt nothing except the heat. She watched the first shovels of earth dumped on the coffin, then turned away. The dull sound of earth hitting the coffin continued, but in the quiet here on Mount Royal, away from traffic, Gloria could also hear the droning of bees buzzing around the crabapple trees. Pink-white blossoms covered their branches. It was spring after all.

"A nice time of year to pass," Mrs. Meade said. "Gives you hope for the life everlasting."

No one appeared to hear. Gloria's mother opened her handbag and put her handkerchief away. She smiled at Gloria. "At least that's over," she said.

Gloria took a step forward, ready to turn away from the graveside, but her high heels had sunk into the grass, and she had to lift her leg awkwardly to free herself. James tried to steady her and she took his aid without a word. She saw when she glanced sideways at him that he was looking at her with concern. "Are you all right?" he whispered in her ear.

She nodded and pulled herself away from him. She began to wonder how she could tell him she didn't want to go out to dinner with him, as he had offered, that she wanted to leave Mrs. Meade and her mother as soon as they got back to the apartment and return to the Chopin étude she had started to work on. The music was waiting for her, she could lose herself in the effort of trying to make the instrument approach what she heard in her head when she read the score.

The sound of a car roaring up the incline intruded on the quiet. Gloria saw the eagerness with which her mother turned toward it, stepping away from the relatives. She seemed to have no trouble with soft grass, her high heels didn't hinder her stepping toward the future.

The car was a Lincoln town car, driven by a man in his fifties, with a full head of greying hair and a cigarette in his hand. When he stopped the car, he tossed the butt out the window before he opened the door. By then Gloria's mother was next to it, leaving Gloria and Mrs. Meade behind.

Brief introductions followed. The man was involved in advertising; Gloria recognized the name of the agency. Mrs. Meade stood beside James's car and waited for him to open the door for her. Gloria opened the door for herself, sat, and watched the town car with her mother in it pull away.

That was when she cried a little, tears she had not shed on the nights when she lay awake and waited for her mother to come home from work. Tears that had not come when she visited her father upon her return from France. Tears she had tried to control after the baby was born.

James was opening his door. She quickly wiped her eyes with her fingers. He saw what she was doing and took a handkerchief out of his breast pocket, as he had done when she met him, as Pierre had done. She looked quizzically at him. He smiled, reaching over to take her face between both his palms and turn it toward him. "Cry if you want to. I'm here to take care of you."

But she didn't want that; she told herself she couldn't. She kissed him lightly on the lips when they got back to the apartment. "No," she whispered. "I need to be alone." She followed Mrs. Meade upstairs without speaking, shutting the door to her mother's flat in the old woman's face.

The heat broke in the night with thunder and heavy rain. When Gloria awoke, she knew her mother hadn't come back, but also knew that there was nothing strange in that. Mrs. Meade knocked on the door when she was getting ready to go to Lotte's service, and she noted how the old woman looked for signs of her mother's presence.

"Just wanted to make sure you were all right, my dear," she said. "Such a stressful day yesterday, and you've got more today too. Would you like me to come with you?'" she asked.

Gloria laughed. "No thanks," she said. "I appreciate your concern, but I'm a big girl now. Remember I spent all that time on my own in Paris."

"But you didn't have such trouble there, I'm sure," Mrs. Meade said. "It is so good that you came back in time. That must be a comfort."

"Thank you for writing me," Gloria said. "But I must be going." She fled outside as soon as she could into the brilliant, rain-washed day, where high clouds scudded across the sky and the smell of unnamed flowers scented the air. She called James from the corner telephone and told him that this time she'd meet him in the cemetery.

It wasn't a long walk, but she had to stop about halfway up the slope. A stream flowed down from the cemetery, past a convent and a few elegant houses including a couple that were under construction. She was tempted to sit down on a pile of paving stones that had been unloaded in front of one half-built house, but she knew that her dress — not black, but a red one that Lotte had particularly liked — would be dirtied. And for this ceremony she wanted to look nice, in Lotte's memory.

The message from the nursing home said that the burial would be at two p.m. in the Jewish cemetery, next to the one where her father had been buried. Nothing about a service, which didn't surprise Gloria. She couldn't remember Lotte ever talking about religion or God. She'd never even been certain that Lotte had been Jewish, although the timing of her flight from Europe suggested that she'd been among the many who left because of the Nazis. Lotte had never said. Perhaps she found it too depressing to talk about. Certainly she preferred talking music to talking politics. And Gloria had been too focused or stupid or naive or self-centred — she didn't quite know what would be the right term — to wonder about what terrors Lotte might have faced.

Church bells at the base of the mountain began to chime

the hour, and Gloria realized she should hurry. A robin sang its clear, trilling, spring song. Lighter and happier than the church bells, it was music for Lotte. A taxi passed her, and she thought she saw inside her other teacher, the Pole. She had not seen him since she got back; she should have reported on her lessons in Paris, thanked him again for arranging for her to meet pianists there.

Later, she told herself. *I will do that later. But first I must go and pay my last respects to Lotte, who would have understood what happened and why I did what I did.*

James had parked his car outside the gates to the Jewish cemetery. He stood waiting by the wrought-iron fence. He didn't see her at first, so she was able to take stock of him without his awareness. He'd put on a little weight over her year away, and his hairline had begun to recede. But he stood erect and alert, still a young man, still full of energy that seemed completely unaffected by whatever he'd seen during the war, still full of hope. As he turned and saw her at the corner, she saw that clearly he was still full of love for her. His face turned joyous, and he raised his arms, ready to embrace her, even though she was half a block away.

Life would be easier if she loved him.

She smiled and waved, but then composed her face when she saw the little group of people gathered around what appeared to be a grave not far from the gate. The Pole had arrived. He stood, arms folded in front of his chest as if for protection. Next to him stood two men wearing yarmulkes, and three women who looked vaguely familiar to Gloria.

The drill was much the same as the day before, only there were no prayers. After the coffin was lowered into the grave, one of the men in yarmulkes turned to Gloria. "We spoke on the telephone, I believe," he said, taking her hand. "She was extremely fond of you, and at your convenience we must talk about your legacy. Will you be free to come to my office later this week?"

Legacy? Lotte had practically nothing. Gloria knew that whatever money she'd had had already been spent on her nursing care, that some of her bills toward the last had been paid by the same Jewish charity that seemed to have arranged her funeral. Gloria didn't know what to say, except, "Of course, of course, whenever would be convenient." And then she turned to James, who was ready to put his arms around her and lead her back to the car.

The Pole stopped her before she'd taken half a dozen steps. "Yes," he said, "she thought a great deal of you. You were her spiritual daughter. She said this when she wanted me to take you on. Be sure to talk to the man, he's got something for you that you will like." Then he bent over her hand, and almost clicked his heels like the Polish aristocrat he had once been.

James made the call to the man's office the next day because Gloria couldn't bring herself to pick up the telephone. The weather turned sultry again, and the emotion that she had been holding at bay pressed down on her. She struggled to breathe. She wanted no more than to hide in a darkened room and balance on the brink of tears. Her mother was somewhere in the Townships; she'd left a message with Mrs. Meade while Gloria was at Lotte's funeral. There was no one to bother her except James, who called every hour.

"No, I don't want any help," she said. "I just want to lie on the sofa and rest." Her voice wavered; she knew her tears would flood uncontrollably if she didn't get rid of him. "I need to be left alone." She let her voice drift off.

"You haven't started drinking?" he asked.

"Of course not," she said. "I'm exhausted and not at all ready to go out to face some old man in an office."

"You need all the help you can get," James said. "Don't you want to go back to France? Don't you want to continue working on your music? Look," he said, "I have no idea what this legacy might be, but you don't want to turn your nose up at any help and not to go would be an affront to Lotte's memory." His voice was stern, he sounded like a lawyer, he sounded like his father's son. "I thought you were more adult than that."

She could see in the mirror by the front door just how terrible she looked.

"I thought you were more adult than that," he repeated.

"Okay, make the appointment, I'll go."

WHEN SHE SAW the necklace, she was glad she'd worn the red scoop-necked dress again. The box the necklace came in sat on the lawyer's desk when she arrived. It was flat, and covered in maroon leather with a bright, gold-coloured clasp. The inside was lined with slightly darker maroon satin so that the brilliants dazzled as soon as the box was open.

Gloria gasped.

The lawyer held it up with both hands and smiled. "Frau Gruber's will says you should wear this frequently. It always brought her good luck." He moved the necklace back and forth slightly so that the stones danced. A flat band two stones deep made up the basic necklace, and three stone-studded filigree pendants hung from it.

James reached out to touch it. "The stones aren't real, are they?" he asked, while Gloria tried to remember if she'd ever seen Lotte wear it. Once, perhaps shortly after Gloria had started her lessons with her, and Lotte had given her complimentary tickets for a recital she gave in 1941, 1942? The hall in the Ritz-Carlton Hotel was full and because Gloria was late she had to sit in back. In the low light from the overhead spots, she remembered seeing sparkles surrounding Lotte as she swayed with the music she played.

The lawyer did not answer James directly. He smiled more broadly. "Are they real? That's not the question to ask. They're real something, of course. But no, I'm afraid their intrinsic value isn't high, it's more like they're real imitations." He handed the necklace to Gloria. "Try it on."

The clasp was complicated, and James had to help her with it, but when she looked at the little mirror the lawyer handed to her, she could see just how lovely it was.

"If the stones were diamonds you can be sure that Frau Gruber would not have ended her days as the beneficiary of the Jewish charities," the lawyer said. "It would have been sold long ago, and she would never have been able to leave it to her favourite pupil."

Gloria held her hair up and back: if she wore the necklace she'd do better to wear it in a chignon to show the necklace off properly. It would look even better against black concert clothes: it was just the thing to wear when she wanted to shine. She smiled at her reflection and then at the lawyer. "How wonderful of her to save it for me," she said. Then she caught James's eye, and saw his judgment reflected there before he said "Terrific."

"She kept it in a safe deposit box," the lawyer said. "I understand that she was always afraid it would be stolen, not because of its great value but because a thief might think he could sell it for a fortune. You probably ought to do the same."

"A very good idea," James said. "But if I remember correctly you said on the phone there were two things from Lotte."

The lawyer snapped the box shut and handed it to Gloria before he turned to the other papers on his desk. "The other legacy has some real worth. It is the piano that she brought with her when she came to Canada fifteen years ago. Do you remember it?" he asked Gloria. "For a long time it took up nearly all the space in her sitting room. That is, until she had to move to smaller quarters."

Gloria nodded. Yes, she remembered. At the very beginning there had been two pianos, a small one Lotte's students played on, and the grand piano — a seven-foot Bechstein.

"It has been in storage for several years, one of her admirers paid the fees for a while, but he died three years ago and now I'm afraid there's a bill of nearly two hundred dollars to pay. The new owner of the space is willing to keep it, but wants compensation. So you have a choice: pay the bill and take the piano, or renounce the gift, so the man can sell it."

Gloria's hand went to the necklace, and she felt her heart thump twice. There was no way she had that kind of money; it was more than the cost of passage back to France. "I remember the piano," she said. "I never played on it." She looked down, catching a glimpse of the brilliants in the necklace. "If I sold this," and she fingered the flashy pendants, "how much would you think I'd get?"

"Not nearly enough, I'm rather sure, even though there is a market for costume jewellery of this quality," the lawyer said. "But you could take it to a good store and get it appraised." He looked questioningly at James. "She doesn't have to make a decision today, although we'd like to get matters settled as soon as possible."

"And of course, the piano would have to be examined and repaired and certainly tuned," James said. "If no one has been playing it for years, it's bound to need work. That will cost." He pulled his small notebook from the breast pocket of his suit coat, and began to write. "Then there's the question of where you'd keep it." He smiled as he said it. Gloria knew he'd resume the talk about their understanding as soon as they were alone.

She touched the necklace again. "I can't make a decision today," she agreed. "There are too many things to consider. And I'm overwhelmed by the confidence that Lotte had in me, to leave me two of her most precious things."

The lawyer sat back and spread his arms out in front of him as if embracing the world. "She loved you and had great hopes for you," he said. "I'm pleased to be able to help."

"We all have great confidence in her," James said. He put his arm around her. "But you'll take the necklace with you now, Gloria, won't you?" He grinned at the lawyer. "I'll take her out to dinner."

"Do that, young man," the lawyer said. "There will be a few things to sign, acknowledging that you've taken the necklace. The rest can wait a few days."

Gloria was sitting at a desk in the outer office when Mike came through. She hadn't seen him since her return from Paris, and it was quite clear that James hadn't talked to him for a long time either. But Mike had heard about the bequest.

"Gloria, I can't wait to hear you play on Lotte's Bechstein," he said. "You'll keep me informed about your concerts, won't you? I want to be able to say one day that I knew you when."

"Of course she will," James started to say, but Mike cut him off.

"Your letters to all of us were greatly appreciated."

James looked at him sharply. "I didn't know you were on the list."

"Of course, he was," Gloria said. "Everybody who contributed to my study fund was. The letters were forwarded from one person to the next. Everybody knew who was next."

"I was the last on the list," Mike said. "Got the news a little late, but I got it." He laughed. "And I suspect I was the first to know about Lotte's will since she had me write it up for her when I had just joined the firm."

"You knew?" Gloria asked. "And you didn't say anything?"

"Tell her," Mike said to James. "She ought to know by now that lawyers have professional secrets. Privileged communication and all that." He grinned again at Gloria.."It won't do for beneficiaries to know what they'll get beforehand. Might be tempted to speed along the process."

"Hardly likely," James said, holding out his hand to Gloria, who had finished signing the papers. "Not our girl."

"No, indeed, not our sweet little girl," Mike said.

It was only after they were sitting in Chez Pauzé that Gloria remembered she should have asked about Mrs. Mike. Then she was glad that she hadn't, because to hear about a happy family and new babies from someone who thought she was so innocent would hurt.

SHE WENT TO see the Bechstein a week later. Summer-like weather had settled in for good, but the inside of the warehouse was still cool. The instrument was in the far corner, protected by a huge, rough wood box and wrapped in quilts inside. The owner supervised while a workman pried off the front end of the box and rolled the piano out so Gloria could take a look. James and Robert stood behind her, ready to give their opinion on the quality of the instrument. Gloria had her doubts about how much they could tell, and wondered — too late, she realized — that she should have asked a musician or a piano tuner to give an assessment. Her first reaction when she saw the shiny black lacquered surface was a delight even more intense than when she first saw the necklace. The instrument was made by C. Bechstein of Berlin at the beginning of the century; it was the best-made piano of its day.

A bench was supposed to go with the piano, but it wasn't immediately visible, so Robert found a couple of boxes nearby and manhandled them over for her. The warehouse owner looked annoyed, but Gloria was ready to play. "We tried to take good care of it," he said. "I know how much the old owner thought of you."

For just a second, Gloria hesitated. What should she play? Something Lotte had loved, certainly. One of the Germans, of course. Mendelssohn, the "Spinning Song." She'd given it to Gloria to play near the beginning of her lessons because it was so cheerful. Gloria could remember working on it and working on it, trying to get the rollicking rhythm right. The notes were still there, she just had to find them in corners of her brain as dusty as this warehouse.

But when she did, and she struck the first notes, she could hear immediately that there was no way she could play to Lotte's memory that day. At least half a dozen keys no longer sounded, and the notes that were produced were far from true. She stopped after a few bars and looked at the boys. Robert looked shocked and James was frowning.

"A lost cause?" Robert asked, looking around at the others.

"We tried to take good care of it," the warehouse owner repeated. "But it has been years."

"We'd need a piano expert to say," Gloria said. "I don't know, but to repair it will cost a lot, I'm sure." She looked down at her hands. "And I certainly don't have the money or any place to keep it. Particularly if I go back to Paris." She stood up and ran her hand lightly over the lacquered wood. She hadn't noticed before, but there were places where the finish was bubbled a little, water damage from a long time ago. "Given the shape it's in, I don't even know if selling it would fetch as much as the storage fees."

She smiled at the warehouse owner. "I'm sorry," she said. "I think I'm just going to have to leave it here, for you to do with what you want."

"Lotte would be disappointed," Robert said.

"Lotte had a lot of disappointments, not the least giving up this instrument which was really lovely," she said. "I remember," and she hesitated. "But she was someone who loved music, and the fact that she wanted me to have the piano shows just how much she believed in me. If I have to give it up in order to continue, she would understand."

Robert turned to James: "We could take up a collection ..."

"No," Gloria said. "The music and being able to play it well are what's important. A piano is only an *instrument*," she said, putting an emphasis on the word. "If you want to collect money, help me pay for more study in Paris. That's what Lotte really would want." She turned to flip the wooden keyboard cover back into place, and suddenly she found her eyes watering up. "It's the dust," she said, wiping them with her fingers as she stepped away from the piano. "Let's get out of here before I start to sneeze." Then, to the warehouse owner: "Do you have the papers I need to sign so you can try to sell it for the back rent?"

"We'll take care of that," James said. "Now, let's go get lunch someplace interesting."

Good, Gloria thought. I won't have to be alone with him, and as they left the warehouse, she linked her arms through both his and Robert's.

ROBERT WHO CAME to Gloria's rescue; kind, gentle, bumbling Robert, with the offer of another season on the cruise ships. He excused himself when they got to the restaurant, saying he had to make a few phone calls. Upon his return, he was beaming. "All right," he said, sitting down at the table where James and Gloria had already drunk half the bottle of champagne James had ordered. "You know how everybody loved you last summer, called you the musical angel, and all that? Well, I just gave *mon oncle* Hector a shout and he's arranged it all. You'll leave on the first cruise in June, and we'll see that when the summer is over you'll have sufficient funds for another year."

Gloria beamed. "Such good friends," she said. She fingered the necklace. "Lotte would be so pleased."

She felt light, restored, happier than she had been in months and months. She held out her glass for more.

James wanted to take her off that afternoon to some place private, but she hinted again that it wouldn't be a good time. He looked hurt and a little puzzled, but didn't push her. At the end of her first cruise, she acquiesced, but by then she could arrange things so he — a man whose experience with women wasn't vast — hadn't noticed a thing.

JAMES CAME TO Paris to visit her in May of the following year. She hadn't planned to go back to Canada that year; she had a series of concerts in small towns arranged by a friend of the

Pole, a woman who had turned impresario. If Gloria were careful with the proceeds, she'd have enough to stay in Paris another year, although she knew that this level of touring did not translate into much money. The woman behind the tours was quite clear about that. In fact, the reason she had gone into agenting was because there was more money in it for a musician of her calibre than there was playing on tour. But at least — and here she leaned over and tapped Gloria lightly on the forearm — she could launch some careers.

But the boys wanted Gloria to return to Montreal. James was on a mission. His firm had some business in Paris, and he'd campaigned for the assignment. There was something like the European small-town concert tours developing at home, he told her. Gilles Lefebvre and his friends had brought together several musical groups for the concert series, in Quebec and across Canada. James and Robert had assurances that Gloria would be a shoo-in for one of the touring spots. She'd be terrific, James said. When she didn't answer, he was ready to plead with her in person.

Gloria listened to James without reacting to his declarations, not even when he reached for her hand and brought it to his lips. She felt his eyes on her, but she looked straight ahead into the gathering night. She suspected she'd betray her disquiet at his touch if she looked at him, and she knew enough not to appear repulsed.

Birdsong bubbled up in the darkness; the song rose and fell, the notes tumbling over each other achingly.

"A blackbird," Gloria said. "Such a difference from the blackbirds at home. Did you know that Messiaen wrote a piece for flute based on it?" A response off-subject, but the best she could do.

Another blackbird called. The song was subtly different, obviously part of some long-enduring ornithological conversation linked to spring and love.

James listened. "It's lovely," he agreed. "But we have birds at home. We don't have you." He kissed her hand. "I miss you terribly," he said.

When the birdsong ended, the night was nearly silent except for the distant rumble of traffic. Above their heads, the sky was a pale blue. Something flashed green on the other side of the square: a cat's eyes.

James stood up. "Shoo," he said. He took a couple of rapid steps toward the animal. It scurried out of the park and across the street, where it disappeared through a high gate guarding another courtyard.

James turned back to Gloria. "Birds don't come around when cats prowl," he said. "All makers of music need protection."

She stood up and went to James, wrapped her arms around him, and burrowed her head against his chest. "Yes, they do," she said. Then she stepped back and looked at him. "I'll come back this time next year. You set things up for me, I'll do whatever you want to help, and then I'll come back. Everything is organized here for the next several months."

A YEAR LATER Gloria moved back to Montreal. Her mother had moved from their small apartment into a much bigger one in a building on Sherbrooke Street near the Museum of Fine Arts. She was engaged, she said, and her intended had invested money for her in real estate. "It wasn't much," she told Gloria, "but he's so smart and we've made a bundle."

Gloria thought that her mother's offer of a small rental in one of the buildings she now owned was a recipe for trouble.

The old upright piano had been sold while she was in Europe —
"It was just sitting there collecting dust," her mother excused
herself — and Gloria wanted a place big enough for a better
piano. She also wanted her privacy.

Robert came to her rescue. He, too, had put money into the
postwar construction boom and now owned two new apartment
blocks. If she wanted to take one of his apartments, he'd set the
rent so she could handle it. "That'll be my contribution to your
career. The only string attached is that you'll have to play for
me, and me alone, now and then." He winked at her. "James
here will just have to put up with that."

James laughed, but downed the rest of his brandy quickly.
They were sitting in Chez Pauzé again, finishing up dinner, and
going over the schedule that Jeunesse Musicale had set up, as
well as the plans for a New York concert. The Knickerbocker
music society had invited Gloria for the following spring,
and because the fee they were prepared to pay was laughable,
Robert's great-uncle had agreed to bankroll her expenses.

"But now I've got to take this lovely lady home," James
said. "She has to get up early tomorrow to practise at the
Conservatory."

"Ogre," Robert said. "I don't know how you put up with him."

When she bent over to give him a farewell kiss on both
cheeks, he held her hand just a little longer than necessary.

Strings. There were many but usually invisible. The apartment
was big enough for a grand piano and Gloria could pay for the
rental of a baby grand. The flat was larger than any she'd lived
in by herself; three rooms with a view of the side of the mountain. She had little furniture: a bed, a kitchen table, one chair,
and the piano. The lack of a sofa for a guest to sit meant that
she would continue to discourage all possible visitors.

When it came time for the tour she said quite firmly that she didn't want either James or Robert trying to follow her itinerary. "I've been on my own for a while now. I got around France last year by myself. I ought to be able to handle some train rides in Canada, for heaven's sake. Everything's set up, I just have to get to where they want me. The only thing that could go wrong is that the piano someplace is a dog, and there's absolutely nothing you could do in a case like that. It's up to me to make the best of it."

So she set off to hit a dozen towns on the Gaspé Peninsula, and after that La Tuque, Chicoutimi, and Alma north of the St. Lawrence, and then two dozen places in Northern Ontario, Manitoba, and Saskatchewan. She played crowd-pleasers: Chopin waltzes, a Liszt sonata, a piece by Vincent d'Indy for Canadian content, and Bach. The reviews were positive, she was interviewed on several radio stations, and by the time the tour ended in Toronto, she had attracted the attention of two agents who wanted to represent her. She chose the one who had connections in Canada as well as New York, and gleefully told James on the phone that the sky was the limit.

But three times during the tour she shared the bill with a singer. One of them was Pierre, called to fill in at the last minute for a concert in Saint-Boniface. The tenor who'd been scheduled to perform got laryngitis, and Pierre was in the city — his grandmother was dying.

Gloria was sympathetic when he told her. She tried to be cool, tried to make this picture of a dutiful grandson come to pay his last respects jibe with the man whose touch was electrifying. She knew she couldn't trust herself, that she should stay away from him. But she didn't. Early the next morning as he left her hotel room he told her that for them to be together would never be anything more than madness. It took all her strength not to make a scene, not to cry and carry on. The only positive outcome was the way she found she could touch that sadness when she played.

THERE WAS PLENTY of time to think about what lay ahead that winter, days when she sat on the train or in a small hotel room with her scores on her lap, and no piano to practise on. When she touched base back in Montreal, James was always overjoyed to see her. He didn't push, he handed her the mail that had come in her absence, told her how he'd had his secretary answer some of her letters, how he and Robert were looking forward to attending a few of the performances which had begun to fill up her calendar for the next year. In his eyes she read what he really wanted: the commitment to a date to get married.

On the train down to New York City for the Knickerbocker concert, she decided that when she returned to Montreal she'd marry James. He'd been patient long enough, and she owed him so much.

SHE PLAYED THE Fauré beautifully, she could feel it; she was not at all surprised that the audience rose to its feet and gave her a standing ovation. She stood in front of the hall of what had been a great New York mansion and felt bathed in glory. At the far end of the room she caught a glimpse of herself in an old mirror, and through some trick of light and aging surfaces, it seemed as if her head was encircled in brightness. *I must remember this*, she thought. *If I never play as well again, at least I'll have this memory.*

Pierre was there to congratulate her; he waited until the

effusive society members had presented their congratulations, until she'd been toasted with sparkling wine in the reception that followed, until she'd been asked if she could come again next year.

She was ready to agree to anything; she realized that there were few evenings when she would able to allow the river of music to carry her away so magically. When Pierre appeared at her side, she smiled and told him where she was staying when he asked. She was not at all surprised to see him sitting in the lobby when she arrived, escorted by Robert's uncle and aunt. She saw him watching her as she bid them a good evening, and she knew he was behind her when she waited for the elevator to take her up to her room. She did not turn around until they both had stepped inside and the doors were shut.

In the morning, after he'd gone, she told herself that this had to be the last time. She called James and told him her concert had been a wonder. She asked him to meet her train, she was missing him a lot.

He had a huge bouquet of red roses, ferns, and white orchids that must have cost a fortune. She knew as she took it from him that this was the sort of bouquet one kept, not one that was tossed out in the garbage the next day the way the standard posy was. She cradled the flowers and leaned forward to kiss him on the mouth. "Thank you," she said, and she meant it.

Once they were in the car, with her suitcase stowed in the trunk and the flowers laid on the back seat, he brought out something else: a large box from Birks. He handed it to her and then busied himself starting the car.

"Careful," he said. "It's breakable."

He didn't watch while she tore at the paper, but began to move the car away from the curb.

"Breakable," she said. "Sounds interesting." She shook the box inside the wrappings. Nothing sounded. "Not crystal bells or anything like that."

He laughed. "Getting close though," he said. He glanced over to see how she was progressing. "Take your time, there's more where that came from."

By then, Gloria had the box open and was struggling to pull out what was inside. It was wrapped in several layers of tissue paper. A vase, she thought. A crystal vase, big enough to hold the bouquet, the kind of thing she remembered seeing once when she and her mother went to visit her father's mother.

"Do you like it?" he asked. "My mother picked it out. She said it was just the thing that a young woman needed when she started out."

Gloria looked over at him. *Starting out what?* she wanted to ask. Not starting out a musical career. What would she need crystal vases for? But she didn't ask, because she knew this was a roundabout way toward something.

She was right. He was saying, "Look to see if there isn't something inside the vase."

She turned the vase upside down. She knew before she saw the small box what it was. A diamond solitaire, an engagement ring. The starting out would be starting out as James's wife.

She said nothing. Of course, that's what she'd meant when she called him from New York. This what he'd been wanting for a long time.

ROBERT WHISTLED WHEN he saw it on her hand. "A diamond as big as the Ritz," he said. "The boy does know how to do things."

Her mother told her to take it to the other carriage trade jewellery store, Mappins, to get it appraised. "Make sure it's the real thing," she warned her. "Remember how lovely that necklace is, the one your old teacher left you. You can't tell sometimes."

Then there was the question of the slight change the ring's weight made in her touch. She'd never worn a ring, and Lotte had been quite emphatic about not wearing jewellery on hands or arms during performances. "Distracting," she had said. "Can throw you off. If you want glamour, wear a necklace."

But this ring was a special case, and she knew James would be very disappointed if she did not wear it for concerts, particularly the next one she was scheduled to give in Montreal in a couple of weeks. That meant she would have to wear it constantly, practise more than usual, try to see if there was any difference in her reaction time, if her hands worked together in the same way. Making music, Lotte used to say, should seem effortless, and no listener should realize all the work that came before that ease.

The weight turned out not to be a problem. Gloria did a few extra finger exercises, working on the ring finger, left hand, to compensate. Nor did the feel of the band bother her after the first couple of hours of playing while wearing it. What did disturb was the way it looked. She hadn't realized just how much she looked at her hands — those familiar, intimate extensions of her deepest and most authentic being. Her teacher in France believed in regular practice with eyes blindfolded — it was supposed to make you concentrate more intently on the music — and, once Gloria had a score in her head, she found the exercise not difficult.

So she was surprised when her eyes kept returning to the ring on her finger. It glittered in whatever light there was, and when the sun shone on the keyboard the refractions danced around the room. There was no way for her to avoid them. On the third day, she closed the blinds in her living room to keep out excess light, even though it was hot and she wanted the window open to let in the air. When that didn't stop the distraction, she slipped the ring off and, feeling a little guilty, she worked on the most difficult part of the program with bare fingers.

James arrived at the apartment about six-thirty that evening to take her someplace "glacially air-conditioned" for dinner. She laughed when he said that, and didn't protest that she had so much work to prepare the Fauré for the concert a week away. The prospect of a little coolness at the end of the day gave her an additional spurt of energy and it was only when he buzzed the front door that she realized she hadn't put the ring back on. She felt in the pockets of the summer dress she wore to practise to see if she'd slipped the ring in there. But it wasn't, nor was it on the piano itself or on the shelf where she kept her scores. She tried to remember what she'd done with it this time, all the while listening for James's footsteps to turn the corner on the stairs and echo up to her apartment. It had rolled off the piano, she decided; she was down on her hands and knees, sweeping the floor with her hands when he knocked on the door.

"Just a second," she called. "I'll be right there." He'd been asking for a key, and she had been thinking that maybe he had a good claim on one now, but she was very glad that he wouldn't see her as she was. Could the ring have rolled into a crack in the floor? Had it ended up under the radiator, out of sight and out of reach? But, no, there was a glimmer coming from halfway across the room. She scrambled to her feet, swooped over to pick it up, and settled it on her finger by the time she opened the door for James.

"So pretty," he said after he'd taken her in his arms and kissed her. "Such lovely pink cheeks. You are completely ravishing."

She smiled; there was no way she would explain that her high colour had come from fear. "Let me change my dress," she said. "This one is all sweaty from practice."

He followed her to the bedroom door and stood, watching while she pulled out another cotton dress. He didn't step into the room; he still was hesitant enough in his status as fiancé not to enter without an invitation. But the sight of her stepping behind the closet door to put on a clean dress was a thrill he felt he could claim as a right. And to offer him compensation for the way she had been careless with his ring — not that she had any intention of telling him — she asked him to slide her zipper up.

He leaned forward and wrapped his arms around her. "Maybe I should just slip the zipper down now," he whispered in her ear. "Maybe we should just stay here."

She laughed, pulling herself out of his embrace. "No," she said. "You promised me air conditioning. It's just too bloody hot here."

"At the moment," he said. "Leave the windows wide open and maybe when we come back it will have cooled off a bit."

She nodded, although she didn't like the suggestion in his tone of physical entanglement later. "You do that, and I'll finish getting ready."

He took her hand and gave it a little squeeze. "Of course," he said. Then he folded her hand over his and brought it up so he could look admiringly at the ring. "Such a lovely hand, such a privilege to see my ring on it."

She wanted to pull her hand away. He wasn't going to own her. As they ate, she found herself thinking about his generosity and openness. She began to wonder if she could possibly spend a life with him without confessing at least part of the shadows in her own.

When they lingered over coffee — despite James's eagerness to get back to Gloria's apartment, he also appreciated the coolness of the restaurant — he inadvertently gave her an opening. "Robert's offered to do the marriage contract for us," he said. "I'm getting some stuff together so he can see just what my assets are and we can work out an equitable arrangement. You ought to make a list too."

Her first reaction was to laugh. "I'd forgotten about the marriage contract business. Is there really any need to have one? I haven't got anything valuable except Lotte's necklace and your ring. The piano I'm using doesn't belong to me. I know the law here requires a contract, but really, on my side it's just a formality."

"But you don't know everything about me. What if I have a family hidden away somewhere who might come forward when I die and try to claim what I have after I'm gone? With a contract, you're guaranteed certain things, no matter what."

"Oh come on, you don't have a secret life..." she began.

"I've told you all my secrets. The biggest one was about the Italian woman during the war."

Gloria remembered the conversation when they were beginning to plan out her career. She put her hands on the table, palms up. "And you said that I had a very long lifeline, and only one true love."

He picked up her hand again. "Did I say that? Well, if I remember what she told me, that's about what you've got in store for you." He traced the lifeline, then squeezed the hand shut the way he had done that other time. "One true love and two lesser ones, I'd say. But I'm no expert, and as long as I'm the true love I don't mind."

"You are," she said. And she put her free hand up to touch his cheek. "But there is something I must tell you."

He listened. She said nothing about meeting Pierre this last week, she didn't even mention his name, but in the briefest of outlines she told the story of the lost child. He didn't move while she spoke. He held her hand, and stared at some point halfway between them. When she finished — after no longer than five minutes, she kept to the bare facts — he sighed and covered his eyes.

In the background she could hear a recording of music from *South Pacific*, a song about meeting a stranger on some enchanted evening. The arrangement was full of strings, overplayed, over-blown, too much orchestration for what had been a rather nice song about a man finding a woman to love in circumstances that surprised him.

"Never let her go," James repeated the line from the song to himself. He reached in his pocket and pulled out a ten dollar bill that he dropped on the table. "I don't intend to," he said to Gloria. "But I've got to think this over." He rubbed his eyes again as he stood up. "No, now that I've found you, I don't want to let you go. But listen, take a cab home, and I'll call you in the morning. I've just got to let this sink in." He turned to summon the waiter, and did not look at her when she reached up to kiss him on his cheek.

"You are my one true love," she whispered. He didn't reply.

IT NEVER WAS clear exactly what happened. Robert arrived at ten a.m. when Gloria was practising the Fauré. Ordinarily she wouldn't have answered the buzzer because she didn't like to be interrupted once the work was going well, but she did this time, since she thought it might be James, come over to continue their conversation. She picked the engagement ring up from the little dish on the kitchen drain board where she'd put it this time for safekeeping, then pushed the buzzer to let him in. She turned the ring around, admiring the diamond, as she waited for James to climb the stairs.

But it was Robert who arrived. "Darling girl, I'm afraid I have some bad news for you. Let's sit down." He led her to the kitchen.

The accident had occurred in the small hours of the night on the road that curved along the north shore of the island of Montreal. James's car was found upside down in a ditch and burning. His body lay not far away where it had been thrown by the impact.

His death had probably been immediate. The police contacted his parents in Toronto. The super of the apartment house where James lived had no better idea of who might be next of kin.

"And they called me," Robert said. "I came over as soon as I could." He let the sentence hang in the air, watching Gloria's reaction.

She didn't say anything. Tears welled up in her eyes, but she wouldn't have been able to say just what she was crying over — poor, dear James, or herself, who had, she was absolutely certain, sent him to his death.

"Had he been drinking?" Robert asked gently. "Did you have a disagreement? The police wanted to know if he'd been depressed, and I said that, on the contrary, I'd never seen him in better spirits since you agreed to marry him."

"Had he been drinking?" she repeated because she wanted to say something, felt she had to say something. "No, no more than usual when he left me last night." And then she sobbed, because she knew she must tell at least a little bit. "But after that I don't know," she said. "Oh, Robert, I don't know what to say. Yes, we had a little disagreement. I don't want to tell you what it was about, it's none of your affair. He was not pleased."

"It will be all right. Don't worry. It will be all right."

Neither of them noticed the absurdity of his words, but Gloria remembered them the rest of her life.

She dedicated the Fauré concert to James's memory, and when it came time for an encore — the audience reaction was enthusiastic, how could it be otherwise? — she explained she was going to play a song from *South Pacific* that they'd heard that last evening. "I promised never to let him go ... and I won't," she said before she sat down to play. At the end the applause was deafening. She bowed once, wiped her tears away, and then allowed Robert to hustle her out of the hall and into his car. There was no party, no shaking hands, and no kisses. Just the silence of her apartment and the shadow hanging over her life.

James's parents kept their distance. They'd never approved of his relationship with Gloria. Underneath their sadness they were glad not to be entangled with a woman entertainer. There had been no wedding, no marriage contract, his will did not mention her. Whatever he possessed would go to his family unless she contested it, Robert said. But what was the point?

Her own mother had advice. He loved her, he had money, she should get something. "It's sad what happened," she added. "But men are like streetcars. There's one along every five minutes." Gloria laughed, not pointing out that streetcars were being replaced by buses, not saying that she'd never felt right wearing the ring. She put it in the satin-covered box that held

Lotte's necklace and hid the two pieces of jewellery at the top of her closet.

When the contracts came for two concerts the next fall in Toronto and Kingston, she asked Robert to help sort out the clauses. She threw herself into new repertoire. She never wanted to play Fauré again. The music was like a life raft on the great river. She could often forget everything; she was transported beyond the aching muscles in her hands and the aching heart in her chest.

It might have gone on like that, with a new season in prospect and a growing reputation as an excellent musician who was not only beautiful but courageous. Toward the end of July, however, the signs became unmistakable.

GLORIA INVITED ROBERT to come to visit her for a private concert as soon as she realized. She sent him a note, written on special paper she bought at Ogilvy's. *You once said that all you wanted from helping me was a small concert all for yourself. I think you mentioned that you were afraid James might be jealous, and he just laughed. Well, I know that he would be very pleased if I offered you that little recital now, because I can't think of any other way to thank you for all you have done for me since the accident.*

He sent flowers with his reply: a bouquet of roses and ivy so large that it didn't fit the crystal vase that James had given her. The accompanying note was short: *Yes! Whenever you like!*

Because she knew that time was pressing, she set the date for the following Sunday. They talked on the phone about what the program should be. Bach, of course, a Chopin étude, and the Debussy that she was preparing for the fall concert season.

"And would you mind if I brought a little supper for us too?" he asked.

She began to say that she was not equipped, that her apartment was more a studio than a home. He cut her off. "It'll be a little fancy picnic supper, really. Don't you worry about a thing, I'll borrow my mother's *fête champêtre* equipment. She has whatever we might need."

Gloria worried a little about getting Robert's mother involved at this point. It was bad enough that James's parents were relieved that they would no longer have to deal with her. Given what she was going to ask of Robert, she expected an even worse reaction from his family.

He arrived, as they'd agreed, about six p.m., laden down with goodies. Bringing the picnic hamper upstairs took one trip, while the transport of the wine and other drinkables took a second. Sweat was rolling down his face when he finished and he asked if she minded if he took a moment to wash his face. "And maybe take off my tie?" he asked. "If this were a concert in a hall, I wouldn't ask, it would be an insult to the performer, but given the circumstances maybe you'll forgive me."

Gloria laughed. "Don't worry, take off your shoes too. That'll maybe make up for the uncomfortable chair." She'd thought about trying to find something better than the straight-backed chair, but there was no easy way to do that. Besides, not having one might help her case.

The windows were open; outside, the shadows from the edge of Westmount had begun to gather on the hillside. In an hour it would begin to cool off, but Gloria had decided it would be best to play her program through before then. Afterwards they might relax in the beginning of the coolness, then, as they picnicked on the floor of the apartment, she would lay everything out for him.

In many respects Robert knew music better than James had; he had a more instinctive feeling for it, he could more easily allow himself to be carried off by it. Gloria had always known that, but she hadn't thought of the implications. As she played, she saw that he was touched by the pathos of the Chopin and moved by the Bach the way she liked to see her audiences react. He had brought scores with him, and held them on his lap like a very serious *mélomane*, but he didn't follow them. He let her carry him into the river of music. He was buoyed up by her effort, her intelligence, her skill. In between her selections she looked over to see him staring off into space, his good eye as unfocussed as the bad one; he was somewhere else.

James had always wanted to touch her when she practised; when she paused, he would stand behind her and knead her shoulders, which sometimes felt good, but more often was annoying. Now she realized with a pang that she'd never have to risk hurting his feelings by being cross about his touch again.

Robert was the very best sort of listener.

When she finished the last selection, the Rachmaninoff that he'd asked for, he didn't smile or applaud or thank her immediately. He just sat there, still wrapped in the music. She had to rise from the piano and come over to him, before he moved.

"Bravo," he said hoarsely. "I've never heard anything more beautiful." He stood up, looking around as if he didn't know what to do next. "Absolutely terrific." He clasped his hands tightly and rocked up on his toes. "What a pleasure. Thank you so much."

Gloria smiled at him. "I'm so glad it pleased you."

"Pleased me? Oh, you can't imagine ..." But then he seemed to remember that he had brought something to share with her too. "Oh, yes,'" he said, getting down on one knee to pull a small oriental carpet from one of the sacks he'd brought. "My mother insists you must have something like this to make a meal *al fresco* agreeable," he said, spreading it on the floor. Then he turned toward another sack — an insulated one — in which he'd stowed the champagne. Two flutes materialized from the picnic hamper while she wondered if there were something she should do to help. But when she took a step forward and knelt by the hamper, he waved her away. "No, no, darling girl. It's my turn to do something for you. That was simply wonderful."

First they toasted her playing and the memory of James. Then they ate what he'd brought — cold roast chicken, a green salad, potato salad, crusty bread, a raspberry tart, and a bottle of a white wine from Alsace. There were big, white linen napkins and a Thermos of coffee to finish things off.

He took her hand in his when they sat, leaning up against the wall and looking out the window at the night. "You have no idea how much this means to me." And he kissed her hand, holding it a moment longer than simple comradeship required.

"I am so glad you like the music," she said. "But I'm the one who should thank you for all you've done."

"Glad to help," he interrupted, dropping her hand as if he remembered that it might not be appropriate. He wiped his mouth with his napkin. "Anything to help you." The words were lost, but Gloria knew that moment had come.

"Actually," she said, "I was wondering if you could give me some advice. I'm badly in need of it."

He listened carefully. She made it simple. She'd learned her lesson with James. She made no mention of the first baby, nor did she mention the possibility that the baby she was carrying wasn't James's. There was no need to. He jumped to the conclusion, and to her pleased surprise she didn't have to suggest a course of action.

He looked at her, a whole range of emotions playing over his face, from shock to bewilderment to a slow, delighted grin.

"The answer is obvious," he said. He took her hands in his and held them tightly. "If you'll have me, we could get married."

She looked at him steadily. "You know what it would involve, don't you? People will talk, they'll figure it out, they might be quite cruel."

"Let them," he said. "What can they say that I haven't heard already? But you know I've loved you for nearly as long as James did, only I could never say so, not when he had a prior claim on you. Because I loved him too, in my own way; he was my best friend. I cannot think of a better thing to do than marry you and be a father to his child."

"Think it over," she said. "Remember: 'Marry in haste, repent at leisure.'"

"Darling girl, leisure with you has been my idea of heaven for longer than you can imagine."

SO IT WAS decided. The only argument they had as they worked out the details was whether they should tell James's parents about the baby. "He was their only son," Robert said the night they sat down to go over the marriage contract. "They ought to know that the line will not die out."

"Nonsense," Gloria said. "I mean, I can see how they might like to know. But we have to think of the child. It has to grow up believing that you are the father. You said yourself you wanted to be the father. Maybe, when it's older, when it's ready to start out in life on its own, we can tell it the true story. There will be people who'll put two and two together and always assume that's what happened. But let me tell you, I know what it's like not to have a father around, and I wouldn't want to wish that on this child. It deserves to be loved by you, to have you present to encourage it."

He picked up the contract, and pretended to look at its clauses, but when he looked back at her she could see the tears in his eyes. "Don't worry about that," he said. "I will be a very good father."

There were banns to be published, the contract to be filed, documents arranged so Gloria could add Murray to her professional name, a small reception to be organized. With the help of contacts in the Anglican diocese the wedding was set for the end of August, nine weeks after James's death. Not many of Robert's friends and family were in town as it was summer; they were at Métis-sur-Mer, or Tadoussac, or in the Laurentians. Robert's great aunt and uncle and aunt sent their regrets from Ste-Irénée. His mother had a gastric attack. The wedding party was tiny: Mike and Mrs. Mike, Gloria's mother and her intended. Gloria and Robert agreed this was good, as there'd be less gossip.

The one thing that remained to settle was the matter of sex.

Robert was a man of the world, of course. He was thirty-six, going on thirty-seven. He'd been in Paris shortly after the Liberation; he'd been swept along on that glorious wave of joy; he'd had his wartime adventures. The affair with the nurse he met at the field hospital when his eye was being treated was more serious. A girl from the Prairies — her pretty face was the first thing he saw when the bandages were taken off. No one had been sure he'd see again. The doctor and hospital personnel stood around holding their breath. It was clear then that the vision in his right eye was all but gone, never to return, but his left eye saw, taking in the nurse's blue eyes and curving mouth. That she smiled delightedly meant all the more to him when he saw his own face: he'd bear the scars for the rest of his life and he was ever after careful to have his picture taken from the left side. She liked his sense of humour too, and even though she was engaged to someone in the RCAF, they sought each other out until it was time for him to be shipped back to Canada.

In Montreal, he'd "played the field," as he explained to his mother, who always had a nice girl of good family to introduce to him. But partly because of his worry that his appearance put people off and also because he wanted sympathy from no man, woman, or child, he never trusted a woman who appeared to be attracted to him, a fact he had confided to no one except James.

He was in demand as an extra man at dinner parties, and more than once he was mentioned as "one of Montreal's most eligible bachelors" by the society columnist in *The Gazette*. But at the time of James's death, his name had yet to be linked with a woman in a serious fashion, and a rustle had begun to run through the legal community about his virility to the point a couple of nasty cracks had been made at his expense.

Gloria did not consciously consider Robert's reputation for lack of interest in sex when she invited him for the private concert with the idea of asking his counsel. But it was there in the back of her mind; if she had been asked to formulate what she was thinking, it would have been along the lines of a man who has done without is not likely to be demanding.

Later, much later, when her daughter Frances was pregnant the first time and Gloria had decided that a proper mother ought to read what people were thinking about pregnancy and motherhood, she found an explanation for what had happened next. It was all hormones, just hormones, that made the nipples of her breasts exquisitely sensitive so that on the first embarrassing night she spent with Robert she was astounded to be swept away when he touched them.

They were standing in the middle of the bedroom looking

over the lake of the house Robert's cousin had lent them. It wasn't a honeymoon, they both agreed. Too many things, especially the memory of James and his death, hung over their heads. Gloria, frankly, did not expect much. If their first sexual encounter could be got through with a minimum of mess and disgust, she would consider herself lucky, maybe even luckier than she deserved.

But after dinner in the little roadhouse in the village, and a celebratory brandy on the deck as the twilight gathered in the midsummer night, there was no avoiding it. Robert yawned, and she took the hint. She went inside and took her night-gown — a new white cloud of a gown that her mother had bought for her — into the bathroom. She showered and then, drying herself off, looked at her body in the full-length mirror on the door. It had been a while since she'd taken stock of herself that way; too much going on, a certain shame at what she had done with Pierre and to James, fear at what she might see. What belly she had developed from the first baby was gone and nothing from this one was showing, unless it was the fullness in her breasts, a slightly darker shadow around the nipples. Her shoulders were broad, her arms strong, her legs short but not badly proportioned. She did not look like a beauty contest winner; she was too old for that now.

"All right," she said aloud as she hung up the towel and pulled the nightgown over her head. "It's now or never."

Robert was still wearing his Bermuda shorts, but he'd tossed aside his shirt and espadrilles. He'd turned out the lights and pulled back the covers on the bed so that it looked like a white lake in the moonlight. When he saw her, he stopped unfastening his belt and gasped. "So beautiful," he said. "I never thought I'd see you like this."

She stepped toward him, because she had to, and he met her with his arms wide open. "Darling girl," he said before he kissed her, before he turned her slightly so he could cradle her left breast with his right hand.

The nipple tightened, she opened her mouth wider as the sensation shot through her, running to the centre of her being. So different from James, she found herself thinking amid the flurry of sensations. But Robert's free hand was sliding down her back, to the narrowing at her waist and then to the softness of her bottom. He pulled her to him, she felt his hardness, she allowed her legs to separate to fit around him. There was no turning back now; she realized that she was extremely lucky.

Oxytocin, Frances's daughter Julie said the one time Gloria dared to talk about sex with her granddaughter. "It's behind everything. That and pheromones," she said. "My boyfriend says it's not mysterious. He ought to know. That's what his company is doing research in. Oxytocin is what your body releases when you have an orgasm and when a baby nurses and a whole lot of other times. The pheromones we don't consciously perceive, but they're signals in the air, letting us know that someone is available." When Gloria looked puzzled, her granddaughter added, "Like the harmonics that make a chord affect us."

That conversation was decades in the future; Gloria had only the moment on her mind that night.

"Poor James," Robert said afterwards, moonlight pouring over their naked bodies. When Gloria kissed him once again, she felt his tears.

THEY RECEIVED SEVERAL invitations in early September, once the best people in Montreal returned to the city. By then they'd moved into a larger apartment in another building that Robert owned, one where there was a room for a piano and music and a couple of comfortable chairs where Robert and a friend might sit and listen to Gloria play.

Robert brought with him some furniture from his suite in his parents' house. He'd lived there since he came back, injured, from the war, and his mother had insisted there was no better place for him than there until he recovered. His recovery had taken the better part of a year, but he stayed on afterwards in the apartment above the garage in what had once been the chauffeur's digs. He could come and go as he pleased without being watched; James had teased that Robert found it far too comfortable to be cared for by his family's staff. Robert usually laughed, but he never denied it.

Yet Gloria could see that he'd been thinking of what he'd need to make his own *chez soi*. Within three days he'd organized a double bed, linens, towels, dishes, a handsome Art Deco table and chairs, pots and pans, bookshelves, chesterfield, two armchairs, drapes, and curtains. His large collection of engineering magazines and journals were packed up too. "My dream reading," he told her when she asked why a lawyer would want such technical stuff. "I should have gone back to university and become an engineer when the war was over, but I let my father talk me into joining the firm. And in the end, they're useful," he added as he moved the boxes from the living room into the room that would be his study. "It turns out there's a lot of work in hydroelectricity, and I'm the house specialist."

Gloria nodded, although she had very little idea of what he did all day. He was always busy. He went to court. Talked on the phone. Lunched with clients. Read legal briefs. But to what end? She realized that, after all the time she'd known him, she really didn't know anything about his work. And since her work was the core of her being, she also realized she should feel a little guilty for being so ignorant about what he considered important.

But he was continuing, getting another box to take in the other room. "Not everybody can do something that absolutely consumes them, the way you do. I just consider myself lucky to be able to help you." He put the box down on the floor and came over to hug her. "We're going to need some more shelving in here," he added. "You could store your music scores on the wall over there along with my journals."

Her music was the largest item that she brought with her, after the rented piano. Her clothes took up one whole closet, but most were for concerts. What she wore for everyday was as undistinguished as her collection of kitchen equipment. Her only truly beautiful possession was the crystal vase James had given her.

"You don't mind having that?" she asked Robert. "I'm sure he would want us to use it."

Robert nodded, and continued unpacking his boxes. "Put it in the back room, we'll decide where to store it later."

So she did, looking around the smallest room in the six-room flat. It had just been painted a pale yellow. Neither of them talked about what the room was intended for; it was hard enough to get accustomed to the idea of marriage, without making the leap into preparing for the baby.

Gloria was hungry all the time. She didn't suffer from nausea with this pregnancy. She had a well-equipped kitchen and an account at the nice grocery on St. Catherine that delivered. For once she found herself in a position where she didn't have to depend on boiled eggs and oatmeal. Not that she could cook much more than that, nor could Robert, but he knew which good restaurants would prepare meals for takeout. They ate in restaurants frequently; perhaps three nights a week that fall she'd meet him somewhere when he was finished at the office and she'd put in a full day practising. They were playing house and money wasn't a problem.

But their assumptions about how to live as a couple were different. Gloria's ideas were more than a little sketchy. Her mother had always been independent — not necessarily by choice — but that was about as far as it went. Robert's mother and the wives of Robert's friends, on the other hand, were all keepers of social lives whose importance was unquestioned. As an "extra man," Robert had been a coveted addition to many dinner parties, and he accepted the first invitation that came to them as a couple without consulting Gloria. A cousin — Oncle Hector's daughter — wanted to give a reception for them as soon as Montreal's social season returned after the summer.

Gloria didn't protest. She didn't know how to say no; she had no ready reason to decline. Her schedule was free of concerts for the moment; her agent had lined up a series of four concerts in October and a possible recording date in Toronto, but they were still weeks away. The cousin asked whom Gloria might like to invite, but she came up with only a dozen musical friends, as well as her mother and her uncle and aunt. She wasn't at all unhappy when her mother said she was going to Florida with her intended and so couldn't attend.

After the reception came a flurry of invitations. All the women who had been hoping to marry Robert off to one of their friends wanted to see close-up the person he chose on his own. Their husbands were also curious to meet her, because of the wary speculation concerning Robert's real interest in women. That she'd been formerly engaged to another well-placed lawyer who'd died tragically added spice to the mix. So did the fact that everyone knew she was making a name for herself as a musician of the highest calibre.

The fellow with whom Robert worked closest in the law firm and his wife organized a cocktail party for them. Another cousin and her husband had a small dinner, which Gloria feared would be as boring as the dinners at Robert's great uncle's estate nine years before. But she'd learned how to behave since then; she had more conversation, and she knew her position was less questionable than it had been when she'd been the entertainment on the cruise ships and, secondarily, James's sweetheart. Now she could talk about Paris and Lyon, the recital halls, the reconstruction of the French countryside, the ruins that remained in Germany. She was unable to name who led these countries or whether they were republics or kingdoms; but she had a fund of observations, stories about people who had hidden treasured instruments during the war, who'd helped transport stained glass from cathedrals to the countryside, pianists who continued to play even though they'd been mutilated by the Gestapo during the Occupation, music lovers who cried when they spoke of the joy they'd experienced when they heard a French or a Polish musician play on the BBC shortwave broadcasts.

She looked up after telling that last anecdote to the man on her right to discover that everyone was listening to her, and she realized that along the way she'd picked up the art of telling a story well. Goes with performing, she decided later, when Robert complimented her on the great impression she'd made with the guests.

The following week an invitation came to join three other couples for an evening at a supper club famous for its floor show. Robert had been there before with clients, Gloria's mother had talked about it more than once, but Gloria had never been in any place like it. It wasn't James's idea of a good time; he wanted to have dinner in a restaurant and then go elsewhere for a quiet evening.

"What's the show like?" she asked Robert, looking through the mail. Presents and cards of congratulation were still coming in from his circle of friends and family. The job of responding fell mostly to Gloria, but he wanted to know what, from whom, and when the gifts were received.

He took this invitation and read it again. "Don't know why she just didn't call," he said, "she's got plenty of other things to do besides write notes." He put it down and smiled at Gloria. "I'll telephone if you like, if you'd rather not call someone who doesn't really know you."

"That would be nice," she said. "I'm not sure just what we should say."

"Whatever you want is fine," he said. "It would be, well, politic to go, but we could find an excuse."

"What's the show like?"

"Oh, the usual: music and a girl singer, and a comedian, ending with their famous *tableaux vivants*."

"Which are?" She was stacking the mail into two piles, one for him and one for her. She looked up to see his face take on a slightly guarded look.

"A scene representing some idea or play or whatever, with people all artfully posed and wearing special costumes and looking very lovely, the women at least."

"So, it's theatre?"

The guarded expression turned more somber. "No. Not really. The whole point is not to talk or move, because if it's just a scene the actors can do things they couldn't do on a regular stage."

"Like?"

He didn't answer immediately and she saw a little panic rise in his eyes. "Well, wear less clothes, for example. Be practically nude, if you want the truth. Very artful, I assure you, but sometimes the scenes can be very suggestive."

"And your friends like to go there and stare?" She laughed. "I mean, are they looking for thrills they don't find elsewhere?"

She held his eyes with hers until he nodded. Then she laughed. "I expect it should be as interesting watching them as watching the show."

IT WAS AN occasion to wear one of the concert dresses made by Marthe, the young dressmaker her mother had introduced her to as soon as Robert's money allowed her to have clothes made to measure. She particularly liked the black dress with a halter top that would be cool on hot nights in halls without air conditioning. The skirt fell straight when she stood, but there was a pleat in back and a drape in the front that meant she could sit easily on stage. The little extra fabric also was fortuitous, she realized, because it allowed a little give at the waist, necessary now that she'd begun to grow rounder. Robert brought a scarlet gardenia home with him, and she pinned it in her hair.

"How's that," she asked, looking at her reflection in the mirror while he changed his shirt.

"Beautiful, as always." He finished tying a fresh tie and leaned in to give her a kiss on the cheek. "Take that red shawl with you too," he said. "We're showing off tonight. It's not you who's performing, so you needn't take a back seat to the music."

Interesting thought — one she hadn't considered before, she realized, as she sat in Robert's convertible and headed east in the early evening. When you are a musician, a really good musician, you are a conduit for the music, and no matter how big your ego, you are its servant. Now she was going to be simply a merrymaker in a pretty dress, a friend of the people who were calling the shots.

To get to the supper club, they had to cross the city from their apartment on the west side of the mountain to the east end, near the foot of the Jacques Cartier Bridge. Gloria wrapped a voluminous red silk scarf over her hair, Audrey Hepburn style, to keep it from blowing out of control in the wind flowing through the car.

"You need sunglasses," Robert said when he looked over at her as they waited for the light to change. "Everyone would think you were a film star."

She laughed. "But I'm on the way to being a star already. Just a star of a different kind."

The club had been built in the 1920s, when Montreal was full of jazz and booze. The mosaics of the lobby floor had worn under the thousands of footsteps, but the red velvet stage curtains were postwar, and the menu had been spruced up two years before as the owner tried to attract a wealthier crowd. Still the Lion d'Or had a reputation of being *louche*. Two tall women in short dresses stood on the corner, one posing with a lot of leg showing, the other with a hip jauntily pushed forward. Looking for business, Gloria thought. She wrapped the red shawl around her as they passed by, and she made a point of looking toward their friends who were already waiting for them at the entrance.

Inside the foyer, lined with posters and signed photographs of the celebrities who had played the hall, they were greeted by another young woman, this one wearing a black tuxedo jacket and shorts with a black satin stripe on the side. Her long legs were encased in black stockings with a lace-like figure woven into the sheer fabric. The garters holding up the stockings peeped out from underneath the shorts as she walked in front of them, the stockings' seams running straight up the backs of her legs, pointing toward a bottom that filled the shorts. Gloria saw one of the men nudge another while their wives pretended not to notice.

She'd met the others at least once, and the couple who had organized the evening had been at both parties given for them by Robert's connections. But Gloria couldn't remember anyone's name; she waded· blindly forward, ready to exchange kisses with the women and shake hands with the men. Then she found herself following the others into the darkened hall, a large rectangular space with a stage at one end, a massive elaborately carved wood bar along one side and a mezzanine on the other side. Their round table sat not far from the stage. The bluish light from the spots turned the white tablecloth a pale blue, and the tan faces of the women looked unhealthy. Their lipstick seemed to suck in the light, contesting darkly with their skin.

They had a round of drinks while waiting to be served, followed by two different wines, specially imported from France. It was served by special arrangement with the owner, even though it wasn't strictly legal. There were lots of things not quite legal about what went on places like the Lion d'Or. There was soup, tasteless and creamy, followed by big pieces of meat sliced from a tenderloin, which the place was famous for.

Gloria drank a martini before the meal and two glasses of wine with the dinner without thinking twice about it even though she was pregnant. Her granddaughter would be shocked to learn this, years later, but if anyone that night knew Gloria was expecting, no one would have commented. It was common to drink and smoke when pregnant.

The food and drink were not really what they'd come for; they would have had better in any of their households. As they talked and ate, a jazz trio played. Then, as they were finishing their meal, a girl singer and a saxophone joined the bassist, pianist, and drummer. The beat and the volume picked up, and it was clear that the music was for dancing.

"May I?" Robert's law partner asked, holding out his hand to Gloria. She shot a look at Robert. She'd never been much for dancing; there probably weren't more than a half-dozen times that she'd found herself in a situation where people were moving to music rather than letting the music move them. But Robert only laughed. "Of course, and I'd love to dance with your wife."

It was a painful experience. The man tried to hold her too tightly and the music was too loud for conversation. Even though she could keep complicated rhythms in her head and transfer them to her hands to create a web of sound, her feet had very little sense of movement. She tried to let the man lead her, as her mother had said she should, back in the days when she was thinking of the things a young woman should know how to do. But Gloria couldn't pay attention to what he wanted her to do because she found it artificial and uncomfortable.

Things were not helped when they had moved around the little dance floor to the other side, and she could better see who the musicians were. Their faces at first meant nothing to her, and she watched their hands instead of their expressions, willing herself into a kind of professional respect for other members of the guild.

Then she realized the pianist was the same one who'd been

on the cruise ship that first summer, the one who had sprained his hand in a drunken fall. He was nearly bald now, even though he couldn't be in his forties, and his face had gone puffy. But she could see that he still loved to play and she smiled at him when his glance came her way.

There might have been nothing more, but when the set was over and the group cleared out so the stage could be set up for the show, the *pièce de résistance*, she saw the pianist search the room for her and head over as soon as he spotted her.

Robert saw the man coming too, and whispered something to her that she didn't quite catch. She stood up and turned to greet the man. She'd forgotten how short he was, how his nose and cheeks were covered with a network of broken blood vessels, how his hands trembled when he wasn't banging the keys. She couldn't resist the warmth of his greeting, though; there were too many things mixed up in her memories of that summer.

"Gloria," he was saying. "I hear that you've become an international star. Concerts in Europe and New York, plus all over Canada. Who would have thunk it when you were filling in for me on the ship?" He turned to shake Robert's hand. Robert stood and smiled politely, although it was clear he had no idea who the man was. "You're Robert Murray, aren't you? Gloria and I go way back to when she was part of the talent on your uncle's cruise ships."

Robert nodded and smiled. The house lights dimmed once, but the heavy red velvet curtain across the stage remained closed. It was clear that this pause wasn't going to last long. "Would you like to join us?" he asked, looking around, searching for a chair. "I think the next act will start soon."

Gloria knew that this invitation was merely Robert's unceasing politeness, that the last thing he wanted was to include the pianist in this party of Montreal's young smart set. "Oh, we wouldn't want to keep you, I'm sure you're hoping to take a break outside, get something to eat before your next set," she said to the man. "Can you give me your telephone number? I'll call and we'll get together to talk about old times."

The man felt his jacket pockets with both hands. "No, don't seem to have a card on me," he said. "That's not good for a free-lance musician, is it? But look, check with the management here, they always know where to get in touch with me." He reached for Robert's hand again. "Nice to meet you," he said. And then he leaned forward to kiss Gloria on both cheeks. "Nice work on your part too," he said softly. "A musician always needs to have somebody ready to help pay the bills. Looks like you've hit the jackpot, dearie."

He turned and headed for the bar where the bartender had a double waiting for him, Gloria saw. When she turned back to the table, she felt everyone's eyes on her. "An old colleague," she said, sitting down.

"What a glamorous life it must be," the woman sitting nearest said. "Meeting all those celebrities and entertainers."

"And late nights, don't forget the late nights," her companion said. "That's what you'd really like, having a good excuse not to get up in the morning."

The woman made a little pouty face and then turned to put a finger on the man's lips. "Ah yes, not getting up in the morn-ing. What I'd give not to have a little voice calling for me at six a.m. every day."

"Not that you have to get up then. Matilda gives him break-fast, and you don't have to stir yourself until noon."

"Shhh," the man across the table said. "Have your little tiff later. The show's about to start."

GLORIA HAD BEEN to perhaps three art exhibitions in her travels. Even in Paris, she never summoned the energy to trek to the Louvre. She only knew about the great works of art through pictures in magazines. "No time," she said to Robert when he was surprised at how delighted she was when he found a book of paintings featuring pianists. "I know they're there, but I was just too busy making music to go looking for pictures of people making it."

But when the curtain went up she guessed that what she was seeing was a depiction of a work of art considered to be famous, partly because the audience let out a collective sigh, as if recognizing something known and admired. To make the point, a little man wearing a beret and a painter's smock stood to one side painting at an easel.

The background was a forest with green grass in the foreground and a picnic lunch nearby. Two men, fully dressed in business suits, appeared to be deeply involved in conversation. Neither was looking at the nude woman sitting next to them, her silhouette turned to the audience, one arm not quite hiding her breasts, her gaze coolly aimed outward.

No one moved during the half a minute they were treated to the tableau, not on stage and not in the audience. The young woman had extremely lovely skin, Gloria recognized. The men looked a little seedy, but she was sure she wasn't supposed to pay attention to them.

Applause broke out and continued until the curtain went down.

"The picture caused a sensation when it was first shown," Robert whispered in her ear. She nodded because she wasn't quite sure what her reaction should be. Offstage the little musical group played a jaunty song that Gloria recognized as a French music hall favourite.

The next tableau showed a woman standing in the middle of a field with three others around her, each holding the end of a garland of flowers. The little painter was closer to them this time, and he made a show of measuring their dimensions and running back to his easel to make changes on the picture he was supposedly painting.

More applause, more music after the curtain went down, some cuddling between couples in the audience. Even Robert slipped his arm around the back of Gloria's chair.

The third time the curtain went up, the tension went up a notch. There were two nude women this time, in chains, lying as if draped over boulders. Each was being guarded by a well-built young man, whose interest in the lovely female forms was graphically evident. The little artist approached the tableau with an amazed look on his face, and pointed to the erections clearly visible beneath the men's togas, just in case any of the spectators missed them. There was wave of male guffaws, and then an echoing trill of female titters.

"How could they?" the woman sitting next to Gloria whispered. "I mean, you'd think a woman would be ashamed. All those people watching. I can't imagine ..."

Gloria also was shocked, but she could imagine. Part of it had to be the thrill of being admired, of being the centre of attention, and that was part of the pleasure of being a pianist. They were on display, as was she when she performed. Dozens of pairs of eyes were exciting, no doubt about it.

The excitement in the air grew with the following tableaux. Each was more graphic than the last, each featured lovely, naked women and men sliding closer and closer to sexual intimacy on stage. It was as if the temperature in the hall had risen ten degrees by the end of the show. Gloria was sweating and Robert's arm held her close. The other couples had moved nearer to each other. She saw that the woman next to her had shifted her position so that her legs were slightly apart and her husband's hand was thrust underneath her skirt. Applause, when it came, was thunderous, but obviously it took a few seconds for the spectators to snap out of their spell before they could move.

When the show was over, Gloria stood up with the others, but she did not speak when the couple who had organized the evening asked if everyone would like to come back to their house for a nightcap. "We'd hate to think that anyone went to bed tonight without being completely satisfied," the man said. "We might even try our hand at a few tableaux ourselves." His wife smiled broadly.

Robert looked at his watch. It was only eleven p.m. on a Saturday night; there was no good reason they couldn't party later. He seemed to be searching for what to say. Gloria had had enough of people who gawked at naked bodies and then wanted to play a little sexual game or two. She knew that if for any reason she took off her clothes, her round belly would give her away, and she had no desire to announce that she was pregnant in front of this crowd.

"We must get up early tomorrow," she said. "Robert has a million things to do to prepare for next week, and I'm supposed to work on a new program." She decided to smile. "No rest for the wicked, you know."

Indeed. The others wouldn't rest soon either, she was sure.

"Oh come on, Robbie, don't be a wet blanket," the man who organized the evening said. "Don't let her spoil your fun."

Robert stood silent for a second, before smiling himself. "Oh, don't you worry. We'll have some fun, you know these young brides," he said, and he winked so that everyone might draw lascivious conclusions about what Gloria wanted.

She did not particularly like the impression he was leaving, but she decided it would be better not to protest. So they went through the motions of bidding farewell. Gloria was presented with the cheeks of the women to kiss, and all three men hugged her tight. Robert shook hands with the men, pounded them on the back, then leaned in to kiss the women.

They drove in silence back to their apartment. It was a lovely night, with a hint of fall in the air, and Gloria wished she had something heavier than a shawl with her. When they got back, she fished out a winter nightgown from the bottom of her drawer and pulled it on while Robert was in the bathroom. She crawled in bed before he was ready and turned away from his side. He tried to throw back the covers so they could lie unencumbered side by side, ready for intimacy of their own. But she wouldn't let him. "I'm cold," she said, pulling the blankets tighter and curling up in a self-protecting ball.

He said nothing, although after a moment he kissed the nape of her neck before settling down himself.

THEY DIDN'T TALK about the evening for several days, until Gloria received a call from one of the wives who wanted to gossip a bit about the evening and proposed meeting for lunch on Friday.

"I said no," Gloria told Robert when they met for dinner at Chez Pauzé. "I mean, doesn't she have other things to do?"

"You were polite, I hope," Robert cut in. "Her husband is important."

"Of course I was polite. I'm always polite. A musician at my level must always be polite. But I have more important things to do than spend three hours sitting in a restaurant in the middle of the day talking about people getting their kicks watching imitation sex."

"You don't have to do that, you can make excuses. All she was trying to do was be friendly. You should be flattered."

"She asked about my mother too. She knows all about me, and my crazy family. My uncle who lost all his money. My drunken, misfit father. She's guessed about me being pregnant too. She wanted to know when you and I were starting a family. She said your father can't wait to have another generation carry on the family tradition. She told me you were engaged to somebody ten years ago. I didn't know that."

He laughed, trying to smooth over her rising annoyance. "Not engaged. She's got that wrong. But you only talked to her on the phone for a little? She certainly covered a lot of ground."

"She hasn't got anything else to do; she's very proficient in dishing the dirt. But really, Robert, I don't have time to put up with that sort of stuff. There was a call from my agent too. PolyGram is serious about producing that record."

He reached over and grabbed her hand. "They're serious? Why didn't you say that to begin with? Now that's real news."

That part of the conversation led to a discussion of what was going to happen to them over the next few months. Robert was slated to spend time in Shawinigan. A hole, he said. Much was going on with the power companies. Gloria had five concerts in December and January, plus the recording sometime after the first of the year. Her agent was talking about more touring in the spring. They got out a calendar and started to set out dates. Robert might be able to go with her if she performed in Vancouver in early March. They could make it a belated honeymoon, they could spend time in some romantic little place with a view of the ocean.

And then they remembered why they were together in the first place, and both of them grew quiet because neither wanted to contemplate what it meant.

"So when do you figure?" Robert finally asked. She'd told him, but he never could remember.

"April," she said, and she shivered, remembering that other April. She might have told him about it then, because she felt so close to him at that moment, so sure that they were in accord. But he spread her hand out in front of him the way that James had done and ran his finger down the lines on the palm. No, she couldn't risk it.

"We'll have to work some things out," he said. "You have to do what you want, even if I couldn't." Then he folded her hand in on itself so it formed a fist. "You're right, you can't waste your time."

THE CONCERT IN Vancouver had to be cancelled. She'd be too far along to travel by air, and five days on the train across the continent was crazy. Pregnant women simply were not seen in public very much in the 1950s. "So, where did women hide?" Frances scoffed when her mother told her about the stratagems she went through to avoid appearing to be expecting. "What was the birth rate back then? Twenty for every thousand people? There must have been big bellies everywhere."

There were, but school teachers had to quit as soon as they began to show. Dr. Spock, accused of spoiling generations of North American children, advised women to take it easy during their pregnancies, suggesting that beginning in the sixth month a nap every afternoon was essential.

Try doing that when you're a woman with a career. Frances worked until three weeks before her due date with all three of her kids in the 1980s. After each birth, she took off no more than four months before returning to the office full-time.

A pianist doesn't take time off. Practice continues even when she must stretch around her belly to reach the keyboard. Performance is something else. By November, Gloria was wearing a flowing robe for concerts, a dress that she had Marthe copy from a painting of a pianist in the book Robert had found. They decided make a formal announcement about the baby early in the new year.

"Let people count on their fingers when it's born," Robert said. "In the meantime, keep them guessing." Gloria laughed. It was much, much easier this time. She almost enjoyed the sensation of sharing her body with someone else; she almost forgot to worry about the baby not looking like James.

Thank goodness for PolyGram. No one would see what she looked like when she recorded the Debussy and Ravel. She was sure the technicians sniggered when she had trouble adjusting the piano bench. But they didn't count. The producer liked what he heard through his headset in the control booth. The pieces she was playing had been recorded in Europe since the war by various artists, but no one so far had produced high fidelity versions. PolyGram was particularly proud of this new series of long-playing vinyl disks. While both she and the producer tried to keep the line of the music going during the session, it was rather comforting to know that the recording engineers could cut away small errors and splice in better renditions from another take.

About halfway through the week of recording, her agent called with an added bit of recording-related excitement. The National Film Board of Canada wanted some Debussy played for a feature film they were producing. Called *Photos*, it would feature both English and French actors, and very little dialogue, in a mystery set on the Montreal waterfront. The NFB had a small stable of composers working for it, but the music for this project had got shuffled off the schedule for some reason, so the producers were looking for something appropriate that could be patched in more or less as is. Debussy's "The Girl with the Flaxen Hair," which Gloria had just recorded, was exactly what was needed. The fact that a Canadian pianist had a new recording of it would get around the bureaucratic hurdles to using music not composed especially for the film.

The film came out the week after the baby was born. Gloria and Robert went to see it as their first post-baby outing a month later. The theatre was nearly empty and Robert teased Gloria about making music for a movie that nobody was going to see. But when it was screened at the Berlin Film Festival in early summer it won two prizes, an international film critics' award for its director, and a special award for the music. PolyGram put out a single of "The Girl with the Flaxen Hair," which became the first classical recording to go gold in years, and Gloria was interviewed by the CBC and the major Canadian newspapers.

"So there," she said to Robert after *The Gazette*'s photographer left. "A movie that nobody would see, did you say?"

"I was wrong," he said. "I admit it. But then, darling girl, you wouldn't like me to be infallible, would you? I'm not the Pope, after all." He took the baby from the nurse who was ready to put the child down for a nap. "The only perfect thing around here is Frances, as well you know."

That was the name they settled on after much discussion. Frances, after one of Robert's favourite aunts with Lotte and James as middle names. "Tongues are going to wag, are already wagging about who her father really is," Robert said after he had worn down Gloria's initial opposition. "We won't say anything. We just have our own tribute to our very dear friend."

Gloria said no more and looked at the small being, wondering who she might end up looking like. Light hair and eyes to begin with, at least. Gloria gave a private sigh of relief that all three men in her life had light eyes. James had dark hair, but so did several people in Robert's family. The birth had not been difficult, much easier than her first. This time everything went quicker; she had asked for something for the pain, but before they could give it to her, the baby was on its way.

"This is not your first child," she remembered the nurse saying. Not a question, a statement. How did she know? Gloria was not sure, but she nodded.

But this baby was different from the first, even if not as special as Robert was convinced she was. She deserved the best, and he was persuaded by his mother to engage a nurse highly recommended by friends in Upper Westmount.

"Of course, everyone should have a baby nurse," Gloria's mother said when she came to visit the first time. She'd been in Florida again in the spring and hadn't been around when her granddaughter was born. But that was all right, she told Gloria; she wouldn't be any help, as she never really understood babies. It was a very good that Robert's mother had found such a pearl to help out.

"Of course, everyone should have a nurse," she repeated. "Of course. I wish I'd had one." She bit the hangnail on her right index finger; Gloria hadn't seen her do that before. It was an observation that she put aside to consider later.

She decided to do the same with Mrs. Meade's reaction. "A baby nurse!" she exclaimed when she came to visit and the nurse brought Frances out for her to see. "Now aren't you the one! You seem to have done pretty well for yourself." She took the baby and held her gingerly. "I always got along with children better when they were older. Remember all the times I took care of you, Gloria?"

"Of course," Gloria said. How could she not? Those evenings when her mother had to work, those boring afternoons in the park. This child was not going to have to go through that. Not with Robert as her father, not with family money to buy the necessities of life.

Robert took a week before he got up enough courage to hold the baby. The nurse was right beside him, ready to take Frances should anything look out of sorts. He grinned at Gloria, ignoring the woman. "Just look at her, she's quite happy," he said with obvious delight. "She doesn't seem to mind at all."

Delight was not what Gloria felt about this baby, though. She felt as little as possible. Feeding Frances a bottle the second week, she realized she could hand her back to the nurse, to Robert, to her mother-in-law, to her mother even, and not care if the child disappeared from the face of the earth. Oh, she would go through the motions, carry the child around, present her with smiles to their friends, do what was necessary. But she could not imagine focusing all her energy on this small being.

She did not say this to Robert, Robert who proudly said he was gaga over the little mite. She looked at him, holding Frances, getting her tiny hand to wrap around his forefinger and smile. He crooned tunelessly to her. Gloria felt gratitude. Nothing more. Robert was a good man, she'd always known that, but his adoration of a baby not his own was the proof that he operated on a different level than she did.

Perhaps she had an excuse; perhaps something inside had

been stunted because she'd been forced to abandon that first baby. She didn't like the idea; it came accompanied by a dark-red, horrifying wave of regret. "What could I have done differently?" she found herself saying aloud a half-dozen times when she was alone with Frances. But she was careful not to say things like that when the baby nurse was around because the woman already seemed disapproving.

Gloria would pretend she loved this child. She'd pretended a lot in the past — she could continue. The child deserved it. She had done nothing; she could not help it if her mother had a dead spot in her heart.

No one said what a beautiful baby she was. Not that many babies are anything but miniatures of Winston Churchill, but Frances was particularly unappealing, Gloria thought. It would be easier if she'd been born with lots of hair or if she started smiling early.

No baby smiles before a couple of months, Frances told Gloria years later when Frances's own first child stared stolidly at the world and Gloria said he looked angry. Gloria made no further comment because anything she said then would be considered the wrong thing by Frances, who was determined to do things right.

But Frances as a baby was indeed homely. Her skin was blotchy, her hair was sparse, fading away to nothing in back where her head rubbed against the bed. She was plump, which was probably all to the good. But her face got red when she cried and she cried frequently. Gloria tried several times to rock her into a better mood, tried walking around with her, because that was what mothers were supposed to do. But it didn't work. Only the firm, authoritative touch of the baby nurse or Robert's bouncing cuddle could quiet the child.

Then, about three months after the birth, the family went up to Bic, and settled for several weeks in the big house on the shore that belonged to Robert's youngest aunts. The others, including the nurse, had gone into the village to get provisions and Gloria was left with the baby for the long, hot afternoon. The air was still, as it often is when heat covers the interior of the continent and spills out down the long, wide St. Lawrence Valley.

Because the baby cried when she woke up from her nap, Gloria carried her outside to the swing on the front gallery. At that hour it was shaded and she hoped they might feel a little breeze off the water. The tide was about to turn, and often when the water began running in, the winds shifted too.

The baby, wrapped in a light flannel blanket, began to fuss. "You're too hot," Gloria said, shifting Frances in her arms and pushing the cover aside so the baby's legs and arms were uncovered. "Are you ready for something to drink?" The bottle, filled with formula made that morning by Robert's aunt, sat on the low table in front of her. She shifted the baby again so she could lean forward and pick up the bottle. As she did she bumped Frances's head against the arm of the chair — not hard, but enough, she knew, to be felt.

For a second she watched the baby's eyes grow wide as what happened registered somewhere in the small round head. The eyes narrowed, and the rest of her face crinkled in distress. Her mouth opened and she began to cry more loudly.

"Shh, shh," Gloria said, rocking her body back and forth, trying to quiet the child. "Shhhh, it's nothing at all." A little knock shouldn't do any damage; babies couldn't remember pain afterwards, could they?

There had been nights when the baby cried, particularly

at the beginning, but the nurse had taken care of that. Robert twice hovered outside the door to the nursery, wanting to go in, ready to offer help. But both of them had decided that the woman knew far more than they did, and it would be better to let her handle it. Since then Frances had rarely cried for any length of time, even here at Bic. When the nurse was off, Robert or his aunts were there to pick the baby up. This was, Gloria realized, the first time she'd been alone with the baby. She could count on no help in comforting her.

Gloria ran her hand over the baby's head, wondering if there had been some serious damage. She felt no dents, no bulges, just the shuddering of the little body as the baby gulped for air between sobs. "Shhhh," she said again. "Shhh."

She stood up and began to sway back and forth, hoping that the motion would be soothing. "Shhh," she repeated. "Shhhh." She tried to remember a lullaby, a nursery song, something that might calm the child. The music that rose in her heart was what she'd been working on that morning, Chopin's Étude No. 3, Opus 10. Not what a baby might want to listen to.

But she decided to try. She la-la-la'd her way through the first several measures of the rather melancholy melody that runs within the chords played by the right hand. She had never been a good singer — Lotte had despaired — but as she sang, she noticed that the child quieted. She swayed more, being careful to hold the baby's head steady when the music swooped and she moved along with it.

The sobbing stopped after a few seconds. She felt the baby sigh and relax against her, the little head resting on the slope of her breast. A breeze, no more than a small breath of cooler air, brushed past them. The leaves began to rustle. She put her cheek on the top of the baby's head and smelled the mixture of baby powder and fresh air that emanated from the child. Through the baby's soft cotton shirt, she felt the taut smooth body underneath. She sighed too, and stood still. The melody repeated itself in her head, until she found herself humming it into the baby's ear.

The child stirred, moving its head slightly, pushing back against her hand. She allowed the baby to move until she could see the small, solemn face tipped up toward her. Frances's eyes looked into hers and for a moment there was contact: the child saw her mother. Gloria saw her child. The possibility of something more appeared.

II

"NO," GLORIA, SAID, "I DON'T want to." The window in the dining room looking over the apartment building's inner courtyard was open and a warm breeze stirred the curtain. They'd made it through a difficult winter. Robert had spent much time trying to make up for the fact that he had no technical education even though he'd been pegged by the law firm as their hydroelectric expert, while Gloria struggled with preparing for the Debussy recording PolyGram had signed her for after the success of her first record. The baby nurse was gone, but now they had a live-in housekeeper, a woman from Gaspé whose French was common, according to Robert's mother, but who seemed clean and competent and, most importantly, was willing to live in for six days of the week.

The smell of lilacs floated in from the gardens of the neighbouring buildings, the traffic noises were far away. On the table the second bottle of wine was half empty. Friday night, a moment when, supposedly, they could talk about what really mattered.

That was Robert's idea. But they didn't succeed in having these conversations very often. In principle Madame Beaudry took Sunday off, but often she had a very good reason for leaving for the whole weekend beginning on Friday night. Robert's mother said that Gloria was a pushover for Madame Beaudry's tales of nieces in the hospital or her own asthma attacks.

"But I know what that kind of thing can be like," Gloria told Robert. "I don't know how many times my mother had to scramble to find someone to look after me until she arranged things with Mrs. Meade. Not everyone has a Mrs. Meade." To which Robert would reply: "Madame Beaudry is supposed to be our Mrs. Meade." But he would accommodate to the situation.

This Friday night, however, he insisted that Madame Beaudry be available to put Frances to bed.

He picked up his almost-empty wine glass and looked carefully at what remained. "Why don't you want to? It's just an hour twice a week. And it would mean a lot to my father — he thinks so much of you. And he loves music so much."

Gloria sighed and pulled her hair off her shoulders and up into a knot on the back of her neck. It was still thick and curly. She'd been afraid it might get thinner; there were women who said that after the second child their hair had suffered. She tried not to appear to listen too hard to such comments. This evening the weight of her hair had begun to pull her down; she was going to have to get it styled before she had the next concert, even though Robert would protest. He liked her hair the way it was; he liked the lushness, he said. He didn't mind that she'd kept on some of the weight she'd gained with Frances.

"Really, darling girl, I don't understand what you're objecting to. He's an old man, he's been very good to me, very generous with us, and he loves to hear you play."

To play for an hour twice a week would mean reorganizing the schedule that she was trying so hard to maintain: three hours of practice a day, coaching twice a week, exercise, some time with the baby.

"Late morning would be best, Maman says. You could bring the baby along. She would look after her; it would be a treat for *ma mère*, and a break for you and Madame Beaudry. Take a cab, all you'd have to do is have a standing order with Westmount Taxi and there would be a car at the door so you won't have to wait around. You'll be home by early afternoon, time for the baby's nap, time for you to practise."

Gloria shook out her hair again. "No," she said. "No."

"But why?" he asked. "I don't think it's asking too much."

How to explain? Part of it was disgust — there was no other word for it — at the decrepit state of Robert's father. How to say to Robert, who didn't want to admit his father was dying, that she'd had enough of entertaining the mortally ill when she went to play for her father and the other men at the veteran's hospital, when she saw Lotte struggle to speak after her stroke.

It wasn't as if she could just play anything she happened to be working on. Lotte used to say that music touches listeners in ways that they frequently can't explain, but something about it finds resonances in the human soul. Every society makes music, only the form varies. While Robert's father had dutifully attended many of her concerts, now that his life was ending he might want to hear songs from his childhood, or show tunes, or drinking songs. She'd have to ask what he liked, she'd have to ferret out his tastes. It would take time and energy and heaven knows she didn't have a lot of that in excess.

She didn't respond immediately. She picked up her own wine glass and looked at the dregs.

Robert watched her, but then threw down his napkin as he stood up from the table. "Jesus, Gloria," he said. "Jesus, you'd think I'd asked you to do something immoral." He thrust his hands in his pants pockets and walked over to the open window. He jingled his keys and bounced lightly on the balls of his feet for a minute or two. Finally, he whirled around, his good eye boring into her, his bad eye staring off into space. As always when he did that, she felt dizzy, but she realized that to look away would be make matters worse.

"You don't get it, do you?" he said. "You don't understand at all. This is the man who stood up for you when my mother said I was a fool to get involved after James died. He's the one who said you were a talented, charming young woman with a good heart and that if I loved you I should do what I thought best, no matter what might have happened in your past. He wouldn't listen to *ma mère's* rants. You didn't hear what she called you, thank goodness."

Gloria startled at that. She felt her face grow red.

"Father said she was being unfair, that you were a courageous girl who was battling against stiff odds, who needed every break she could get." He stopped, his voice breaking. "Goddammit," he said as he pulled a crumpled handkerchief out of his pocket and blew his nose. "Doesn't anybody see that the laundry gets done?" he asked as he looked at the sorry state of the handkerchief. "I mean, you've got all the help any woman could ask for, all you have to do is send things to the laundry, and still I never have clean things." He balled it up and threw it across the room, then wiped his eyes with the back of his hand.

"Your mother," Gloria began, although she wasn't quite sure what she should say. She wasn't surprised to hear this, she'd suspected as much. Robert was his mother's only child, after all, her fair-haired boy, her darling.

"We're not talking about my mother now," he said. "We were

talking about my father and his very simple request that his daughter-in-law, of whom he is very fond, play some lovely music to ease his pain. She should come to visit regularly with his granddaughter — yes, yes, don't forget that he can count too, he knows what happened, but he's nevertheless glad to accept Frances as his own." He paused, his good eye once again looking directly at her. "Do you understand?"

"Yes," she said. "I understand very well. I see that what I am going to have to do to stay in the good graces of your family is play: play a role, play so you can trot me out when you need me." She'd never formulated the idea so clearly before, but that's what it was. She was an ornament for them, an accomplished plaything for Robert.

He sat down. He was crying, his nose was running, his good eye was red with emotion and his bad eye stared somewhere to her right, impassively. "No, no, you don't understand. I love you, he loves you. We just want your help, a kind of help that only you can give us."

Gloria shut her own eyes to avoid his. "I have a recording contract," she said. "I have to perfect twenty-four works by Debussy. I have to reach a point where I can play them better than anybody else. How can I do that if I am constantly distracted? There's the baby and now this."

He didn't agree, of course. She had lots of help with the baby, everyone wished her well with her career. He was so proud of her. He supported her career one hundred percent. But the bottom line was this: the Murray family wanted her services, and if she didn't provide them, there'd be the devil to pay.

Not that Robert actually said "the devil," but the idea was there. So were more tears and heated words that prompted Madame Beaudry to look in on them, blinking accusingly. But by midnight Gloria had come around to agreeing to the schedule Robert had obviously thought about in advance. Monday and Wednesday mornings from eleven a.m. until noon.

After he went to bed, she sat up in the dining room, looking into the darkness beyond the window and remembering what Pierre had said when she quarrelled with James that first summer: "We're the hired help, and don't forget it." And: "They pay us the way they pay for masses for their souls." Ah yes, souls; more death, more duty.

The rest of the spring and the early summer weren't easy for anyone. Robert's father died in early July. His mother retreated to her sister's country place in Saint-Sauveur, but not before she had a chance to tell Gloria that her husband's dying wish was for a "real grandchild," preferably a son to carry on the line.

By then Gloria had decided she could not afford to let Robert's family bother her. The old man had been pathetically appreciative of her playing, it was true, and unlike her father and Lotte, he remained cogent and in control of his body up until nearly the end. What he did was waste away until his voice was only a whisper and then nothing at all. How he could have conveyed a dying wish was more than Gloria could see, but she understood where the message was coming from. Everyone knew that Frances was not Robert's child, and the Murrays needed an heir.

Robert did not press her. He was very busy all that fall. His firm agreed that he should spend time learning about what was at stake as powerful people started planning the development of hydroelectricity in Quebec. The firm represented private utilities; they needed to know not only the law but the technology. Robert knew that no one would read long reports, but he could make sure that the short reports he wrote were accurate and inclusive.

He told Gloria, as he had before and as he would tell Frances on the afternoons at Bic when they'd do science experiments together, that he should have retrained as an engineer after the war. Gloria refrained from commenting that he should not have let his mother run his life because she knew that saying that would only muddy the waters. And then she laughed to herself, since muddied water was what was going to make the electricity, wasn't it? They even came to a sort of a bargain. Once he'd got his head filled with engineering and economics, he would use everything that came his way to push her career up to the next level. And the child would follow.

PREPARING FOR THE Debussy recording was an undertaking. The composer was a fanatic about strict interpretation. He set out detailed instructions on his scores, and during his lifetime he made the musicians with whom he worked practise arpeggios and chords hundreds of times. When she was in France, Gloria had not worked with anyone who had known the Master, but two of her teachers had studied with musicians who had played for him. As she always did, she tried to recover what they had said, rustling through the annotated scores she had, riffling through the little notebooks she'd kept. She remembered one of them saying that Debussy wanted to write music with a form so free that it would sound improvised. Yet she knew Debussy was far from casual about what he wrote; he said he could spend weeks trying to decide whether one chord was the right one, or if another was needed. There is a unity of tone in his work, too. *Unlike the Romantics*, she found scribbled on one score, *Debussy doesn't contrast musical ideas, but wants the parts to connect*. Another note read: *in this arpeggio, the two hands must come down almost plaited together and then unfurl like the skirt of a dancer.* Hah, she thought to herself; what does that mean exactly? That was one of the problems about trying to put into words how to play something. So much was muscle memory of hands and arms in the right position, plus instantaneous communication between eye and fingers. The result was the invisible current of sound that changed incessantly from instant to instant as the river of music flowed along.

When she became immersed in what she was practising, she was only dimly aware of what went on in the apartment. There were afternoons that winter when she suddenly realized that it was dark outside, that the housekeeper had taken Frances out for a promenade in the carriage, that the day had slipped away from her. But when the two weeks in the recording studio finally came, she felt she had a good hold on the music.

She went to New York by herself. No question of staying with Mike's cousin. The recording company paid for a hotel not far from the studio so she could come and go without difficulty. She listened to the producer; she wasn't worried that the technicians would laugh at her as had happened when she was pregnant and recording that first time. She felt she was playing very well, and she was pleased when she listened to the tapes that were made. After that she went back to Montreal and waited and practised and prepared for a series of concerts designed to promote the recording. In September she'd play with the symphonies in Chicago and Cincinnati and for the University Musical Society in Ann Arbor. There would also be solo concerts in Wilmington, Washington, Charleston, and Palm Beach in November. The tour would end in February when she played in Philadelphia, at the Brooklyn Academy of Music, and in Symphony Hall in Boston.

IN THE SUMMER, as part of that preparation, Robert got friends of his family to open their house at Grand-Métis for a series of little concerts, the way his great uncle and aunt had done for years on the other side of the river in Charlevoix. Gertrude Alexander, the grande dame of the family then pushing eighty-five, liked the idea a lot when he and her grandsons, friends of Robert's from Collège Jean-de-Brébeuf, proposed it. The house was so big, she said, and her grandchildren didn't visit enough, so why not have a little music on a Saturday afternoon?

Three Saturday afternoons; two in July and one in August, when the weather was likely to be good and the gardens at the Alexander house were at their finest. They weren't as nice as Elsie Reford's; few gardens anywhere could rival the ones she started on her estate overlooking the St. Lawrence before the war when she was laid up with peritonitis and her doctor told her she should take up something less strenuous than fly fishing. Mrs. Alexander said she thought Elsie was absolutely mad, but Mrs. Alexander had done a very nice job herself with her own gardens and she wasn't averse to showing off just a little to a select group of friends and music lovers.

The project was designed to showcase Gloria, but she wanted to work at least once with a singer, as three times during the tour she would accompany a young singer who had won a local prize. Robert and Mrs. Alexander hoped at first to get someone whose name had drawing power, and at one point Robert thought that Maureen Forrester would bite; the idea of arranging for a weeklong stay for her whole family was a good attraction. In the end, though, Forrester and family opted for the Muskoka country north of Toronto. Much running around followed — good singers have their work planned out for them a couple of years in advance — but then someone suggested Pierre Boisvert.

He'd be busy later in the summer — his career was going pretty well too — but he could pitch in for the first concert. Robert was so glad to have the problem solved that he agreed before telling Gloria.

"You remember him, don't you?" he said to Gloria the Saturday morning after he got off the phone with Mrs. Alexander. "His agent says he'll do it as a favour for me because *mon oncle* Hector was a big help to him ten years ago." He was shuffling papers, getting ready to go to work; with his *perfectionnement technique* completed, he was now more important at his firm. He looked up at her and smiled. "I haven't heard him sing in a while, but his agent read me a review from *The Globe and Mail*. Sounds like his voice has matured and he's headed for the big time."

Gloria felt her face freeze, and she looked back at the score she had in front of her. As she made notes, she was drinking coffee, and for a second she was afraid her hand would shake and the cup would rattle on the saucer.

"You both were on the cruises for a couple of summers, weren't you? Seems to me I remember hearing you accompany him."

"Ummhum," she said, not looking up.

"What did you think of him then?" He paused in his shuffling of papers while he waited for her reply.

"He has a good voice," she answered quickly. "But I never was sure how serious he was," she added, deciding she had to smile back at Robert. "It's good he's agreed, though. At least that problem's solved." But she was annoyed with Robert for not discussing the matter with her beforehand.

She said nothing more. When the time came for the concert, they quarrelled. She'd been all week in the house they'd just bought at Bic with the baby and Robert's younger acts just two doors away. They helped with Frances some and would do more when Gloria was on tour, but Madame Beaudry had refused to come to Bic for more than three weeks; she was now visiting her brother in New Carlisle in the Gaspé. Gloria had struggled to find time for practising, and she was tired of juggling that with the baby, who was really not a baby anymore. At a bit more than two, she was walking and talking and taking up far more space than she had during the winter. At least her hair had grown out to be blond and curly; Robert sometimes called her his "girl with the flaxen hair."

The night before the concert, Gloria wanted to leave for Grand-Métis as soon as Robert arrived from Montreal so they could have dinner in a restaurant that had recently opened. She'd arranged with the young girl from the village, who worked for several families along the shorefront road, to look after Frances, and she'd called the restaurant to make a reservation. But this was the last thing Robert wanted to do; the drive from Montreal had taken nearly eight hours and he wanted to sleep. She pouted and wouldn't come to bed with him until he promised her that he'd get the aunts to stay with Frances overnight so they could stay at the hotel in Métis after the concert, sleep late Sunday morning, and not hurry back.

Before then Robert had another peace offering: a rose-coloured brassiere and panties set, bought by him specifically to go under the summer concert dress Marthe had made for her. He brought the package out when Gloria was just waking up in the early summer morning, before Frances began to stir.

He put the little box on the pillow next to Gloria's head. "Just something, because, darling girl, you are so special," he said.

She sat up, blinking a little, listening to hear if the baby was stirring in the next room.

"Something so you will feel beautiful all the way to your skin," he said, watching her fumble with the ribbon. Inside, the garments were nestled in tissue paper. She shook them from the wrapping impatiently.

"Lovely," she said, smiling at him. "Just the same colour as the dress too."

He stretched out beside her. "Marthe gave me a little bit of the fabric to take with me when I went shopping at Ogilvy's. She said I ought to make sure. Now try them on to see if I got the right size."

Of course, they fit — a man who checks the colour also checks the size. Then they made love quickly on the floor of their bedroom because the bed squeaked and the aunties would be coming over any minute to take care of Frances. It was not particularly satisfactory for Gloria because she did not like to be rushed. But because she had been so unpleasant the night before she felt she owed it to him.

MRS. ALEXANDER'S HELPERS were setting up her drawing room when they arrived. Robert set about supervising, while Gloria was left to deal with Pierre, who announced as soon as he saw her that they needed to practise.

She made a point of not looking at him directly when she greeted him, holding herself so stiffly as to be almost impolite. There was no time for anything but the music. The afternoon was billed as a concert for a summer day so the program, worked out by Robert and Pierre, included art songs for him, and Debussy for her.

"All right," Pierre said. "Shall we begin?" She felt his eyes on her, but she had to remind herself that he looked at all women like that.

She sat down at the piano, and tried a few scales. Mrs. Alexander had promised to have it tuned again — it hadn't been quite right the week before when she'd come over to talk about the arrangements — and Gloria was glad to see that not only did it sound true, someone had adjusted the two keys whose action had been slightly slow. Where had Mrs. Alexander found such a gem of a tuner? Gloria would have to ask and get him to come to work on the piano at Bic.

The run-through went well. She noticed that Pierre's voice was slightly richer than it had been, that it had lost some of its brilliance, but overall he sang better than he had the last time she'd heard him. With anyone else she would have commented on this, but she kept her attention on her music and when he was finished, she folded his songs up and prepared to play Debussy's "La cathédrale engloutie," "The Sunken Cathedral." There was no other piece which allowed her to plunge so deeply and quickly into the depths of the river of music. "You'll have to excuse me," she said without getting up from the bench. "I need to go over something just once again."

"You won't join me and the others for a little snack?" he asked. There was a teasing note to his voice that in the past she would have smiled at.

But this time she held him off. "No, thank you," she said, not looking at him. "I'm not hungry. I'll get something later with my husband."

"As you wish, Madame," he said, and he left her to her music.

Robert was somewhere taking care of things. That was good. When she was finished she went upstairs and into the bedroom on the back of the house that looked out over the gardens and then beyond to the river, appearing so peaceful and powerful from this distance.

Mrs. Alexander said she should use the room as her bou-
doir. "I'm sure that you may want a moment or two to yourself
before your performance." There was a bowl of the first peaches
on the table next to a low, overstuffed chair, along with a plate
of small watercress and egg salad sandwiches — there would
be similar fare after the concert as well as drinks and tea.
Mrs. Alexander had insisted that no one would leave her house
without receiving proper hospitality.

Gloria probably had time for a nap, but she was too agitated.
She picked up two sandwiches to nibble on and went onto the
balcony, which ran the length of the house on that side. The
day was just beginning to slip into afternoon, the shadows were
slightly longer. A breeze carried with it the smell of roses and
salt water, the perfume of gardens and the sea. She saw Robert
standing on the lawn with the Alexander brothers and two
other men she didn't know. One of them was carrying a brief-
case and, as she watched, he opened it and handed a file to
Robert. Even from this distance Gloria could tell that he was
annoyed. When he was on holiday, Robert did not like to be
interrupted with work. This summer there had been many more
claims on his time as the new provincial government began
its plans for great projects. Gloria had not paid much attention
to the details, but this afternoon, even from a distance, she could
tell from the way he ranted that Robert did not consider what
was happening to be good.

One of the strangers was speaking, making large, earnest
gestures. Robert flipped open the file, and then thrust it at
the younger of the Alexanders. It looked to Gloria as if he said
"later," before he turned on his heel and headed back into the
house. She looked at her watch: almost showtime.

The doors to the drawing room were already open, as were

the tall windows that looked onto the garden. Gloria went directly to thank Mrs. Alexander for her generosity and support. The old woman was sitting in an armchair to the left of the little platform her helpers had constructed. "I want to sit where I can see you well," she said to Gloria, holding her hands. "You play so beautifully."

Gloria, who was bending over, leaned a bit more so she could put her cheek next to hers. "Thank you so much for everything," she whispered in Mrs. Alexander's ear.

"It is my pleasure," Mrs. Alexander said and squeezed Gloria's hands.

Gloria shut her eyes and smiled to herself. She had been very lucky that so many venerable women looked out for her. Robert's aunts were very helpful, so had been Lotte and her own mother in her loopy way. The last two were gone now — Lotte dead and her mother permanently in Florida — but maybe this lady who smelled of talcum powder and French cigarettes would take their place.

Mrs. Alexander kept hold of Gloria's hands as Gloria straightened up. "Play well," she said.

Gloria nodded, but when she turned away, smoothing the neckline of her scoop-necked dress because she knew that it bowed open when she leaned over, she saw that Pierre had been watching. Their eyes met, and she had no doubt that he had seen the top of her breasts and her rose silk brassiere.

The rose silk underwear indeed. As Pierre looked at her, she almost believed he read her thoughts, that merely by looking at her he could tell about the morning, about Robert, about what she wanted and didn't want. That was nonsense, all nonsense, of course. She pushed the thought from her mind as she smoothed the dress. She and Pierre were professionals who needed to concentrate on what came next. They had music to make, and that was what was important.

Gloria went forward so she stood next to the older Alexander brother who was going to welcome the fifty or so guests and introduce the program. As she passed Pierre, she made a point of leaving enough space between them so there would be no chance she might brush against him.

The concert went well. Sixty-five minutes of art songs by Debussy and Mahler, ending with Gloria playing Lucien Garban's transcription for piano of Debussy's *La Mer*; works chosen well and performed well. She was not at all displeased with the way she played.

She had to take Pierre's hand when they took their bows, and then they stood side by side as the guests came forward to congratulate them. By now the shadows were longer in the garden, and a light breeze had begun to blow in through the open windows from the river. The sweat that had accumulated as she played was now cool in the fresh air, and she felt herself shiver. Pierre leaned over and pulled her to him. "Can't let the star catch a chill," he said to the little group gathered round them. "We have to look out for such talent."

Gloria smiled because that was expected, but slipped out of his embrace. Nevertheless, his touch carried some of the electricity she remembered, and she looked around for Robert, the way a gambler might look for a lucky charm. He had been sitting in the back, she was pretty sure; he'd been there when she sat down at the piano. She didn't see him now — the chairs had been shifted to allow easy access to a drinks table set up just inside the door from the entry hall to the drawing room. But there he was, coming toward her, with two glasses in his hands. He was smiling, a big grin full of pride in her, in the fact that he was her husband.

"Darling girl," he said, sweeping her into his arms, balancing the drinks behind her back. "You were wonderful."

Darling girl: lately he hadn't used the pet name often, and she wondered if something was going on, but she smiled nevertheless. "You were pleased?" she asked, taking a gin and tonic from him. "I enjoyed it myself."

"Which is just the way it should be," he said. Then he turned to shake Pierre's hand. "Masterful," he said. "I don't remember ever hearing a finer performance of the Mallarmé poems."

Pierre smiled back. "Praise from someone who knows music as well as you is always a real compliment." He turned back to Gloria and draped an arm around her shoulders, casually, as if they'd been pals forever. "And it was such a pleasure to sing accompanied by a truly great pianist."

"Flattery, flattery," she said, stepping away from him, taking Robert's arm, to show just where she stood.

"No, no, completely true," Pierre said. "I only speak the truth."

"You both were wonderful," said one of the ladies who had come forward to fawn over Pierre. "I was quite swept away." She turned to her friend: "Didn't we agree that we were overwhelmed?" Pierre beamed, and Robert allowed the conversation to begin swirling around Pierre before he leaned over to say softly to Gloria, "I must talk to you. There is a little problem."

Lately he'd said things like that often, and, remembering the scene she saw earlier, she had an idea what he was going to say. The pleasure of the afternoon began to drain from her, like air from a slow leak in a party balloon. She wanted his company this evening, she wanted to enjoy the success of this project — as much his as hers — with him. She wanted, oh how she wanted, their evening alone in the hotel with time enough to make up for their hurried encounter that morning. He'd promised. She stopped so he couldn't lead her the few steps away where they could talk without being overheard.

"What do you mean?" she asked. But she knew. She took a big drink of the gin and tonic as he began to tell her. Then she emptied the glass and reached for another as a waitress passed with a tray.

At issue was one of the power companies Robert represented, some arcane provision of a stupid contract that the new government, feeling its oats, wanted to revoke. They couldn't do it — not without going all the way to nationalizing the company and others like it — but until that was recognized there would be much legal manoeuvring that required Robert's attention. "I can't help it," he said. "If I work this weekend, though, I should be free and clear by the middle of the week. We'll still have our holiday — the concert next weekend won't be affected. We can have our little night out next Saturday. You understand, don't you?" But it wasn't a question; he expected her not to mind. "I have to go to Quebec City as soon as I can get out of here politely. You have dinner with the Alexanders and Pierre, you invite them all to the hotel for dinner, the reservation's already made. Make sure Pierre has a good time, he gave an excellent performance and we should be grateful for the way he came in on such short notice."

As Robert spoke she watched Pierre, who was now listening attentively to what Mrs. Alexander was saying. The old lady had made her way slowly from her privileged seat to the front so she could hold Pierre's hand in both of hers and smile up at him with the smile that everyone said had made her the most charming woman in Grand-Métis before the war. He seemed to listen carefully — Gloria remembered how he had told her it was essential to make the rich think whatever they said was important. Nevertheless his attention shifted when Robert spoke his name. He looked over at them and flashed another of his own special smiles.

"Dinner?" Robert said in a stage whisper over the women's heads, and Pierre nodded.

The men sorted things out, deciding who would take whose car, that one of the Alexanders would take Gloria back to Bic in the morning while the other would take Pierre to catch the train. No one asked Gloria her advice, which did not please her. Someone handed her another gin and tonic, and she went to sit by herself just outside the open door on a wrought-iron bench placed to invite contemplation of the garden. She did not feel much like contemplation. What she felt was tired and disappointed and angry. And afraid.

"Make sure Pierre has a good time," Robert repeated as he was leaving forty-five minutes later. "You let me know if she doesn't play the perfect hostess," he told him.

Mrs. Alexander did not join them; she said she was far too old and infirm to stand in the way of young people enjoying themselves. The Alexander brothers brought two young women who seemed far more interested in Pierre than in Gloria. Given that the men were also more interested in the girls than in her, Gloria found herself on the margins of the conversation. She drank another gin and tonic while they waited to order, and because the others weren't great wine drinkers, she finished off both the white and the red that Robert had ordered when he called about their reservation. By nine-thirty, when the dining room was emptying and the band in the bar by the pool had begun to invade their space, her mood had not improved.

She wanted to be done with them all. Good hostess to the end, however, she suggested coffee and cognac or a digestif to finish the meal, but the Alexanders and the girls begged off.

"Why don't you come with us to the bar?" the younger Alexander suggested. "We won't tell Robert or your little girl if you'd like to go dancing with us."

His date giggled, as if the idea of Gloria dancing was preposterous. His brother added, "the music may not be up to your standard," letting his voice drop off, as if there were a world of insinuations possible, about popular music, and art music, about the tastes of the young and succulent versus those of people well into their middle years.

Gloria knew for a fact that he liked classical music and that, more importantly, he was at least fifteen years older than the girl he was with and three years older than Gloria's thirty-two. She was tempted to make a remark about men who play in the nursery, but Pierre cut in before she had a chance.

"Of course, let's go dancing," he said. He reached over to pick up Gloria's hand. "You may not know it, but Madame Murray won dance contests the summers we worked the cruise boats together.

Gloria was surprised. "Dance contests?"

"My dear Gloria, you haven't drunk so much that you've forgotten, have you? The rumba and the samba."

"Nonsense," she said. "You may have, but I didn't. I was too busy working. Pianists have to play for their supper, whereas tenors have nothing to do when the dance music starts but have a good time."

He winked at her. "Oh, maybe you didn't win, but you could have. Why don't we show them how it's done?"

She stood up, still holding his hand, ready to say good night.

Then she saw the maître d'hotel heading over with the bill for her to sign. "A moment, just a moment, my friends," she said, taking the clipboard. When finished, she turned back to the others. "Good night," she said, but they were gone already, and she was left with Pierre. Across the room she could see how the younger Alexander was letting his hand rest on the rounded hip of his date, casually, as if it were acting independently of his will. "The bastards," she said aloud to herself. "The lecherous bastards."

Pierre heard her and laughed. "Indeed," he said. "Come, just one dance, I know you're tired, but you can't let them dismiss you so easily."

Not much logic there, but at the time it seemed to rhyme with the irritation she felt. She started toward the bar, but she had to stop to steady herself on the back of a chair before she reached the halfway mark. She turned to look to see if he were following her. He was. "All right, one dance," she said.

They had never danced together before, no matter what Pierre said, but they did it well. The band — piano, bass, guitar, and pretty girl vocalist — wasn't bad. She held herself a respectable distance from Pierre at first, but as he led her around the dance floor she allowed herself to come closer until she felt his hardness against her belly and her nipples grew stiff in anticipation. Between numbers they did not touch, maintaining the pretense of propriety, but when the singer began a torchy version of the Bobby Darin hit "Beyond the Sea," they found themselves looking directly at each other.

"Debussy," Pierre said. "*La Mer.*"

"Of course," Gloria said. "Is nothing sacred?"

"No," he said. Then, after a few moments as they moved to the tune slashed from the music she'd played that afternoon, music she'd recorded and she felt she owned, he said, "You go up to your room, and I will stay down here another fifteen minutes."

She nodded, and when the band stopped she shook his hand and made a show of saying good night to him. From across the room, she waved in the direction of the Alexanders. And she left, calling for her key at the desk, and then climbing the stairs from the lobby slowly, as if she were very, very tired.

He spent the night, returning to his own room — paid for by Robert and Mrs. Alexander, she remembered later — only after the sun had come up. The rose panties were ripped, she noticed when she was packing things up, waiting for it to be late enough to go to the desk and ask if a taxi could be found that would take her back to Bic. She did not want to wait around for the ride pre-arranged with the Alexanders. The damage to her underwear was a small price to pay. What she must do, she decided as she sat by the window in the early morning light and realized just how stupid she'd been, was suggest to Robert that Pierre was too attentive. Say nothing more than that, just let it be known that she didn't appreciate it. A lie, of course, but there were times when lying is the only thing that can be done, and anything is justifiable in self-defence.

SHE SAW HIM once more, two summers later. He called her at Bic. It was the middle of the afternoon when Alexander was still asleep. Frances not taking a nap exactly, but in her room. Ordinarily Gloria wouldn't have answered the phone because those afternoon hours were precious — she played through Debussy, Ravel, and Poulenc, searching for work for her next recording, her next series of concerts. But it was so hot that her sweaty fingers were sliding on the keys and she needed a drink of water.

The first time the telephone rang she told herself she had a good excuse to stop.

"Hello," she said, wondering just who might be calling at that hour.

"I keep track of you," Pierre said without identifying himself. "I can count too. Those children of yours, they could be mine."

His words took her breath away, and for at least half a minute she could not speak. "No," she said, when she recovered a bit. "You're mistaken." And she hung up.

The second time, she hesitated. She stood next to the telephone, knowing it would be him again. She picked up the receiver, then set it down again quickly, breaking the connection.

When the phone rang a third time, she considered just letting it ring. But if she did, Alexander would wake up and Frances would want to know what was happening. She couldn't face that.

"I'm up in the village," Pierre said as soon as she picked up the receiver. "I'm coming down the hill in five minutes. I know you're alone, you don't need to worry about me confronting your husband." Then he hung up.

Gloria saw Frances was standing in the doorway, watching. She had her thumb in her mouth, the way she did when she was worried or afraid. Her big blue eyes — such lovely eyes, thank God everybody in the family had blue eyes — did not leave Gloria's face for an instant.

"Maman," Frances said. "The baby's awake."

Gloria forced herself to smile at the little girl. "Is he crying? I don't hear him." She looked around. She had to get out of the house. She didn't want to see Pierre.

"Look," she said to Frances, making an effort to sound cheerful. "Why don't you run in the kitchen and get us some peaches from the bowl on the table. I'll go get Alex and then we'll go for a little walk down to the cove. How'd that be?" Robert was in Quebec City — he wouldn't be back until midnight — and the aunts had taken the other car to Grand-Métis for tea with Mrs. Alexander. If Gloria and the children left, the house would be empty.

There is very little sand at Bic. Farther east, when the Rivière Mitis empties into the St. Lawrence, there is a beach. Farther east still, toward Métis-sur-Mer and Grand-Métis, the coastal plain is deeper, the hills farther away. But at Bic the cliffs rise behind a narrow shore, marking some ancient fault line. The highway, the village, the farms, and the peat bogs lie above, on the plateau that once, thousands of years ago, was the bottom of some ancient sea but now is a hundred feet above the St. Lawrence.

Their house sat about halfway between the point where the road winding down the hillside arrived at the littoral, and the road's end by the Catholic chapel. The location meant something in the social hierarchy of the village, but Gloria was not attuned to the nuances. Robert's branch of the Murrays had built their summer houses here at the beginning of the twentieth century, and not at Métis-sur-Mer, Rivière-du-Loup, or another of the places frequented by the Anglo establishment, probably to show their independence. Indeed, Robert said, they'd crossed the river precisely to get away from the summer people in the Charlevoix region, where there had been Murrays since the days of Montcalm and Wolfe. Probably marriage into Catholic Francophone families had played a role in their wanting to get away — unlike the handful of Protestant churches in the Métis villages, on the Bic shore there was no Anglican chapel to match the Catholic one. But friendships among younger folks of subsequent generations had blurred the lines: Robert's mother had met Mrs. Alexander during the year the latter spent learning French and embroidery at the Ursulines in Quebec City.

Later, much later, Frances realized that she had no idea what language they spoke at Bic. Her mother and father always spoke English, but when her father took her to the village in the car, and people asked whose pretty little girl she was, she thought she answered in French. She didn't get the languages straightened out herself until she was about nine. To avoid that confusion, she insisted that everyone speak only French to her own children, a requirement that Gloria thought was completely unnecessary and which she subverted all the time.

That afternoon Gloria's thought was to walk east along the road to the place where a small stream comes down to the St. Lawrence. Then she'd put the stroller behind a rock, and, carrying Alex, walk with Frances to the place where the stream widened out. There were pools to throw stones into, and several big logs that had washed down from the highland that would shelter them from view.

But first of all she had to get Alex up, change him, get his things ready; she had to wrestle the stroller down from the veranda and to the road. She did not hear the baby as she climbed the stairs to the nursery, but when she opened the door, he was standing up in his crib, singing to himself. His face broke into a big smile when she entered the room, and he held his arms out to her.

She picked him up and snuggled her face against his neck. He smelled of Ivory laundry soap and little boy pee — half delightful, half disgusting. At sixteen months, he was running more than walking, although he liked to sit near her, listening to music. In her embrace he hummed the first five notes of the theme from the Ravel she'd been working on that afternoon.

"You are wonderful," she whispered to him. "Your sister is

all very well and good, but you are just about perfect."

For a while he had submitted quietly to having his diaper changed if she allowed him to play with a small windup music box, designed to hang from the edge of a baby's bed. He would hold on to the loop and wave it around in time: Beethoven's "Für Elise." The mechanism was wearing down; the tune's rhythm lurched along. The day before he had thrown it across the room in annoyance, but Gloria was sure that music filled his soul, and that he would be as consumed by it as she was.

She sang to distract him, as she struggled with his waving legs. He didn't like her to sing, she knew; she'd never sung well. Frances had told her so when she was two and a half, which had irritated Gloria at the time.

Finally, though, she had Alex changed, and his bottle and a snack for both children arranged. She had Frances hold Alex by the hand while she bounced the stroller down the steps to the road. Early in the summer the road surface had been oiled, but a week of summer thunderstorms had left it full of ruts. Pushing the stroller was not easy. Frances wanted to run ahead, but even though there was practically no traffic on the road, Gloria insisted the little girl stay by her side.

"Listen for cars," she told Frances. "You must help me, so we won't be surprised." Her daughter looked up at her; she was well aware that her brother was her mother's favourite. She seemed to decide that it was worth obeying her mother this time in order to win a little praise. "What's that?" she said almost immediately.

Gloria paused in her struggle with the mud and ruts to listen. "I don't hear anything," she said, but she remembered that children often can hear frequencies adults can't hear. "Let me listen a second."

"There," Frances said. "Up at the top of the hill." She pointed almost directly up the cliff, where, Gloria realized, the road began its switch back down to the shore.

"Hmmm," Gloria said, not sure she heard anything at all, but deciding to trust the child. "Let's hurry up so we'll be off the road before it gets down here."

The tide was out; the flat strata of stone that bordered the fault line were visible. Up ahead, the rock Robert and Frances often walked out to — "the castle," he called it — stood guarding the coast. There was a place that always had water in it, where rushing water had cut a deeper channel in the rock. Robert had let Frances jump over it several times, but Gloria didn't want her to try it this afternoon.

"No, we're not headed that way today," she said when she saw Frances looking in the direction of the castle. "We're going to see what's at the cove. Look, up ahead, by the cove. There's some nice driftwood to climb on." Not that it could be seen yet; they were just at the point where the oiled road ended, and a track turned up the smaller stream. It would be hard going, but Gloria was pretty sure she could make it to a place where they wouldn't be seen from the road.

"Listen," Frances said suddenly. "There's a car coming. Didn't I tell you?"

This time there was no doubt about it. A car had made it down to the road at the bottom and was grinding its way toward them.

"Quick," Gloria said. "Let's hurry up ahead."

"Why?" Frances asked. "It won't hurt us here, we're at the end of the road."

Out of the mouths of babes. Gloria didn't want this to happen; it shouldn't happen.

She could hear the car stop, but its motor continued to run. She didn't dare turn around, but she knew he was there, looking for them. Had he stopped at the house? He must have, how otherwise would he know to go looking for them farther along the road?

"Gloria," she heard him shout above the sound of the water and the wind.

"The man is calling you," Frances said. "Do we know him?"

She stopped, because there was no point in going any farther. She wasn't going to escape him this time. "He's a singer," she said. "I accompanied him a few times."

"Oh, a musician," Frances said, disappointed. "What does he want?"

"I don't know," Gloria answered. She began to struggle with the stroller. "But I suppose we ought to find out."

He met them halfway along the track, and she was pleased to see that his well-shined dress shoes and his trousers were wet and muddy. She did not lean forward to give him the customary kisses on each cheek, she didn't hold out her hand.

"These are the children?" he said.

"As you see," she said. "Frances and Alexander."

He knelt down. "Hello," he said to Frances, who had slipped behind Gloria and was holding on to her skirt. "Won't you say hello to an old friend of your mama's?"

When she said nothing, he turned to Alex. "And you, young man. What's new with you?" Alex stared gravely at him also, blue eyes round, face solemn.

"I have heard through the grapevine that you are very musical," he said. "Is that true? Do you like singing?"

"He doesn't like it much when Mama sings," Frances said.

Pierre looked up at Gloria. "He doesn't? Shows what good taste he has."

Gloria did not laugh. "We were going for a walk," she said.

"And I would be very pleased to accompany you."

"But I would not be pleased if you did so," she replied. "Frances," she said, "do you want to run up ahead and see what's happening at the cove?"

Frances looked from her to Pierre, and then nodded her head before she began picking her way along the edge of the track, bouncing from big stone to big stone. Alex saw her and began to fuss, waving his arms and leaning forward in the stroller.

"I was over in Charlevoix, singing for all that crowd, and I heard that you spend your summers here. I just had to see them once," Pierre said when the little girl had gone beyond earshot.

Gloria didn't answer. She wondered exactly what he wanted from her now. He knew that Robert was wealthy man and she had had considerable success.

Frances called, "Maman," and began running back to her. Gloria knew she was going to have to shut him up. But as she opened her mouth to say that he would have to leave immediately, she made the mistake of looking directly at him.

He caught her glance, and while he began to speak of concert tours and music lessons for children, he smiled. She smiled back; she couldn't help herself.

He saw. Without stopping his flow of words, he put out his arms and drew her to him. "They are beautiful," he said in her ear. "Robert is a lucky man."

When she pulled away she was crying, tears flowing down her face, obscuring her vision so she did not see Frances dash past her until the little girl was back where the road ended.

"Watch me," Frances called as she headed out over the rocks. "You don't think I can do it by myself, but I can." When she arrived at the edge of the little channel she hesitated, looking at the water rush back after a wave. Some spray from a wave sluicing into the channel shot up in the air as she prepared to jump. Her left foot missed the rock completely and she fell with her chest and shoulders flat on the rock, her legs dangling in the rushing water. From a distance, Gloria could see her struggling to find a ridge to wedge her fingers in, but she began to slide.

Then another wave splashed over her. "My God," Gloria cried. "Do something."

Pierre was already moving, jumping in, bracing his feet against the opposite sides of the channel, in water up to his waist. He slipped his hands under the girl's arms and hauled her up, lifting her onto the rock ledge on the shore side. As she lay sputtering, he pulled himself out and knelt beside her, clearing her hair away from her face, making sure she was breathing, running his hand up and down her back as she forced air in and out of her lungs.

Gloria, who had grabbed Alex, hurried forward awkwardly pushing the stroller. Alex howled, but once Pierre had brought Frances to Gloria, she put the baby back in the stroller and folded Frances in her arms. They rocked back and forth, as Gloria crooned a nonsense tune.

"We have to get back to the house," she said to Pierre when Frances stopped crying. "I will tell Robert that you just stopped by — and that you were a hero."

"All right," he said, reaching out to take Frances. He held her close. "But I'm claiming this one for my own, this little girl with the flaxen hair. I saved her."

Alex cried harder when he saw that his mother was no longer holding Frances, and Gloria reacted mechanically to stop his tears by picking him up. She didn't know quite what to say to Pierre, but she couldn't let him get away with thinking that.

For a moment they stood, staring at each other, each holding a child. Then he leaned forward as if he might try to kiss her.

"No," she said, turning away from him. "I can't allow that."

"I'm cold, Maman," Frances said before Gloria could say anything more. Her teeth were chattering.

Pierre looked at her, and then at Gloria and Alex. "He's a good father, is he?" he asked.

"The best," she said. She touched Frances's cheek with her free hand. "Isn't Papa the best?"

Frances nodded and then squirmed around so she could look at Pierre. Her big blue eyes stared solemnly at him.

"All right," he said. "I'm just an old friend of the family, one of your musical buddies who happened to stop by."

He stayed at the house long enough to have a cup of tea and to meet *les tantes* when they got back from Métis-sur-Mer — *les tantes* who had heard about how wonderfully he'd sung two summers ago when the Alexanders got up that series of little concerts.

III

THE CONTRACT TO RECORD MUSSORGSKY'S *Pictures at an Exhibition* was all but signed in the fall of 1973 when Gloria got the word that the recording company wanted to postpone the project. Her agent called her with the news just as she was getting ready to go to Toronto to teach a master class and see Alex. It was his first year at the National Ballet School; he insisted he was fine, but she worried anyway — he was only eleven. Her suitcase stood by the front door and, next to it, a box of cookies made by Madame Beaudry and another box with a present that they'd promised him if his grades were good: a Sony Walkman with a dozen tapes that Gloria had selected for him.

"You've got to be kidding," she said. Her flight was in an hour, and she'd already called the taxi. "What's going on? If we don't get into the studio it won't be ready for the hundredth anniversary."

"That's just it. They've decided that nobody really cares. He's an old Russian composer; they're saying it won't sell — they're trying to rationalize their list. "

The doorbell ring, the cab was at the door. "I'll call you from

Toronto," she said. Not what she wanted to think about on the way there, but how could she help not?

It was the mention of "rationalizing the list" that bothered her the most. She knew what that meant: dropping artists and work from the catalogue. She had a dozen recordings with three companies now, almost all French music. True, her most recent hit dated from three years before, a record devoted to the music of Erik Satie, the haunting, deceptively simple pieces of the eccentric French. composer. But it had done very well, especially in Canada, in part because it was featured in a movie. The soundtrack for *Goin' Down the Road*, the saga of two men who leave Cape Breton to find work in Toronto, was mostly folk and country music. But in a short scene one of the men is attracted to a girl in a record shop and the record she's listening to is Gloria's recording of Satie's haunting *Gymnopédie No. 1*. For a moment quite different worlds touch. In the weeks following the film's release, Gloria's recording of Satie's work made the Canadian charts.

Since then, attention to classical music in general had declined. In fact, Gloria's last record — more Debussy, a sort of greatest hits, the suggestion of the record company — had been reviewed only in two magazines. Her playing was "exciting as always," one of the critics wrote, but he questioned why she wasn't exploring new musical territory. "We haven't heard this fine pianist play Chopin in a long time. Her interpretations would be worth listening to."

Gloria did not keep a scrapbook. Later, when Julie needed encouragement, Gloria set her to work putting all the clippings in order so they could talk about music and musical careers. But she did have copies of all reviews then, because her agent had a clipping service. Occasionally she read the critics' comments.

"Don't believe an artist who says he doesn't care about reviews," she told Julie when they sat in the garden room with the stacks of loose pages cut from magazines and newspapers. "Everyone wants to know what is said about them. The trick is to learn from that, not to be destroyed."

As it happened, Gloria had thrust the latest envelope of clippings into her carryall two weeks before, where they had stayed until she was seated in the plane. By then, she had run through all possible reactions to the contract cancellation. Robert would know how to determine where she stood legally; that was one of the advantages of having a really good lawyer in the family. If he didn't have an answer he put one of his clerks on the question. As for playing Mussorgsky, she had to admit that one of the reasons the project appealed was the critics' insinuation that she was sticking too closely to well-beaten paths.

The stewardess brought coffee and croissants. Gloria brought out the envelope with the clippings. She had already noted that it was thinner than usual. Ten years earlier, when she had started touring after Alex was born, she was reviewed in all the cities where she performed, as well as in at least half a dozen magazines for her records.

The first clipping she pulled out was good-sized: two columns of a standard newspaper page with a photo of her holding a bouquet of flowers. It was from the *Kingston Whig-Standard* when she played in the music series at Queen's University two months before. Not a bad concert, as she remembered it, although the hall was only two-thirds full. But Kingston, she'd been told when she played there several years earlier, was not a big classical music town.

What she was not prepared for was the tone of the review. "If you like concerts given by remote control, then you might find la Gloria's performance interesting. The last time she played here, she dazzled with freshness and skill, her renditions of Debussy were sheer delights to hear. But something has happened in the last few years. Last night she was going through the motions. The audience might as well have listened to a robot whose battery was running down."

She gulped her coffee and swallowed quickly, because suddenly it seemed she had something stuck in her throat. Who was this person? Some kid trying to show off? But no, he — and yes, it was a male name — had heard her play before. He couldn't have been someone who had never heard a concert.

Her impulse was to crumple up the clipping, tear it into little pieces, stuff it in the pocket in the seat in front of her. Then she caught sight of the picture again, which was not the usual publicity still her agent sent out. No, the photo had been taken that night, from the side so that shadows fell across her face, highlighting every wrinkle. Her eyes looked haggard, her jawline sagged. The flowers hid the front of her dress so that she seemed not to have a waist, only shoulders as massive as a football player's. There was nothing graceful about her. She had never seen a picture of herself so ugly, so ungainly. So old, much older than the forty-five she could not deny.

She sucked in her breath, and the air collided with whatever had stuck in her throat before. The coughing took her by surprise. Suddenly she found herself fighting for her breath, the whole upper part of her body bent over, her throat burning. Tears sprang from her eyes, her nose ran, all thought was chased from her mind by the convulsions of her body.

The stewardess, who had been standing a few feet away, quickly came over to pound her on the back. The man next to her moved her plate and cup from the fold-down table. The clippings fell to the floor. She left them there when she regained control.

But they remained on her mind the whole day in Toronto. She disliked teaching intensely. On the one hand she felt an imposter — who was she to tell anyone else how to play? She who felt so out of control herself once she found her way to the right place. Technique might be taught, exercises for practice could be suggested, areas for reflection counselled. But the music itself came or did not come; it had a life of its own, and she could only point the way for the young, she could not lead.

And if she were successful as a teacher, she was only creating competition for herself. Not that she ever said that to anyone; it was an idea that seemed too base, too egotistical to share. But it was true. How many opportunities were there for musicians? Each accomplished student was someone who might be offered concerts that might otherwise be offered to her.

Lotte had taught seriously only when her concert career was over. She taught because she had to in order to live, and poured her ambition and love into her students, especially into Gloria.

Gloria held this line of thought at bay during her master class, and when she swooped down on the ballet school to carry Alex off for dinner. His choice was a fancy pizza place that had opened not far from the school's residence and where the kids all wanted to eat.

When she was with her son, it was not difficult to forget the ugly newspaper photo, the terrible review, the cancellation of the Mussorgsky contract. Although he feigned nonchalance when she arrived at the rehearsal hall at the end of the afternoon, she knew he was pleased she was there — and not only because of the gifts she brought with her. His eyes danced when she was recognized by the head teacher, he allowed her to put her hand on his shoulder when she listened to a report on his progress, and when they left he briefly took her hand himself as they walked down the street.

His energy was still enormous despite the hours of ballet class and the weight training the boys began very young. The academic schedule was as full as ordinary school. During dinner, he talked non-stop about the friends he'd made, the residence counsellor who bugged him because he talked after lights out, and the problems he had with the science class. "I thought that would be the easiest part, after hearing Papa and Frannie going on and on about all that stuff. But here they get us to do experiments and to write things out, and it's boring."

Gloria laughed, as she had a flashback to the summer afternoon when she saw exactly what her children's future would be. A rainy day at Bic, with Robert and Frances, nine, making an electric circuit for lighting the performance that Alex, six, had put together to a record he'd found in one of the cupboards of the old house. Both Robert and Gloria had laughed at the performance he gave to "Rum and Coca-Cola" by the Andrews Sisters. Obviously he had no idea what the words signified, but he loved the beat and he ran and kicked and attempted leaps to it.

Now Alex's reactions to science sounded exactly like what her own had been, but she thought it wise not to mention this. So far she'd not told either of her children that she hadn't graduated high school. She supposed that Robert hadn't said anything about it either.

Alex chattered all the way back to the residence, continuing to talk even when walking down the street on his hands. He did not allow her to kiss him goodbye, so she had to content herself with blowing kisses at him from the taxi.

"My son," she told the driver as they watched Alex spring cartwheels back inside the building. "There are times when he's not very restful to be around." But she knew she sounded proud.

The good feeling lasted until she'd checked her messages in the hotel and ordered up a bottle of wine and an order of roast chicken. It was the kind of meal she often craved after a concert, when she'd eaten earlier but still found herself ravenous. This time she'd let Alex eat his fill of the pizza, and she'd merely pecked at her portion and her salad. The restaurant wasn't licensed and now she felt she really needed a drink.

The room service man opened the bottle for her, let her smell the cork, and then poured her a small taste. It wasn't bad, and she eagerly drank a glass as soon as he left. Her hands and face felt grimy, so before she continued, she went into the bathroom to wash. She didn't flip the right switch, and instead of warm incandescent light, the bluish glow of an ultraviolet disinfecting bulb — the latest thing in hotel hygiene — lit the room. She stared at herself in the mirror above the sink, looking worse than she had in the newspaper. Pasty white skin pockmarked with imperfections, eyes ringed in black from makeup, a nose that cast long shadows. Wrinkles everywhere.

"Pictures at an Exhibition," she said aloud. "More like a horror show."

What she should have done then was immediately flip on the right light, chasing away the exaggerations of the blue. But she was held by the vision of a woman no longer young, certainly no longer a rising star. It had been an uphill struggle since she was sixteen or seventeen; she'd fought so hard, made so many sacrifices, killed part of her life. Yes, the baby had lived, but he was dead to her.

The phone rang. It would be Robert. She hadn't called him yet to report on Alex, and he'd want to know what she thought about how he was doing. Then there was the matter of the contract: she hadn't called her agent back either, but that could wait.

It seemed that Robert had taken a call from the agent at the house shortly after he came home, and had heard the whole story. So after he'd listened to Gloria's thoughts about Alex — he'd seen him himself at the beginning of September, just before the boy started his first academic year, and was pleased to learn his good impressions then were confirmed now — he told her he thought she had a case.

"They can't let you go. They're stupid to think they can," he said. "It's a very foolish business decision on their part, to say nothing about what it means in artistic terms."

"Right," she said. "But I'm so tired tonight I don't really want to talk about it. I'm supposed to have breakfast with Alex at the school, so I've got to get up early, and then there's another of those deadly classes to teach. I'll be home by early evening. If you want, we can talk then."

"If I want? It's more what you want, it seems to me, darling girl." She could hear him start to spiral off, slipping on his hero's cape, ready to protect her.

"Shhh," she said. "We'll worry about it tomorrow."

There was a pause.

"How's Frances?" she asked to change the subject. "You haven't said anything about her." Frances was his sweetheart, even if he refrained from saying so.

But he was thinking about other things. "Fine," he said. "Fine, fine. She came back from wherever and had dinner before I got home. Madame Beaudry made spaghetti again."

Gloria laughed. "That's what the girl likes," she said. And before he could respond, she staged a yawn. "We'll talk tomorrow. I need to go to sleep now."

But she didn't. She picked at the chicken and drank the rest of the wine and then stood at the window, looking out at downtown Toronto. The view was like that from many hotel windows she'd stayed in over the years. The chicken was a little drier, the wine more flavourful, and her day had been both better and worse than many others. Master classes were the pits, seeing Alex do cartwheels was the greatest.

But something was changing. She wasn't sure what it was. She turned on the television. She opened the mini-bar. She had a nightcap. She did not think of music.

DRINK ALWAYS HELPED, but given the example of her father she'd been aware that she had to keep it under control. Robert liked his Scotch and water, as well as good wine. The summer Gloria played a series of festivals in France and Italy, he, the children, and the aunties came along for part of the tour; he arranged to buy four cases of various *appellations contrôlées* and have them shipped back to Montreal. That was the beginning of his serious wine collecting, the start of his cellar.

With Alex in Toronto and Frances busy with science projects, volleyball, and student government, Gloria and Robert had the occasion to spend evenings alone together frequently, evenings which usually featured wine. Often when waiting for Robert to come home, Gloria found it congenial to have a drink in front of the television. No new recording possibilities were being suggested, despite the fact that the industry was switching over to the new digitally mastered format. Part of the problem, her agent said, was that she'd developed a reputation for being difficult after the legal back and forth over the Mussorgsky project, even though, once recorded, it sold reasonably well. But, said Robert, how could she not have pushed back when the company shoved? To act otherwise would have been foolish, sending out the message that she would take whatever was offered.

She began to worry more about Frances. In the usual order of things, younger children leave the nest first, but Alex had flown off before he hit puberty and now he was soaring. He presented problems, but they were of a completely different order than the ones that crowded Frances.

The girl had no marked talent, Gloria decided when she made an inventory of Frances's attributes. She might have some small musical aptitude, but she had refused when Gloria tried to start her on the piano at five. She adored Robert, which was to the good, and she pleased him by doing all the silly science experiments he suggested. She got reasonable marks in school, she liked volleyball and basketball, but she appeared to Gloria to lack the passion needed to be more than average. She wasn't even pretty enough to be assured a future as someone's wife.

These were not opinions that Gloria shared with Robert, or with any of the women who might consider themselves her friend. She had few friends; she realized this the winter after the Mussorgsky business. Pianists who aspire to concert careers tend to be loners, unlike string, woodwind, or brass players who are always making music with others. The fact that she had children and a husband who needed a hostess meant she spent less time cultivating friendships. When there was time to spare from practising or performing, she knew she should spend it accompanying Robert, or attending to the children.

From the beginning, Gloria had avoided teas and luncheons organized by the wives of Robert's colleagues. She didn't volunteer when the mothers of Frances's friends called her for help on a school bazaar or field trip. In the summer she spent no time on ferrying the children around to pool parties or tennis lessons. She was asked to serve on boards of music schools and foundations, but so far she had pleaded family obligations. She saw no contradiction there; she did what she could.

Marthe, her dressmaker, said she understood. Marthe had been the one who convinced her that she needed to spend more money on her regular clothes as well as concert dresses. Marthe, who saw she was pregnant with Alex before Gloria was sure herself.

"This one will be due next spring," Marthe said that rainy September afternoon when Gloria came to her studio to discuss two new dresses for the winter season. "Shall we do what we did when you were pregnant with Frances? That worked pretty well, don't you think?"

Gloria stared at her. Until then she hadn't mentioned the possibility to Robert — she'd been afraid to go for a pregnancy test. "It's that apparent?" she asked. She'd begun to undress so Marthe could take her measurements, but she clutched her dress to her chest as if it would protect her.

"If you know how to look," Marthe said. She glanced up and saw the tears rising in Gloria's eyes. "Don't worry," she said. "Your husband will be delighted."

"My husband," Gloria said. For a second she teetered on the brink of telling this smartly dressed woman only a little older than she was all about Pierre. But no, as sympathetic as Marthe appeared, Gloria knew this was not the place to go into the details of why she might feel ambivalent about this baby. Nevertheless she couldn't stop her tears. "My husband ..." she repeated between sobs.

Marthe took the dress from Gloria and pushed her gently toward a chair. When she was sitting, Marthe took her by the shoulders. "Don't worry," she said. "It will be all right. It almost always is for people like us." She winked. "We make sure of that."

After that, Gloria never knew just how much Marthe knew or how much she guessed. But she came to enjoy her sessions with the dressmaker: the afternoons they looked at photos of the latest collections and the publicity stills from movies. Standing for a fitting with Marthe, Gloria talked about what she liked in a dress, about the problems of travel, about diets and makeup. It was rare that she said much about Robert, her career, or the children. Marthe would nod, light another cigarette, and listen. Over the years Gloria was sure that Marthe came to know her better than anyone else. So she was the logical person to consult when Frances was graduating from high school.

The girl had been accepted at MIT. "Why not try for the best?" Robert had said. "We can pay for it. If you want to be an engineer, begin at the top." He was so proud of Frances, so pleased she was doing what he wished he had done.

"At least she won't have to wear made-over things like I did," she told Marthe at the fitting for the dresses she wanted for the two concerts she was giving in Atlanta and Charleston that April.

Marthe nodded but said nothing as she concentrated on the darts under Gloria's bust.

"Then there's the matter of the dress for her graduation," Gloria looked down to see exactly what Marthe was doing. "There's a reception with the parents, and then a dinner and a dance. She'll need something nice for that. I thought I'd bring her in so you could suggest ..."

Marthe broke in with her deep laugh that disintegrated into coughing almost immediately. "You think she'd agree to anything I'd suggest?" she said when she recovered. "Not many of my clients can persuade their daughters that what they'd get here would be better than something off a rack at Le Château or one of those boutiques on Crescent Street." She took a sip from her tea, which her assistant kept topped up. "Go buy some fashion magazines. *Seventeen* and *Mademoiselle* and *Flare*. Let her do some looking. Don't push them on her, just leave them lying around. When she's had a chance to look at them, maybe she'll want to come by."

Gloria was skeptical, but she got the magazines and left them on the counter in the kitchen. Frances was always hungry. She might have a weight problem later, but one thing at a time. Gloria knew to choose her battles. When she heard the refrigerator door open, she got up from the piano in the adjoining room and unhurriedly walked to the door.

Frances was looking at the magazines, but she hadn't picked one up yet. "Hello, sweetheart," Gloria said. "Come give your old mother a hug."

As Frances looked over at Gloria's smile, a small frown wrinkled her forehead. She didn't move, but made a little kiss face before she opened the refrigerator door to take out the milk.

Gloria decided to ignore the rebuff. "There are some good apples," she said. "Madame Beaudry got the kind you like." She walked over and put her arm around the girl's shoulders.

Frances continued to forage for something to eat.

Gloria waited several beats until Frances pulled out bread and peanut butter and put them on the counter. "Could you take out an apple for me too?" she asked.

The girl did so without speaking, but she glanced over at her mother, who smiled broadly. "Many thanks, my sweetie," Gloria said. She bit into the apple vigorously and wiped her mouth with her hand. She laughed. "What a mess."

But Frances did not find it amusing. She was spreading peanut butter on the bread, pointedly not paying attention.

Gloria took a couple of more bites, before deciding she should be more direct. She picked up the *Seventeen*. "Did you take a look at this?" she asked. And when Frances said nothing, she said, "There are some nice party dresses in it. Have you given any thought to what you're going to wear to your ball?"

More silence. Gloria picked up the *Mademoiselle* and leafed through it, holding it carefully so as not to get juice from the apple on it. "There are predictions for fall in this one." She hesitated a second and then lunged, "And while you're thinking about clothes, it might be a good idea to start planning what you're going to take with you when you go to Cambridge."

Frances looked up, peanut butter sandwich in one hand, glass of milk in the other. "They don't wear uniforms at MIT?" she asked, with a show of innocence that Gloria knew was only to annoy her. Frances hated the uniforms she had to wear at Villa Maria. She'd been given a detention three times for changing into jeans the moment she was out of school.

"Of course not," Gloria said, forcing a little laugh she hoped would pass for charm. "But I suppose that part can wait. What's important now is making sure you have what you want for graduation."

Frances folded her arms and leaned against the counter, pointedly looking away from her mother and the fashion magazines. "Maybe I don't want to go," she said.

Gloria half expected that reaction and had already decided to laugh it off. "But of course, you want to go," she said. "You've done so well, and there will be all those awards handed out at the ceremony beforehand. It's a chance for you to shine."

"Maybe I don't want to go," Frances repeated, stuffing half the sandwich in her mouth. When she'd chewed enough to speak she added, "It won't make any difference to anyone if I'm there. If I win any prizes, they can send them afterwards. Or you can get them." She polished off the rest of the milk in the glass. "Yeah, that's what we should do. You should go, and you can pick up any awards I might win, like they do at the Oscars. I can write a little acceptance speech for you, and then I can go do something interesting as soon as exams are over. Plant trees, go prospecting, help the aunties move." She'd begun to pace.

Not wanting to take a bow was something that Gloria didn't understand. She knew some people were so shy they simply couldn't stand up and take credit publicly for what they'd done well. But she doubted that Frances was one of them. Nobody who put so much of herself in her science projects and the basketball team, nobody who had to work so hard because she had so little talent, should let herself be hindered by shyness.

"Don't be silly," Gloria said. She reached out to stop the girl as she strode by. "Look at me," she said, but Frances looked away. "Your success has meant a lot to your father, and you owe it to him to go."

Frances stopped, and Gloria smiled to herself because she had won at least part of the battle. Frances did not look at her mother, but she said softly, "Oh, I don't think he thinks it's all that important."

Gloria took her right hand from Frances's arm so she could cup the girl's chin and look directly at her. "Oh, my little sweetheart, you have no idea how important it is. He is so proud of you."

For a long moment they stood there, with the kitchen clock ticking behind them, and the sounds of birdsong coming through the open window. "In that case ..." Frances said, letting the words trail off.

But her capitulation on that point did not solve the problem of a dress. She continued to refuse to leaf through the magazines, so Gloria tore out a half-dozen pages with what she considered possibilities and handed them to Frances at breakfast a week later.

"Tell me what you like and we'll get Marthe to run something up for you," Gloria said. "What about this, maybe in a sort of raspberry? It will look great with your hair, and you can put roses in it to bring out the colour."

"No reds, no pinks. Never," Frances said. Red had become Gloria's signature colour, her concert clothes always had a splash of it, and for ordinary wear she chose red as frequently as she could. "I want something different."

"But with your colouring, it's a striking choice."

"You didn't hear me: I want something different." Frances grabbed the loose pages and leafed through them. The third sheet had a photo of two girls, one wearing a pink strapless number whose organza skirt floated like an inverted tulip. The other dress was deep purple with a halter top and a skirt cut on the bias so it flared out to end a couple of inches above the girl's knees. "Sugar and spice" was the caption, and the smiles on the two girls' faces repeated the message.

"I don't call organza 'different,' but the shape is quite unusual." Gloria said.

Frances interrupted, "Not that floaty stuff. You don't get it at all," she said. "If I have to get dressed up, I want one like the other one. Purple. Sexy. Short."

Gloria looked at Frances, her expression questioning, and then turning almost amused. "Sexy?" she asked. She was pretty sure that Frances knew she did not look like the girl in the picture. She weighed a good fifteen pounds more, she had a bust, and her waist was thick. A solidly built girl, her father said once. "A girl with some meat on her bones."

But Gloria decided it would be folly to mention the fact that Frances did not look like a fashion model. "I don't know what the nuns would say," she began. The school had strict regulations about length of uniforms, which the girls contravened regularly by rolling up their skirts at the waist as soon as they were off campus. "Isn't there something about what will be considered appropriate in the bulletin about end-of-the-year activities?"

"Who cares?" Frances said. She thrust the pages back at her mother. "It's that one or none at all."

Marthe nodded when Frances arrived with the photo. "Purple, sexy, short, indeed," she said. "I think I have some chiffon exactly that shade, not enough to make a dress from. I'd have to order more, that's not a problem. But enough to give an idea of how it becomes you." So Frances stood before a three-way mirror and Marthe draped fuchsia chiffon over her bare shoulders, letting the fabric swoop low over her bosom.

Gloria watched as Frances rubbed the chiffon between her fingers and smiled. Marthe used fabric that felt good to the hand. But even arranged artfully, it was clear that fuchsia was not Frances's colour, her skin appeared yellow, her light hair looked dirty.

"Not purple," Marthe said. Even Frances had to agree. The

dressmaker winked surreptitiously at Gloria, as she turned to look through her stock of samples. "Not red, you say, so what about green?" She held up a dark, forest green silk with more body to it than the chiffon, but which was supple enough to swirl. "We'll trim it with gold braid and you will be truly beautiful."

It wasn't quite as simple as that, because Marthe had to convince Frances that she should wear a good brassiere underneath. The model in the magazine had looked braless. "But when you have such a lovely bosom, you should take advantage of it."

Frances blushed, but agreed after she tried the dress on. As for the length: the Sisters thought the girls would be wearing long skirts, so they hadn't issued a directive about length. Nevertheless, Frances agreed that a skirt hemmed just above the knees would do more for her sturdy legs than one hemmed at mid-thigh.

GLORIA THOUGHT SHE looked as lovely as she could, and Robert was obviously proud when he swept her out onto the dance floor at the ball during the first father-daughter waltz. The dress's real success became evident that fall at MIT when Frances ran into Daniel, who been dragged to the ball as the escort of a friend's sister. Frances, like many of the girls, didn't have a date, so after that dance with her father, she stood on the sidelines.

Gloria considered it a measure of how much starting MIT had matured Frances that she told her what Daniel Marcoux said when he met her at a mixer given by her residence. He came across the hall as soon as he saw her, she reported when she called at the end of September. He remembered her name and he told her how terrific she had looked the night of the ball, "standing in the doorway, sort of silhouetted against the garden outside, and the setting sun shining on my hair. 'Shiny, curly, really lovely,' is what he said, and he told me he almost came over and introduced himself then."

Gloria refrained from commenting that this was proof that clothes do matter, and refrained too from wondering aloud why this young man was so backward he hadn't done something then. "Good," she said simply. Then Robert cut in because he wanted to hear about her classes.

Gloria only learned later that by then Frances had ditched most of the clothes Marthe had made for her: the plaid A-line skirts with matching sweaters and blouses, the forest-green tweed pantsuit for special events, the peacock-blue wool dress with the long, full sleeves and the short, swingy skirt. Frances pushed them to the back of her closet where she wouldn't have to mess with them. The three white shirts and the two pairs of bell-bottomed jeans along with the denim jacket and the short leather, fleece-lined coat hung in the front: that was what she wore.

The shirts presented a problem at first because Marthe had made them in fine cotton that needed to be ironed. But after a couple of weeks of wearing them wrinkled, Frances discovered that if she put them on when they were fresh from the washer and wore them until they dried they looked all right. It was much easier than ironing, and sitting around wet didn't seem to matter either, at least at first. When she mentioned what she was doing to her mother on the phone, Gloria immediately told her take them to the cleaners, have them done professionally, but even that turned out to be more trouble than Frances wanted to take with her appearance.

Frances had a lot of other things to think about. She'd graduated at the top of her high school class, but she found the math at MIT much harder. She was unprepared. Three times in

September she called home to talk to Robert about her problem sets. He told Gloria rather proudly that he really didn't know much about the subject, but he could tell her how to approach the problems. "Poor little sweetheart, what she's got to learn is that she has to proceed systematically, review her notes, and relax. There're not many problems she can't solve that way. I told her everything was going to be all right."

Gloria looked up from the score she was studying and nodded. For a fleeting instant she felt something that she'd tried to guard against — a twinge of jealousy over the fact that whatever happened, things would turn out right for Frances. But then she dismissed the thought as unworthy. "She always was a good student," she said, because that was the truth.

Frances probably would have done well that term, in part because of Robert's proud assistance. She soon got the knack of studying at MIT, and not the way the Sisters had taught, with a premium given for neatness. In mid-November, though, she got a cold, and then a fever and then swollen glands and it was all she could do to drag herself out of bed. She didn't say anything about it when she called home the first Sunday, but on the second she said she wasn't feeling well, which was why she couldn't talk very long.

"You suppose she's all right?" Robert asked Gloria when she hung up.

Gloria, who was deep inside a letter to her agent in which she wanted to propose two new projects for concert tours, nodded. The girl would be all right. Hadn't they already established that?

But the next week Frances sounded extremely weak when they called. Yes, she'd had to skip some classes, but her roommate had gone in to explain to the profs.

"Take care of yourself," Robert said. "Go to the health services. Are you sure you're eating enough?"

"Losing a little weight probably wouldn't hurt her," Gloria said when Robert signed off that conversation. "And surely she has enough sense to get herself to the doctor if she's really feeling low."

Robert couldn't resist calling in the middle of the week to see how she was doing, but when no one answered, Gloria argued that was a good sign. "She's feeling better, and she's probably at the library studying."

She could tell from the way he set his jaw that he wasn't convinced. "With Alex, I've got more confidence that somebody is always looking out for him. They really have to care about the health of dancers, particularly the boys. But at MIT ..."

"MIT is for young adults, the cream of the cream. It's not a boarding school," Gloria said. Yet she listened carefully every time the phone rang to see who might be calling, even though she did not jump to answer the way Robert did when he was there.

Daniel called on Saturday. He had to explain to Robert who he was but as soon as Robert repeated the name, Gloria placed him among the people that Frances had mentioned. He was the backward boy from Montreal.

"Yes, yes, young man," Robert said. "What is it that we can help you with?" He looked quizzically at Gloria, and mouthed "a boy." Then Gloria watched as panic crossed Robert's face. "She's in hospital?"

Daniel, it turned out, was a lab assistant for a course that followed one Frances was taking. He overheard her roommate tell the prof she was sick and couldn't hand in the assignments. When the prof said if she was that ill she should go to health services, the roommate said she felt too bad to go out. Daniel said that was the point he decided he should see how she was.

Frances never told Gloria how glad she was to see him, how he seemed to arrive in a wave of light when he opened the door to her room. Someone laid a hand on her forehead and she tried to open her eyes but they rebelled against the brightness.

Daniel said, "She's very hot. She's got a fever." The hand disappeared and the voice seemed a little further away, troubled, worried, urgent. "We've got to take her to the clinic. Where's the phone?"

And that was the beginning of the rest of their life, although neither of them knew it at the time.

On the phone, once the diagnosis of mononucleosis had been made, once she seemed safe in the hospital, Daniel gave Robert the telephone numbers for health services and the doctor in charge of her case.

"He said he'd been with her all day, running interference with the doctors," Robert told Gloria when he got off the phone. "It sounds pretty serious — mono with possible complications. I'm going down tonight, if I can get a flight." He began to dial the airline. "Are you coming too?"

Gloria hesitated. What did a mother do in such circumstances? Run to her child? That's what a good mother did, what she would have done for Alex without hesitation. But her agent was passing through Montreal and had agreed to talk about projects on Sunday; it was a meeting Gloria had worked for weeks to set up. She didn't want to cancel.

"Well?" Robert asked. "Do you?" Then someone answered on the other end and he started to speak into the phone. "I want a flight to Boston tonight ... Dammit! She put me on hold."

Gloria stepped over and took the receiver from him. "What

you're going to do is get your things together, and I'll stay on the line to make the reservation. You go down alone; you can handle it without any problem. If necessary, I can come down tomorrow night, but by then you will probably both be on your way back."

He looked at her sharply, as if that wasn't the reaction he expected.

"Go. Get ready," she said. "You're better at this sort of thing than I am, and if I'm here, I can see about getting her admitted to the Royal Vic as soon as you get back." And besides, Gloria thought to herself, Frances is his favourite. He should be the one to look out for her.

"HE'S A NICE young man," Robert said when he called the following day. "He was in her room when I arrived. The nurses thought he was her sweetheart so they let him hang around, but he says he's just a friend." He laughed. "Our Frannie needs more friends like that. We really owe him something, because if he hadn't come along she would be in a much worse way, I'm afraid."

It took three days to get matters sorted out, to make sure she was stable enough to travel. She went directly to the Royal Vic, where she stayed for ten days.

By then it was clear that she'd have to withdraw from MIT. Robert got the necessary forms for the doctors to sign; there was danger of serious damage to her spleen, a not uncommon side effect of mono. She needed to rest, and she shouldn't be too far from home; it was out of the question for her to take final exams. And, since there wasn't much chance of retaking the first semester courses next semester, given the lockstep that MIT insisted upon for its freshmen, the best thing would be to start from zero later.

Gloria and Robert did not talk to her about that until she'd been home from the hospital for more than a week. Christmas had passed. It was a very strange holiday, with Alex coming back for only two days, as he had a major role as one of the children in the National Ballet's *Nutcracker* in Toronto. Gloria performed her usual Christmas benefit concert with musicians of the MSO for a group of charities, but either she or Robert were with Frances every evening. Not that the girl reacted very much: she didn't even want to talk to Daniel when he called the first two times. When she agreed to take the phone when he called to wish her *Joyeux Noël*, Gloria saw the worry lines between Robert's eyebrows relax. She recognized that she, too, felt lighter than she had in weeks. They'd been lucky with their children's health, she now realized; this was the first time there had been serious illness or injury. Even Alex had escaped the usual sprains that seemed to go with ballet training.

The Saturday morning after Christmas, though, as she and Robert sat in the music room drinking coffee and looking out at the snow falling in the garden, he brought the subject up. Without a preamble he began: "But she's only seventeen, remember."

Gloria nodded and looked down at her hands. She'd had them manicured the week before, and the polish had begun to wear away. As always she kept her nails short, the better for playing, but she liked to keep her hands looking elegant nevertheless. She knew she should take the polish off herself, and make an appointment to have it redone the following week.

Robert appeared not to notice that her mind was wandering. "They finish secondary school here so young now," he said. "There's no grade twelve anymore. Maybe we shouldn't have let her go away so early. Maybe she should consider continuing in Montreal."

Gloria took a deep breath and clenched her fists. The prospect of the girl lounging around the house for months, doing nothing, appalled her.

"Well, what do you think?" Robert asked. "You seemed to enjoy having her here. Sitting beside her and listening to music together. You looked so cozy."

They probably did. Frances once woke up and mumbled about how the smell of Gloria's perfume was comforting. She loved the child, of course, that went without saying; it went with the territory. But, once Frances was healthy again, to have her in the house for an undetermined amount of time would be trying. Gloria found herself remembering just how hard she'd had to work at seventeen. She suspected it was unnatural for her to be tempted by resentment, but she had to put her cards on the table, present what she'd been thinking for some time.

"It was your idea to encourage her to aim for the top," she said after she stared out at the snow for several moments. "The girl is hard-working, and she seems to genuinely like mechanical things, so I suppose your idea of engineering for her was a good one." She paused. What she had to say next wasn't going to sit well with Robert. "But is she strong enough? There aren't many women in the field. It won't be easy."

"There is not much that's worthwhile that's easy," he said. There was a pause before he continued in a very small voice. "You know that perhaps more than most."

It was time to speak some truths, Gloria knew. "Well," she began, "times have changed and Frances will never have the kinds of struggles that I did. I imagine she could make a life as a good engineer. If she's not the best, she might not feel like a failure."

Robert said softly "You are far from a failure."

"Perhaps. But I have not done all I set out to do."

"Nor have I," he said. "And yet we are still in the game."

She nodded. "But I'm not sure our girl is going to be strong enough for what she thinks she wants to do. Look what just happened. She can't take the pressure."

"She is young, maybe too young. We weren't wise to send her there, so far away from home, without anyone to guide her."

"When I was her age I was pulling my own weight. And you were only a few years older when you were in the war."

"Four years older," he interrupted. "That's a big difference at that age."

"You're making excuses for her."

"She's a sweet and intelligent girl."

"Oh, come now, Robert. You're blinded to the facts. And she isn't even your daughter."

"Don't say that," he said. "She is more my daughter than James's."

There was a clatter from the kitchen, and both looked up. It was Madame Beaudry's day off. Frances was supposed to upstairs in bed.

"Is that her?" Robert whispered.

Gloria shook her head, but she really didn't know. She was afraid it was Frances.

They'd always been upfront about one version of the story and it was part of family mythology. Gloria had been engaged to someone named James who died in a car accident and Robert married her because she was so sad and because he had always loved her. There was a photo of James with both of them, all three smiling, looking young and handsome, that Robert kept in his office. He was a very good man, Robert always said. His misfortune was Robert's happiness. But they'd been carefully vague about what year that had happened. Certainly they'd never said anything as blunt in the presence of either of the children, nor had they made serious comments about the children's capacities in their presence.

Robert got to his feet and headed for the door. He hesitated before opening it, but Gloria knew what they'd see when the door swung open. Frances was there, holding a piece of bread in one hand and a knife covered in peanut butter.

"What are you doing up?" Gloria said. "You haven't any slippers on, you'll get sick again." Frances's face was white and her mouth was open, as if she were in shock. "Come along, sweetheart," Gloria said coaxingly, fearfully, guiltily. "Let Papa help you upstairs and I'll bring you some cinnamon toast and tea."

Toast spread with butter and sprinkled with sugar and cinnamon was one of the few things Gloria made, but that afternoon she couldn't get the toast done properly. She burned the first two slices and had to begin again. Robert got Frances upstairs and sitting up in her bed by the time Gloria had found a tray, and placed the teapot, cup and saucer, and the small plate with the toast.

Gloria put the tray down on the dresser and brought the cup over to the bedside table. She handed Frances the plate with the toast, and settled herself in the straight-backed chair Robert had pulled next to the bedside. She looked at him as he leaned against the wall at the foot of the bed, his arms folded across his chest.

He nodded. "Let the girl have something to eat," he said. "She needs sustenance."

Frances looked at him and took a small bite of the toast. "Would be more nutritious with peanut butter," she said.

Gloria laughed — not the charming, lilting one she used

to impress, but the genuine laugh that came out when she was surprised by pleasure. "Nutrition isn't the only thing that food is about," she said.

Frances took a bigger bite, but didn't say anything. When she'd finished the toast, Gloria took the plate. "Well?" she said to Robert.

He sat down on the end of the bed, and put his hand on the bump that was Frances's feet. He cleared his throat. Seconds ticked and the late afternoon sun shone as if nothing was happening.

Finally, he said, "You heard us talking, didn't you?"

She nodded. Gloria noted that she did not look at her. Then Robert began.

"We've never hid the facts from you." He paused, watching to see if there was any reaction, but Frances simply took a sip of her tea, avoiding looking at either him or Gloria. "You remember how we've talked about James," he continued. "He was your mother's first, great love, and they were going to be married." He stopped and cleared his throat. He attempted a smile as he put the handkerchief back in his pocket. Frances was looking at him with an expression on her face that Gloria couldn't read. "As I was saying, they were going to be married, only he was killed — he died in a car accident on a country road. It was a tragedy, a fine young man who didn't get to live happily ever after with the most beautiful, the most talented girl in Montreal." He coughed. "We were all devastated. You can imagine how we felt, not the least your mother. But — and this is a miraculous part, for me at least, and maybe for you too — his tragedy became my good luck. You knew that, didn't you? We've never hid that part."

Frances nodded.

Robert took a deep breath. "But what you have not known," he said, grasping her foot harder through the covers, "is that your mother was pregnant with you when she and I married."

For a moment the girl looked blankly from Gloria to Robert and back. "I was born April 17, 1957," she said. "And your anniversary is at the end of the summer. When we were little we used to go up over Labour Day weekend to your cousin's place in the Laurentians to celebrate, right?"

"We were married in August 31, 1956. You can do the arithmetic. You're going to be an engineer." He paused. "There is not a night that goes by that I don't thank my lucky stars I was able to marry your mother," he said. "I had loved her for years, and I have always considered that you were my daughter every bit as much as Alex is my son." He scooted forward on the bed so he could reach over and stroke her hair. "I have always been so proud of you. I've been overjoyed to see how you've grown to love so many of the things I love. You are and always will be my sweetheart."

He made an awkward movement, standing up, holding out his arms, and Gloria stood up immediately too. They stood with their arms around each other for a moment. Frances watched them. "Papa," she said, making her voice as loud as possible. "Papa, don't worry. You are my Papa forever."

He turned away from Gloria, his face covered with an immense grin. "Oh, the sweetheart," he said. He leaned over to prevent his daughter from struggling to her feet. "Relax. Don't strain yourself," he said, easing her back down on the bed. "It will all turn out well, like in a fairy story."

He turned back to Gloria. "Won't it, darling girl? Doesn't everything turn out well?" he said, wrapping his arm around her shoulders. He nuzzled her under her ear. "You are magic," he whispered so only she could hear.

There was no question of challenging that. Gloria knew just how wise it was to let people believe what they wanted. She smiled, but was worried about the second part of what Frances must have heard: Gloria's assessment of Frances's prospects.

Gloria waited until after they'd had dinner, a casserole Madame Beaudry had made from the Christmas turkey that only required warming up. Frances was sufficiently recovered to come down and sit with them at the dining room table. When Frances had gone upstairs to shower and put on a clean nightgown, Gloria went in to say good night. There was nothing unusual about this; every night since she'd come home, both Robert and Gloria had checked to see how she was doing. But Robert had an urgent phone call, and Gloria took this as an opportune moment.

After she bent over to give Frances a kiss on her forehead, she sat down on the bed, and tried to take the girl's hand. For a second Frances stared at her, and then pulled her hand away.

Gloria let her, but there were things she had to say. "You heard the part that came before the talk about James," she began. It wasn't a question; it was the opening point of a discussion, if Frances wanted it to be.

But she did not want it to be. She turned her head and began to fiddle with the bedside radio, seeking a station that played rock 'n' roll. Another thing to annoy her mother, Gloria thought.

"No, don't get involved in listening to that now," she said. "We have to, I have to, make clear what I meant when I was talking this afternoon about courage and all that. I didn't mean it the way it may have sounded." She paused, thinking that, no, that wasn't what she wanted to say either, but having started, she had to continue. "I only want the best for you. You must know that. It's just I don't want to see you hurt."

"I wasn't hurt. I got sick." Frances pushed herself to sit up in bed. She ran her hands through her hair, cut short without her consent during the days when she was in the hospital. She hadn't complained about that, but Gloria knew she resented the way they'd taken control of her body. "Lots of people get sick. Mono is very common, even bad cases like mine. Mono is no reason to think that I can't do what I want to do."

"Which is?"

The question had been asked before. She'd even written an essay on it when she applied to MIT. But as Gloria watched, she seemed to be searching for something new to say, as if the days when she wallowed in terrible fatigue had allowed reflection on a level deeper than consciousness. How else could she have come up with the words which came out so easily, which had such an effect on Gloria?

"The best. I want to be the best, and I want to matter in the world. I want to have it all: career, money, lovers, children. I'm not going to be like you. I'm not going to be second-rate, still trying to make a name for myself even though nobody wants what I can do anymore."

Gloria took a big gulp of air as if she'd been slapped by a giant wave and pulled under water, but she continued to smile.

"What are you talking about?" Gloria said. "I have a very good career. I have engagements set up for the next year and a half. I'm very much in demand." She knew she sounded like her agent making a pitch for a concert series or a new record deal. But it wasn't that easy, and she wondered how this girl, this daughter of hers, had figured out through the haze of her illness and her adolescent self-absorption just how tough it had been for Gloria lately.

"Why are you here this time of year?" Frances said. "Other

years you'd be off doing great things in early January, you were always on the road then. But you're here."

"Possibly the fact that you've been ill has something to do with it," Gloria said. She took a deep breath and ratcheted up her smile. "Well, what I really am glad about is that you're better," she said. "And I'm glad you want to go to the top. You do that. I am behind you every step of the way." She stood up and turned toward the door. "It will not be an easy life," she said. "Remember that I warned you." She turned back at the door. "And, by the way, my career is not over."

It was Gloria who arranged for Frances to enroll in calculus and chemistry beginning in two weeks at Dawson College. It was strictly irregular, but it helped to have contacts, to have admirers, to have pull. She told Frances she would argue with Robert if he protested the idea of her going back to MIT in the fall. But by then Frances had decided to stay in Montreal; Daniel was coming back to work on an advanced degree at Université de Montréal.

THE SUMMER OF 1979, Daniel and Frances took their engineer's tour of Europe. By then she'd finished her degree and worked for SNC-Lavalin for the better part of a year. Daniel had obtained his Ph.D. and he was going to work in the field before he started teaching. In the fall they both were going to be posted to the big hydroelectric project at James Bay — she estimating concrete needs, he several grades up the corporate ladder.

"We didn't do anything cultural the whole three weeks," Frances said when they came by with a couple of presents for Gloria and Robert. "No concerts, no art museums, no old churches, nothing like that." She was grinning. She knew exactly what Gloria's reaction would be.

This was not news to Gloria, as they'd outlined their plans

before they left. At the time she hadn't said anything — there was no point, Frances had her own ideas — but she didn't think they'd spend that amount of time without succumbing to the attraction of something beautiful.

"It was terrific. We started out looking at the dikes in Holland; we took the sewer tour in Paris, we saw the new cantilever bridge in Switzerland, we checked out the aqueducts in Italy, and that was the best, the absolute best ..."

"For sure," Daniel said. "All that concrete and engineered stone. I knew the Romans were great builders, but to see the Pantheon and roads and the aqueducts that are still standing ... It's amazing, absolutely amazing."

There was more, which Robert listened to avidly, finding an atlas to consult as they spoke. Gloria, who brought out beer, white wine, and a bowl of peanuts — Madame Beaudry had the day off — listened too, but her attention wandered when they began pouring out statistics about catchment basins, rates of flow, and Roman concrete recipes. Frances, she noted, looked good; her hair had bleached out in the Italian sun to nearly the flaxen colour that it had been when she was a child. Her skin was clear and sprinkled with freckles across her nose. But it was her smile that made the difference. She glowed with happiness.

"Come, take a look," Robert said to Gloria, holding the atlas open to the spread on Italy. He smiled, obviously pleased that his girl and her friend had seen things that he would like to visit. "How many times have we been to Rome and never visited the Pantheon?"

Gloria laughed. "You always said it was a tourist thing to do, and I was always working. But," she added quickly, "next time we must get you to make an itinerary for us."

"Madame Murray, I'd be pleased to do that," Daniel said.

"And we could add some of the architectural wonders, with notes about their construction. That way you'd be able to see them with new eyes, and you won't miss out on any fine music."

She had no idea if he knew anything about music. Frances certainly had said something about what was listened to in this household. Daniel sounded as if he were trying to impress Gloria, to butter her up, but she decided to give him the benefit of the doubt.

She got up and brought out another bottle of white wine and two more cans of beer. When she retrieved the corkscrew from the table next to Robert so she could open the wine, Frances shot a questioning look at Daniel. He nodded briefly. "No, Maman, we've had enough to drink this afternoon. We have to go by Daniel's parents' house too."

"You're not leaving so soon," Robert said. "I've got more questions."

"They'll have to wait," Frances said. She got to her feet and held out her hand to Daniel. He stood up too, and put his arm around her. "We have something else to say."

"Yes?" Robert said. It was a question, but Gloria began to think she knew the answer even before Daniel began to speak.

"We want to get married," he said.

"We'll both be at James Bay beginning in October and we'd like to live together," Frances said. "You have to be married to do that."

"But we'd want to get married anyway," Daniel said. "After all we went through this summer."

"We'd like to have your blessing."

Robert reached for his handkerchief. Gloria felt herself standing straighter. She spoke before Robert could. "Of course," she said. "We would be pleased."

Her reply gave Robert enough time to jump ahead to the next step. "Wonderful," he said. He hugged first Frances, then Daniel, then both.

"The wedding will have to do be in October, over Thanksgiving weekend, because Frances has to go up to LG-2 week after next, and won't get back before then," Daniel said. "But that should be all right, don't you think?"

"Don't worry," Robert said. "Leave everything to us."

"A big wedding," he added, after the pair left the house. "A big wedding, that's what we'll give her. We need a party. This is something to celebrate."

"Don't get your hopes up." Gloria stood looking out the window as the young couple walked down the path toward Daniel's car, holding hands. Frances said something, Daniel laughed, and grabbed her around her waist, pushing her in front of him. She resisted a little, her hair coming loose. He continued to push. She turned around quickly and pretended to knee him in the groin. He took her by the shoulders, but not before their legs were intertwined and she was forced off balance. Laughing, they fell sideways onto the lawn where they lay for a moment, gazing into each other's eyes before exchanging a long kiss.

Robert looked over Gloria's shoulder. "Well, why not?" he said. "They're young." His arm crept around her, and his hand brushed her breast.

"Yes," she said. And, because she still loved his touch, she turned to kiss him. "But," she said, breaking away, "your daughter may have other ideas about weddings. She has a mind of her own. You know that."

Robert laughed. "Good thing too. But we'll see."

Gloria didn't have much time for planning. In the fall she would be artist-in-residence at Bard College, giving master classes

and headlining a concert series at a number of American col-
leges. It would require commuting from Montreal for a week
every month, but her agent had convinced her it was worth
doing. In addition, she'd agreed to serve on the board of the
foundation that was converting the old Murray place in Charlevoix into a music centre and camp. Meetings, too much travel,
and not enough time to work on developing new repertoire.
But Alex was in New York now, dancing for the American
Ballet Theatre, and Frances was more than ever glad to be on
her own.

Gloria would be free Thanksgiving weekend, and Robert
wasn't joking about taking charge. A big wedding would be
a chance for him to entertain all the members of his family,
his business associates, his friends in politics, and — not inci-
dentally — show off his lovely, accomplished children. Gloria
never refused when he announced they needed to have a dinner
party, but she had made it perfectly clear years before that she
had better things to do with her time than plan one. When his
only daughter got married, Robert almost had an obligation to
make up for hospitality not returned. Daniel's family was large,
and if not well-connected, perfectly acceptable as in-laws. They
should be feted as well.

Gloria was in upstate New York the weekend Robert and
Frances thrashed it out after polishing off Madame Beaudry's
pâté chinois. She knew that had she been there to advance any
suggestion, Frances would have got up from the table and
walked out despite her great affection for her father.

By the time Gloria arrived back in Montreal on Monday
evening, the basic outline had been agreed to. The wedding
would take place the afternoon of the second Saturday in October. A religious ceremony at Église Saint-Viateur in Outremont,

Daniel's family's parish church, but no communion. A reception afterwards at the Ritz-Carlton. The guest list maximum would be three hundred and fifty.

"I'm not to bother her with any details. She's got too much to do," Robert informed Gloria. "I said you'd help her find a nice dress, but that's the limit of your involvement. I'll see to the rest. I already have my secretary booking the Ritz."

Gloria smiled; secretaries helped a lot when doing legwork. As for the dress, she'd talk to Marthe.

"ONE HOUR-LONG session before you go up to James Bay and then a fitting that last week," she told Frances. "Having Marthe make it will be quicker than going shopping in a lot of stores. You don't have time for that. And neither do I. And remember what a success Marthe's dress was for your ball."

She told Marthe to put aside Wednesday afternoon for Frances, and Tuesday she and the dressmaker spent another couple of hours going over possible models and fabric. Long sleeves, sweetheart neckline, full skirt, no train. Simple, in a white silk brocade. But Frances wanted a white tuxedo, if she had to have something made to order. "I'm a woman in a man's world," she said. "I wear jeans and workboots and a hard hat most of the time when I'm on site. Something frilly just isn't me."

Marthe nodded her head in agreement as she brought out the stack of sketches and swatches she'd prepared. "But your mother said it was a church wedding, and I don't imagine the priest would approve of pants on the bride."

"They're worse than the nuns in high school," Frances agreed. "But it's what I want," she went on. "I knew I should have insisted on a civil ceremony."

"But as I understand it, that's what you agreed to," Marthe said, riffling through a magazine. "It would be more trouble than it's worth to renegotiate that part of the deal." She looked up at Frances. "If it means something to your young man's family, and you've already said all right, my advice is to let sleeping dogs lie. One thing'll lead to another ..."

Gloria wanted to jump in and say something about how brides should look like brides; even in operas they did; there were thousands of girls who would trade practically anything to have a custom-made wedding dress, and didn't Frances realize just how lucky she was? But Gloria had learned something from their other fights. The most she allowed herself to say was "Maybe Marthe has some ideas. She's dressed hundreds and hundreds of brides."

Before Frances could snort a retort to that, Marthe found what she was looking for. "Here," she said, "here's the solution. A suit, but with a long skirt, not trousers. And we can make a lovely little blouse underneath that you can wear when the dancing starts and it gets too warm."

"Dancing," Frances said, "I don't think there's going to be dancing." But when she saw the design that Marthe proposed — a tailored jacket and a long, bias-cut skirt in heavy ivory silk — the girl had to agree it just might do.

"Can you put a little green trim on it somewhere?" she said, once she'd stripped down so Marthe could take measurements. "I mean, it was your green dress that started the whole business off."

Marthe looked up at her and smiled: "It's not customary, but I really see no reason not to. Let me think about the best way." Which was why the collar and cuffs on the blouse were piped with green, while the topstitching on the skirt's hem was green too. "Just a touch," Marthe said. "Enough for symbolic value."

Neither Gloria nor Frances had expected Robert's reaction, though. "No ruffles, no train? But you won't look like a bride at all," he said when they came back with the sketch Marthe had made. "I've been looking forward to you being dressed like a princess."

"She'll look lovely," Gloria said. "She'll look regal and that's better than looking like a princess."

"It's what I want," Frances added, which was enough to shut up her father.

Then there was the matter of the engagement ring that James had given Gloria. It sat in its box on a back shelf in Gloria's closet. She had forgotten about it. Robert hadn't.

"If James had lived, he might have wanted his daughter to wear it," he said to Gloria when he was filling her in on the latest wedding details. "Maybe we ought to offer it to Frannie — you know, as a link with the past."

"No," Gloria said without reflection. "She is your daughter, period. Sell it, put whatever it brings into bonds for them. She'll get the benefit and we won't have to bring up old stories that shouldn't be repeated now. Let sleeping dogs lie." She thought *let lying dogs sleep*.

A more serious problem developed over the music. Not the organ processional — the church had a list of suggestions and Frances rubber-stamped Robert's choice.

"But we want a soloist to sing too," she said.

Robert nodded and smiled. "A couple of vocal selections would be very nice indeed. Where's the list? I saw several things that would be appropriate. "

"No, nothing from that list," Frances said. "I already looked.

Not one of them means anything to me. What we want is an Italian song that's important to us. It's called '*Rondine al nido*.'"

"That old warhorse?" he said. "It's not even a song about happiness. You know the lyrics are about love flying away like a swallow, don't you? That's not suitable, it seems to me. Does it to you, Gloria?"

She had vowed not to say anything, so she allowed herself only a small, noncommittal nod of her head.

"It means something to us," Frances insisted. "There's a story behind it." She looked down at her hands, at her square fingers with the nails cut short, as if looking there would make it easier to explain.

"Of course," Robert said, "we'll have to get a local artist to sing it," Robert's secretary came up with Pierre Boisvert's name.

"You remember him," Robert said to Gloria. "You accompanied him at that concert together at Métis and he dropped by once when we were at Bic. Since then he's made a bit of a specialty of bel canto and Italian songs. Comes very highly recommended, and even more importantly, he's free the weekend of the wedding. I went ahead and signed him up. Good tenors are always busy."

Gloria knew what Pierre had been doing, she'd made it clear to her agent that there were several artists that she didn't want to work with for one reason or another, but nevertheless every couple of years there'd be a gig offered that included him in some way or another — a concert in Ottawa was the most recent one, eighteen months ago. Because the organizers of the series were people she'd worked with for fifteen years, she wondered then if she were far enough removed that she could see him again, but in the end she decided she wouldn't take the chance. But now, like that summer concert, there was no explanation she could give that would make sense and not jeopardize her carefully constructed life.

She was so busy she didn't listen to Robert negotiating what else might be sung at the wedding, or deciding with Frances and Pierre what accompaniment he should have. Pierre suggested Neapolitan guitar, given Daniel and Frances's great love of Italy, but the priest said no when Robert asked. After that came discussion with the organist. What Italian composers wrote good wedding music? Pierre wanted to be part of that, as well. But Gloria managed to avoid seeing him until the Thursday before the wedding, when she came back from Bard.

She was gracious; she shook hands with him when they gathered at the church to look things over. Both Robert and Pierre wanted to have a musical run-through. "It's your daughter, darling girl," Robert said. "It just simply won't do if the music is any less than terrific."

The organist — a man she knew had studied at the Conservatory about ten years after she'd come back to Montreal from France — was appropriately pleased to meet her in person. The priest laughed and took her hands too, saying "I'm your greatest fan."

Gloria smiled warmly at them, but ignored Pierre.

Marthe had made her a tailored suit in burgundy crêpe de Chine with a knee-length skirt; proper attire for the mother of a bride who didn't want flourishes. Daniel's mother wore a dark mauve tunic over a dress that camouflaged her ampleness. The two friends who were Frances's attendants had long-sleeved forest-green shirt dresses and carried bouquets of purple asters, deep red and dark gold chrysanthemums, dark green leaves. The flowers on the altar were clouds of autumn colours.

"It's all quite pretty," Gloria heard Pierre say in her ear when she stood in the vestibule, waiting for Alex to escort her down the aisle. "But not very Italian."

She turned around in spite of herself. "Shouldn't you be up in front, in the vestry waiting for your cue?" she asked.

"I'll slip up in a moment, but I wanted to see how it all looked beforehand. It's not every day one's daughter gets married."

What he said could be interpreted at least two ways, and she looked carefully at him to determine which he intended. His grin told her all. "I wanted to see the boy too," he said. "I heard he was a dancer and I couldn't imagine how that could happen." He nodded toward Alex, standing near the doors to the sanctuary with his arm around the girl he'd brought from New York. She was a dancer too, thin and nearly as tall as he was but with an aura of provocativeness about her despite her boyish figure. Audrey Hepburn, Gloria had thought when she first met her, not a dancing corpse like some of the girls in the company.

Alex was tall, like both Pierre and Robert. His eyes were the same bright blue as Gloria's, and his dark brown hair was as curly as Frances's. So handsome, so talented; Gloria could not help but be proud of him. She watched him kiss the girl, his hand slipping down her back to cup her bum and draw her closer.

Pierre, too, saw and laughed softly. "A man after my heart, I'm glad to see. There are advantages to spending all your time with dancers. So many lovely girls and so few real men."

"Shut up," Gloria said. She kept her voice low, but she suddenly was so angry she wanted to shout. "If you say one thing more along that line, I don't know what I'm going to do but it will be drastic."

"Gloria, my dear," Pierre began, but she reached over and

took his hand, digging her nails into it. As usual, the nails were cut short, but pianists have strong hands.

"Gloria." He yelped, and pulled his hand back. "I didn't mean anything. You know that."

She did not look back. She walked toward Alex and the girl. "Excuse me, Alex," she said. "But I think it's time."

Alex gave the girl another kiss on the cheek and let go of her hand, watching as she was escorted to the front by one of Daniel's cousins. Then he turned to Gloria. "Ready to make our grand entrance, Mom?" he asked.

She held out her hand to take his arm. When Pierre called something after them, she ignored it.

THE NEXT YEAR Robert had his first heart attack. He was sixty-one and in good shape; he played squash regularly despite his vision problems. But he was scared sufficiently by his first three days in hospital, by the machines hooked up to him, by the concern on his doctors' faces, that he vowed to quit smoking. "And I think I'll start cutting back on my workload," he told Gloria. "When I get back home, you'll see."

Gloria nodded, and told him that whatever he wanted to do she was behind him one hundred per cent. Then, because he was supposed to stay in hospital for at least a week more, she took the train down to Hyde Park to teach her master class at his insistence. "I'll be fine," he said. "Where could I get better care? When I go home, though, that's when I'd like you around."

She told herself she could look after Robert, they'd be fine. But she felt very tired her second night at Bard. It had been a long day; in addition to the class, she had audition tapes to listen to, and her agent to argue with about what she should do next year and the year after. The fatigue and worry showed on her face in the mirror in the bathroom of the small on-campus apartment. She needed to take a bath, she needed to take the time to do something about her pasty skin.

Gloria poured herself another glass from the excellent Gewürztraminer she'd found in the liquor store in the village. Sipping her second, then third glass of wine, she waited for the hydrating mask to do its work.

Looking at the small wrinkles around her eyes, she decided against plastic surgery. Three of the wives in the circle of Robert's colleagues had already lost their smiles to a little nip here and a smoothing there. Better to live with her face, making sure that it was properly creamed and protected, but counting on a lifetime of professional smiles to give her face lines that meant character, not age.

It wasn't egotistical, she was pretty sure, to think that her smile was still charming. Her teeth didn't need work, as she'd had the front ones capped when the children were small. Her mother had suggested this right after Alex was born. "Nothing makes a woman look more tired or uninviting than crooked, stained teeth," she'd said.

She took another sip of the wine, and thought about Robert.

She should call him before she went to bed. No; she should call him now, because surely they'd be turning out the lights in his room soon.

For a second she wondered again if she should have left so soon after the procedure, but he had insisted. Once her obligations at Bard were over she would be free for two weeks; she'd stay home, she would look after her husband. She'd play for him the way she'd played for his father, she'd try out the repertoire she was working on. She'd ask his advice; there was nothing he liked more than to be consulted about her programming.

The phone rang and as she hurried into the other room to answer it, she dropped the wine glass on the tile floor of the bathroom. Glass and wine everywhere. She stopped for a second to compose herself before she picked up the receiver. Calm. Collected. Been working too hard.

"Hello," she said, pitching her voice low to sound calm for Robert. But before she could tell him that she was just about to call, she realized it was not Robert, but Frances.

"Maman, you'll never guess," her daughter said. Gloria could hear someone laugh in the background, and a voice like Robert's saying "that's it, that's it."

"What?" Gloria said, alarmed despite the happy sounds on the other end of the line. Frances wouldn't be calling if things were all right, would she? What was she doing down from James Bay? Robert had not wanted to alarm either of the children and Gloria had played down the situation when she'd talked them earlier in the week. "Is that your father I hear? Aren't visiting hours over? And why are you there?"

This time Frances laughed. "Oh, maybe visiting hours are done, but they've given us special dispensation. And we're here for a very good reason. Come on, guess what. Something terrific is going to happen."

"Give me the phone," Robert was saying. "Let me tell her, if you're going to play coy."

Gloria heard the sound of movement on the other end, before Robert came on with a voice stronger and younger than she'd heard in a while. A good sign; she felt herself relax. "We're going to be grandparents, darling girl. They just came down from James Bay to find out for sure. How's that for marvellous news?"

"What?" she said. *I can't believe what I'm hearing*, she thought.

After Frances, Robert, and Daniel had hung up, with laughter and joy, and Gloria had had time to reflect, she couldn't believe the reaction she'd heard. Having a baby shouldn't be a surprise, after all; people who are married have babies. People who aren't married have them too — as she well knew. But why was Frances the engineer so pleased? Didn't she know things were going to change for her in a massive way?

Gloria saw the broken glass. Mechanically, she went over to pick it up, holding the shards in her hand, being careful not to cut herself. There was wine left in the bottle; after she'd dumped the slivers of glass in the trash, she took another glass from the kitchenette. Then she sat down in front of the window, pulled the curtains back, and, with the lights off, looked out in the night, glass in her hand, bottle by her feet.

She found herself shaking, but with cold or anger, she didn't know. Or maybe it was envy; yes, maybe that was it. She had never been able to welcome any of her children with such a light heart. She had grown to love both — her children; Frances and Alex were very, very dear to her. As for that other, first, ghost child, he had begun to haunt her.

What was Frances doing to herself? She'd have maternity leave — because families were moving to the James Bay settlement, healthcare was not going to be a problem. She'd come back to Montreal for the birth.

But it was so much more complicated than that. She was going to be inhabited by another creature for months. Even if she arranged abundant help, even if Daniel helped — and it sounded like he had already signed on to be the model, modern dad — it was going to be very, very hard. Robert's princess didn't know what she was getting herself into.

The bottle was empty. There was no traffic on the country

roads Gloria saw from her window. She ought to go to bed. But she knew she wouldn't sleep. She had to talk to Frances, now, before things went any further.

It was nearly midnight, so they should be at the house by now, given that they'd been at the hospital at nine p.m.

She dialled and the phone rang six times. She was just about to hang up when Frances's sleepy voice answered.

"It's your mother," Gloria said. She hesitated, trying to think how to approach the matter. She truly didn't want to make things difficult for Frances, she knew just how defensive the girl might be about anything she suggested. She took a deep breath and willed herself to be calm. But she found herself blurting out, "Just what do you think you're doing?"

"Trying to get some sleep," Frances answered. There was annoyance in her voice. "Everybody says to store up now," she continued, sounding more like the good spirits of earlier in the evening, "because once the baby's born, we won't sleep at all." Daniel laughed in the background. Gloria pictured them in bed in Frances's old bedroom, his lanky frame too long for the ordinary double bed.

"That's just it. How could this happen?" It was a stupid question, and Gloria regretted the words as soon as they left her mouth.

More laughter from Daniel, when Frances repeated Gloria's question. "Tell her: In the usual way," Gloria heard him say.

Frances giggled. "We finally got the idea, Maman," she said. "No," she added, apparently turning toward Daniel.

"I'm worried about the consequences. Didn't you give any thought to what might happen?"

"Plenty," Frances said.

"I don't understand then," Gloria began. "It's your life ..."

"It is my life," Frances cut in. "That's just the point."

Gloria could hear that Daniel was saying something, but Frances cut him off. "No, no, she's brought it up," Frances said to him. "I was afraid of this."

Daniel replied, but Gloria couldn't catch what he said. Then came silence, heavy silence, ending only when Frances cleared her throat. When she spoke the playfulness was completely gone from her voice. "Maman, I didn't want to go into this now," she began. "I wanted you and Papa to be happy with our news. I didn't want to hear you tell me about my life and what I should do."

She paused and cleared her throat again. When she continued, her voice was husky, clotted with emotion. "There are things you ought to know, Maman. Maybe you ought to wake up and think about somebody beside yourself. Maybe you thought I didn't have what it takes to get to the top, but I do. I'm proving it. And I can do it while being the sort of woman you never were."

"What do you mean?" Gloria heard the sharpness in her own voice.

"This baby is not an accident. This baby is going to be loved. We're going to have a lot of kids and we'll both take care of them, and I'll be the mother you never were."

The mother you never were! The words stung. "You're twenty-three. You don't know what you're talking about."

"And how old were you when you had me? Twenty-nine. And by all indications you didn't want me, neither you or your famous James."

Frances was sobbing. Daniel was murmuring in the background. "Lucky for me that Papa was there to pick up the pieces."

"Oh, my sweet child, it wasn't that way at all," Gloria said. "I do love you. I tried my best ..."

"And your best wasn't good enough; not for me, not for Alex. Ever wonder why he was so keen to leave home when he was just a little kid? You," she shouted.

Daniel obviously had grabbed the receiver away from Frances. He said, "Madame Murray, this is enough for one night," before hanging up.

Gloria sat for a moment, holding the now-dead receiver. She felt her head spinning; she thought she might be sick. The girl sounded so bitter, and the accusation that Alex had left to escape his mother was so unjust. Frances was being unfair; there was so much she didn't know. All Gloria wanted was the best for her and Alex, that's all she ever wanted.

No, Gloria thought, I can't let it end like that, I've got to explain that I only mean well. She dialled again and got a busy signal. They'd either taken the phone off the hook or were talking to someone else. She waited a couple of minutes, pacing up and down, and tried again. Still the busy signal.

She turned toward the window. The curtains were still open, but now that she was nearer the light coming from the bathroom, she didn't see the countryside beyond the window. Instead she saw her own reflection: a woman alone in a rented space with secrets and sorrows she could not share.

Music — she needed music. The upright piano in the tiny apartment was dreadful: she hadn't asked for a better one because she didn't expect to use it. But she had to play; playing had saved her before. During those awful months, the first year in France when she refused to see what was happening, practice kept her going. She had wrapped herself in a cape of sound and she played until her arms ached and her back throbbed. She played until she was drunk with melody, harmony, rhythm, until the river of music was all that kept her from giving up, completely mad.

She needed to play, so *faut de mieux*, she sat down at the terrible instrument and began with "The Girl with the Flaxen Hair." The action was faulty, the sound was worse. Yet when the first notes sounded, her agitation began to dissipate and, as she moved deeper into the harmonies, she began to cry. In her head, she considered the piece to be Frances's, not only because she had played it time and again when she was pregnant with her, but also because the child had so often floated, self-absorbed, through the world when she was little, like the deceptively simple and calm theme. Even the lone rising notes at the end were like the person Gloria thought Frances had become: heading forward, slightly off-balance, ready to use that momentum to get where she wanted to go.

How wrongly Frances understood what Gloria had done, what her intentions had been. Because at Gloria's heart there always was the child given away, the boy whom no one knew about, who occupied her soul. He was an unacknowledgeable sorrow.

She found herself playing a piece she hadn't performed in public. "Kindertotenlieder," songs on the death of children.

The notes came pouring out. She was accustomed to playing things she'd learned long ago and not touched recently. Every trained musician can do that: after a shaky start, memory kicks in, the pathways laid down between brain and muscle guide the music. The pain of playing was like penance.

Her fingers found themselves playing a berceuse by Chopin that she had played for Alex when he was a baby; then more Debussy; then the "Winter Wind" étude by Chopin she'd played for James at the beginning. The music flowed onward, carrying her with it; Bach in memory of Lotte, the Italian song Pierre had sung at the wedding of Frances and Daniel.

The sky began to grow light with morning. She stood up and walked to the window; outside, the fields were green and she could see the trees ready to burst into leaf.

The boy would be thirty-one in a few weeks, a man wherever he might be.

She put these thoughts away. She had to teach in a few hours. She had new music to work on. Robert was going to need her, and perhaps, if she were persuasive, Frances might too.

IV

THE WHITE PEAK of Mount Baker stood high above the clouds
to the south when Gloria arrived in Vancouver. But, as soon as
the plane ducked into the clouds and began its approach to the
airport, she saw nothing but grey. Her ears began to ache; she
swallowed furiously, trying to equalize the pressure in them.
This was one of the disadvantages of flying when half sick, but
the show must go on.

Mike and Mrs. Mike were in the arrivals area to greet her: still
an enthusiastic *mélomane*, he'd arranged the invitation from the
new recital society in which he was deeply involved. He'd grown
portly since those days right after the war when he'd been one of
the boys, eager to help her career. But Gloria did recognize him
immediately when she entered the luggage claim area; over the
last couple of decades he'd shown up at concerts. His wife was
a different matter. Gloria wasn't sure if she would have recognized her had she not been with Mike. Gloria remembered her
as plump, perpetually rumpled and tired, but now she was sleek
and smartly dressed. Gloria recognized her beige linen trousers
and short, forest green coat as expensive West Coast chic.

"You look terrific," Mike said, kissing Gloria on each cheek.

"So do you," she lied, then added to his wife, quite sincerely: "And you look truly splendid."

Mrs. Mike laughed. "Women our age should take care of ourselves, don't you think?"

"Women any age should take of themselves," Gloria said. "But it seems to me that you've been doing a particularly good job." She caught sight of her own reflection in one of the big windows and realized she suffered in comparison. It wasn't just being tired after a five-hour flight and congested because of the cold. She felt stale.

"My girlfriend here has just received a real accolade for all the good work she's done," Mike said. "She's going to be one of the chief honchos planning events around the World Expo."

Gloria must have looked blank. She'd heard something about another big world's fair, but she had no idea what Mike was talking about.

"Vancouver's going to host the world in 1986, just like Montreal did in 1967," Mike began.

But his wife cut in. "Don't let him snow you, Gloria. It's going to be more work than honour. I got the job because our daughter who's in human resources told me about it."

"Don't sell yourself short, my love," Mike said, hugging her. "I kid you not, she just told me the news on the way over here." He kissed her cheek. "Just goes to show that talent and intelligence get the recognition they deserve."

"Congratulations," Gloria said. "You must be very pleased."

"Pleased? You have no idea," Mike said. "But look, let's get you over to the hotel. Hope you don't mind if we leave you there until morning. It's a nice place and the food is supposed to be extremely good. But there are a few things that we have to get done this evening, among them telling the kids."

"Of course, of course," Gloria said. "Listen, I can get to the place by myself. Why don't I just jump into a cab?"

Mike shot his wife a look. "No, no." But Gloria could see he didn't want to play host this evening and she found herself turned off by the idea of doing anything with them. She had visions of cringing every time she saw the three of them in a mirror: they looking pleased with the way the world was turning and she looking as if she had motion sickness.

"You wouldn't mind?" Mike asked. "You're sure? It's just that this is a weeknight and we want to catch everybody before it's too late. All four have kids of their own and evenings tend to be hectic, so we'd like to make the rounds before bedtime." He picked up Gloria's suitcase and started herding her and Mrs. Mike toward the exit.

"We heard that Frances and her husband have a little boy. You must be enjoying your first grandson," Mrs. Mike said.

But, before Gloria could say they had two boys now, Philippe and Carl, eighteen months apart, Mike continued. "We thought we'd invite people over after the concert on Thursday, you know. Have a late supper with the music crowd. You'd be surprised how many people from Montreal who followed your career from the beginning have ended up in BC."

They were outside the terminal by the taxi stand. Mike raised his hand to summon the next cab in line. "So, we're agreed. The society's assistant director will come by for you at nine tomorrow morning," he said, handing her suitcase and money for the fare to the driver.

She nodded and got in the cab, waving to them as Mike closed the door. Then, as soon as the driver pulled out into the stream of traffic, she leaned back and shut her eyes. This was not going to be an easy trip.

The hotel was on English Bay, but her room looked the other direction, toward the mountains of the North Shore. In the morning Gloria found the clouds had lifted and the day was clear and cold, with snow-covered Grouse Mountain rising beyond the trees of Stanley Park. The sunshine lifted her spirits, but she felt achy and feverish. At the rehearsal, she decided not to exert herself; the program was mostly Debussy, with Bach's French Suite No. 5 in G thrown in for good measure. She had played it a hundred times before; and she saw that the chamber music society people were noticeably subdued as they listened to the run-through, as if they expected more passion from her.

When she left the hall she made a point of giving everyone her best crowd-pleasing smile. "No, no, don't worry about me this evening," she said when one of the organizers asked if she'd like to meet for dinner. "What I need is a bowl of soup and a good night's sleep." She picked up the folder with her music which she'd left backstage while she played. "I'll just spend some time looking over the scores. Anything more exciting would really do me in."

She took a nap when she got back to the hotel and then ordered tea, lemonade, tomato soup, and a small quiche. When she'd eaten — and she was hungrier than she expected — she found little bottles of Scotch in the mini-bar. She settled down in the room's one comfortable chair to look over two of the Debussy preludes. They'd sounded particularly flat that afternoon, and she knew that she needed to do some reflection if she was going to shake that.

The Scotch burned delightfully going down. As she worked her way through the first drink, she began to think she had a handle on a new way into "The Sunken Cathedral," a piece she'd played so often that it had become rote. She poured herself another Scotch, and decided that listening to music would be her reward.

It was shortly after eight p.m. and the FM station was beginning a live broadcast of a new work commissioned for the CBC Vancouver Chamber Orchestra. She didn't catch the name of the composer, but she heard who the soprano would be: Marie-Danielle Parent, who'd sung the summer before at the new music centre taking shape in Charlevoix. A fine voice, well worth listening to, even if the music she'd be singing was an unknown quantity. The title was evocative: "Lonely Child."

It began with a gong struck once, hard. The reverberations were allowed to die out gently, before a theme appeared. The gong was struck again and again, but more gently, sounding quieter and more haunting against a spare, simple melody played by strings. Then the soprano took it up, singing words that Gloria could only partially follow. They began in French — "*Bel enfant de la lumière dors, dors, dors, toujours dors*" — but she lost the sense after that. The sweet sorrow in the soprano's voice pushed anguish beyond ordinary language; she sobbed a series of sounds that the instruments propelled even further upwards.

Like the Mahler "Kindertotenlieder," the emotion behind the piece was almost too much to bear. Gloria found herself wanting to stop the music, but just as she was about to escape by turning the radio off, the timpani pounded out a slow funeral beat leading to the gongs again.

There were more words that she recognized: "*donne-moi la main*," and "*les étoiles au ciel brillent pour toi ... et t'aiment éternellement*." But then the melody was transformed by the strings, to end with the gong striking one, twice, and a third time before it was abruptly muted.

When it was over, Gloria could not move. Nor could the studio audience, apparently, because there was a long moment of silence before applause burst out. It went on and on, much longer than the time allotted in the broadcast's schedule and the program host broke in before it was over.

"This piece by Quebec composer Claude Vivier is not only groundbreaking, it draws deeply on his own experience, doesn't it?" he asked someone whose name Gloria hadn't caught.

"Yes," the other man said. "This is a hymn or an homage to the mother that he never knew. He is an orphan, you see. A true lonely child."

Gloria couldn't listen to any more. She turned off the radio.

She had trouble going to sleep, and when she did she dreamed of walking through Paris with the bells of churches tolling around her, almost like the gongs of "Lonely Child." When she awoke, she saw a connection between those bells, the chords of Debussy's "The Sunken Cathedral" and the haunting gong of Vivier's piece. She spent two hours going over the score of the Debussy, and by afternoon she was not only feeling less ill, but also excited about the coming performance.

As soon as she arrived at the hall for the sound check, she asked if anybody else had heard the concert. The CBC orchestra broadcast regularly on Wednesday nights, and had such a following that no other classical concerts were scheduled in Vancouver then. But the night before, the obscurity of the composer apparently discouraged listeners among the chamber music society.

"Some guy from Quebec, I heard," the woman in charge of publicity said. "But, hey, you're from Montreal. You probably know more than we do out here."

Gloria shook her head. The music community was split between composers and performers — surely these folk knew that — to say nothing of the different poles of action. Toronto was the centre of the universe for music makers based in English Canada, while Montreal had two sometimes overlapping musical worlds, one where the participants usually spoke French and another where they mainly spoke English. Gloria worked in both, but for two reasons she wasn't immersed in either: she had an international career and she had a wealthy husband, which meant she didn't have to scramble. She could afford to be somewhat aloof, and she was.

The result was that she had not heard of this young composer, even though he must have quite a reputation for a Vancouver group to commission a work from him.

"If you want to know more you ought to talk to the vco's programming director," the recital society's director said. "Now, let's get all the final details taken care of and go get something to eat before the concert."

Gloria wanted to make some changes in the order of the program, though, and the director protested. "The programs are printed. It looks amateurish to change at the last minute, unless you've got a really good reason."

"I have a good reason," Gloria said. "It will make a stronger performance. Isn't that what we all want?"

So she finished with Debussy's "The Sunken Cathedral" instead of the Bach. The piece took little more than six minutes, plunging into the depths from the first note. The bells of the cathedral underneath the water rang out, the sound swirled, the melody — as simple as Debussy had written — carried Gloria along. The composer had not intended this to be program music, and even though Gloria had more than once talked about it to students as if it were, the sound had its own logic, its own life. When Gloria arrived at the final chords, each diminishing in intensity until silence returned, the music had produced an effect similar to the final notes of the gong at the end of *Lonely Child*. The effect, so similar, could not be described in words, but everyone in the hall felt it. There was a moment after the music ended when no one moved. Gloria sat immobile at the keyboard, her head bowed, her hands resting lightly on her lap.

The applause, when it came, was thunderous. She was called back for bows twice, and then a few shouts of "encore" went up. But she shook her head at them, smiled and bowed again. There was no way she would be able to play again that night; she'd drained everything she had.

Then Mike was by her side, shepherding her through the backstage and out to the night. Mrs. Mike was waiting in the car by the artists' entrance. "Wonderful, wonderful," she said. "The audience was completely swept away."

He held the car door open for Gloria to climb in the back seat.

"You must be exhausted," Mrs. Mike said from the front seat. "Would you like to go up to your room before we go to supper? We thought you might like to, so that's why we decided to have the supper in your hotel."

"No, no," Gloria said, wishing she'd not agreed to the reception. She felt completely wrung out. But Mike was such an old friend. "I may not stay long, though. You'll understand if I slip out after I've done the usual hellos."

From the silence in the front seat, Gloria knew that was not what they had been expecting, so she decided not to pursue the matter. Instead she put on a smile when they arrived, and stepped out to shake hands with the organizing committee, who must have raced back from the concert hall to arrive before her.

She recognized a few of the people: the dean of the music school at the University of British Columbia, the head of the piano program there, an elderly German man who'd known Lotte and told her straight out that he wished she'd stayed with the Germans and not got into "that French crowd."

She took the glass of champagne Mike offered and stood next to him when he made a speech about how he'd watched her career for three decades and was so pleased that her artistry had grown with time. "Let us drink to Canada's most interesting woman pianist," he said.

He was so generous that Gloria felt a bit embarrassed, particularly given the way he'd been cut out of some of the music activities back at the beginning because he was Jewish. She had not paid much attention back then — she was too absorbed in her own career — but Robert had mentioned the injustice of it when he urged her to accept the invitation. "My great uncle was a real pig. We went along with him, and didn't include Mike on a lot of things. You go and help him and his friends. It's the least you can do."

After the applause, Gloria was supposed to speak. Never good at speeches, and with the champagne making her head light, and feeling destabilized by the experience of "Lonely Child" the night before, she decided she could only manage a smile and brief "thank you," wishing them well in their efforts to bring more music to their city.

"We've got a great series coming up for next year," the director said. Gloria took another glass of champagne and waited until enough time had passed so she could leave. "Look," the woman said, leading her to the buffet table. "Let me get you a plate. You must be starving. I'd like your opinion about who we've got on the roster for next season. We have an empty spot. Perhaps you have an idea who might be good."

She realized that she was indeed very hungry; but for a moment she stood holding her glass and the plate the woman handed her, wondering stupidly how she could possibly eat with both hands full. Mrs. Mike materialized, sized up the situation and held out her hands to take one or both. "Thank you very much," Gloria said, relinquishing the glass. She smiled at Mrs. Mike; even if they'd never been friends, she found herself delighted to be around someone from so long ago. "Are you involved in the planning for next season too?" she asked between bites of tiny quiche. The food tasted surprisingly good, and she remembered that she had eaten practically nothing since morning.

Mrs. Mike laughed. "Only peripherally. But, you know, we do have a problem," she said, reaching for the now-empty plate and handing Gloria back her glass. "Pierre Boisvert was to be our opener in the fall, but he's had to withdraw for health reasons, he says. The society wants a singer for that slot, a good singer, but we're afraid everyone worth having will already be engaged."

"Pierre's ill?" Gloria asked. She looked around to see if the waiter was still circulating with the wine. Pierre? She didn't want to think about him, particularly while she was still raw from "Lonely Child."

"Apparently," the series director said. He was nearby, Gloria neatly signalled to the waiter with the wine. "It's not clear with what, exactly. His agent is being a little vague. Says there's a chance he may be available, but that won't be certain until early summer. That's too late for us."

"Oh," Gloria said, taking a long drink from her fresh glass. "Doesn't sound too serious," she said.

"The rumour is, he's just drying out," Mrs. Mike said. "You remember him from all those years ago: he had quite a reputation then, someone who liked to party. A skirt chaser too." She took a sip from her own drink. "Beautiful voice. I remember going to a recital at Ogilvy's when I was nine and a half months pregnant with our second baby, and going into labour while he was singing 'Nessun Dorma.' I didn't say anything to Mike until the concert was over because I didn't want to miss anything. The baby was born two hours later." She laughed. "He had that effect. Quite a fellow."

Gloria made a polite noise, but found her light head turning dizzily. "There were some who would say he was far too cocky," she began.

"Cocky! Now that's a term I haven't heard for a while," the series director said. "He has such a reputation as a ladies' man that it's probably pretty apt, though. But tagging him doesn't solve our problem. Who are we going to get?"

Gloria shut her eyes. She had no idea and didn't care. What she wanted was escape to her room. That she might dream about the "Lonely Child" and Pierre did not frighten her; indeed, she almost welcomed the possibility. "Listen," she said. "I'm not much good for discussion this evening. Let me think about it. I'll call or write you with my ideas." She smiled and headed for the doorway. She did not look directly at anyone until she almost stumbled into Mike as she was leaving the room.

"Thank you for inviting me," she said as she leaned forward to give him a polite farewell kiss.

"Our pleasure," he said. He embraced her with such intensity that she knew it had truly been a pleasure for him.

IT TOOK HER a week but she did come up with a suggestion: a young baritone from Quebec City who had just finished at McGill and who, everyone said, was going to be great. Then she set about trying to find out more about the composer of "Lonely Child." He'd been in Montreal when the work was presented in Vancouver, it seemed, because he didn't have the money to make it to the West Coast for the premiere. According to a friend of his, who taught piano at Université de Montréal, he was probably back in Berlin, where he'd worked with Stockhausen, or maybe Paris. (What was sure was that he was extremely talented, exuberant, and much better known outside of Canada than in it.)

Gloria thought about writing him a note to say how moved she'd been by "Lonely Child," but she wasn't sure where to send it. When the piece was rebroadcast on the CBC, she listened again, and was even more impressed. In asking around about him, she heard he'd written music for piano. She had played very little contemporary music, but, given the way she had to struggle to bring something new to what she was known for playing, she began to think she ought to explore new works.

Vivier's mentor in Montreal was part of the group of Montreal composers who'd studied in France with Messiaen. They were all younger than Gloria, but she'd met two of them at Montreal events, and they knew musicians she'd known when she'd studied in Paris. She began sending out feelers, asking discreetly just what Vivier had written for piano, who had the scores, and how to secure permission for performing them.

She would have loved to hear "Lonely Child" again, to see the score, to lose herself in it. The more she thought about it the more the music seemed to refer to not just that child so long ago, but also to herself. A lonely child, that's what she'd been, she realized. A lonely child who had found her salvation in music.

And perhaps "Lonely Child" would help her now.

She didn't mention any of this to Robert. Since his heart attack he'd begun to exercise religiously. He discovered workouts with a Walkman were great fun, and he'd begun making tapes of his favourite music. Contemporary music would be out of the question for him, she was sure. Anything composed in the twentieth century, with the exception of Debussy, was trash, he had said once, and she knew he was giving Debussy a pass largely because he was the core of her repertoire.

When help came, it came from Alex, which shouldn't have surprised her, but did. Despite Robert's pressure to take a university course, he'd gone first to New York, and then across the Atlantic to work with the Nederlands Dans Theatre. "Claude Vivier," he said when he was back in Montreal for Christmas 1982. "Yeah sure, he wrote some quite good ballet music. La Compagnie de la Place Royale used a couple of his pieces about five years ago. And one of the guys in Holland says he's written amazing stuff since he got back from the Far East. What's that Indonesian instrument? The gamelan? He's crazy about that."

Gloria felt a shiver run up her spine. Debussy had also been fascinated by the gamelan, after he'd heard it at the World's Fair in Paris. No wonder she felt an affinity. "Help me find him," she said. "Ask your friend if he knows where he is at the moment."

"Sure, Maman." But then he was swept away by Frances's older boy, who wanted to be pushed around on the tricycle he'd received for Christmas. The sight of Alex crawling around the floor while little Philippe called for him to go faster was the highlight of that holiday.

Robert, by then, had come to terms with the fact that Alex was just as committed to dance as Gloria had been to piano. He told Gloria they ought to set up a trust fund for him because he was never going to make any money, and if he was going to have a normal life he'd need their help forever. Gloria agreed. She had no illusions about the struggles of musicians who didn't have the support she had. The implicit criticism in Robert's plan — it was clear he thought men should be more concerned about making a living and being good providers — annoyed her. So did his enormous pride in Frances's accomplishments. Two children already, pregnant with a third, and managing some of the biggest projects in the country. "Our superwoman daughter," he called her when talking to Gloria.

In the end Gloria found two addresses for Vivier: one in Paris and one care of a professor at the Université de Montréal. By then she'd learned that he'd written half a dozen works scored for piano and other instruments, but she'd yet to hear any performed. Nor were recordings available that she could find. The letter she wrote was part fan mail, part a signal that she'd be very interested in collaborating sometime in the future.

There was no future, though. In March Vivier was strangled in his Paris apartment by a young man he'd apparently picked up and who'd robbed him. The story rated mention on the French-language radio and television news in Quebec, but initially only a short notice in the English-language papers. That lack of notice was a measure of both the way the music world was marginal to the greater society and to its fragmentation along linguistic lines.

It was summer before Vivier's friends organized a memorial concert in Montreal. Gloria and Robert were at Bic with Frances's two older children by then, and she didn't hear about it until the day before, too late to get back to Montreal. She was angry that no one had told her earlier, but she felt better when a letter arrived from the woman who'd been Vivier's best friend and who'd been named his executor. Claude had put Gloria's letter in a pile of business to attend to one day, she wrote, but Gloria should understand that he'd been quite agitated for the last weeks of his life, composing frenetically; it was no surprise he hadn't replied.

The woman didn't say so explicitly, but Gloria thought she'd left a door open. Something to work on later. In the meantime, her contact at the Université de Montréal had come up with the score of one of the two works for solo piano Vivier had written, "Shiraz." She didn't dare look at it, because she was trying to dredge up new meaning in the programs she was scheduled to play that fall: Debussy, Bach, Fauré, and more Debussy.

Then she happened upon a short biographical note published in one of the music magazines. It gave a list of Vivier's compositions — forty-nine, a dozen major works written in the last four years. Some information she knew already: born in Trois-Rivières, adopted at age two, educated in Catholic schools and seminaries, composition and piano at the U de M, studies in Europe, the horizon-expanding trip to the Far East in 1976–77. But what she hadn't seen was his birth date: April 14, 1948.

The news reports had talked about him being thirty-four at the time of his death. That had seemed about right. A composer doesn't produce much when he is younger than that, unless he's Mozart, who died at thirty-five. Vivier had been thirty-four. He had been, she realized with a shiver, the same age as her lost child would be.

She was sitting in the music room with the fall sunshine

streaming in the window. The sky was the intense blue of October, bright enough to hurt the eyes. She looked away from the
white brilliance of the page in front of her, and considered. Her
baby had been born in April; she couldn't remember the exact
date. Perhaps that had been her survival strategy, arriving back
in Montreal as if nothing had happened.

How many babies were born in early April in Quebec that
year? Five, six thousand probably; it was the time of the Baby
Boom. How many were put up for adoption? Forty, fifty? And
half of them were boys.

She leaned back in her chair and looked outside as if she
would find answers on the other side of the windows.

It was possible.

The words ran around and around in her head. *It was possible,
it was possible.* It was possible the Lonely Child was her lonely
child.

And he was dead.

She got up, went to the liquor cabinet, and poured herself
a Scotch. She had finished crying by the time Robert called to
tell her to meet her at Les Halles for dinner at eight p.m. That
she was more than a little drunk he gallantly did not notice,
but ordered a double for himself as soon as she arrived.

THE QUESTION OF genetics remained. Talent for music often
runs in families. Consider the Bachs and the Haydens and the
numbers of orchestra musicians whose children become musicians. If this young martyred composer was her son, he would
also be Pierre's child, with a double dose of musical heredity.
The thought haunted her over the next days, the way the sound
of the soprano in "Lonely Child" inhabited her first waking
moments most mornings.

Should she say something to Pierre? No; she'd banished him from her life. And what did it matter, particularly if he were wallowing in his own problems? There were more rumours about the state of his health or rather the self-inflicted torture he was going through as he tried to dry out. Certainly genetics didn't explain everything; look at Frances, as much his child as Vivier might be, for whom music was no more than a part of life, a part that she had been denying since childhood. There also was Alex, who could be Robert's child but might be Pierre's. He had never been able to listen to music without moving; he had the fire.

She studied the one picture of Vivier she had, cut from an obituary in a music review. It showed a nondescript thin face with glasses, a young man who resembled no one and everyone. She had nothing to go on. She should keep silent, and use her doubt to fuel her own efforts.

Julie, Frances and Daniel's third child, was nineteen months when she began to sing. By then, Robert had started his Papi's Saturdays; he cleared his schedule so that the children could come to play at the house once a week. Gloria frequently wasn't there because of the touring that she was doing, but she encouraged Robert. He was taking reasonable care of himself — drinking a lot of red wine, which the latest research said was good for him — but he needed a diversion, particularly since his hearing had started to go.

In winter he had the gardener clear a place on the lawn so it could be flooded for a rink, and had the boys on skates by the time they were two. Daniel joined them when he could, tracking down tiny hockey sticks, so that by Julie's second winter the boys were playing what looked almost like a real match: Robert and five-year-old Philippe on one side and Daniel, a much better skater than Robert, and three-year-old Carl on the other.

Gloria took Julie out to watch, both of them bundled up to their eyes against the January cold. But standing still was boring and chilling; so, after fifteen minutes, Gloria brought the baby back inside.

Gloria didn't know what to do with a child that age. She had never been good with babies; she'd avoided doing much with Frances's boys, and she couldn't remember much about winter afternoons with Frances. Alex had been a different story; he'd listened to her practise from the beginning; they shared a complicity that came naturally. At this age, the age of her grandsons playing hockey now, Alex would crawl underneath the piano when she played to listen and beat time.

Once Gloria had struggled to get the snowsuit off Julie, she sat down at the piano with her. She started out with Chopin's Berceuse, which Alex had liked; but, when the baby got restless and wanted to pound on the keys, she switched to a medley of songs: "Twinkle, Twinkle, Little Star" and "The Skye Boat Song." The baby stopped pounding and listened as soon as Gloria began to sing the words.

Gloria stopped. "Bravo, my darling," she said. "Let's sing it together." She played the melody so that the bare bones of the tune were most apparent. Julie listened carefully, and by the third time Gloria played it, the child quite clearly hummed along for the first sixteen notes.

Gloria turned Julie to look at her; her granddaughter had such a grin on her face. "And how long have you been doing this, little one?" she asked. Children rarely carry a tune before three or four; even Alex had been a little older than this when he started to sing. That Julie was so close on "The Skye Boat Song" was surprising and touching. It had been the song Gloria's father had requested.

Daniel grinned when the boys became too cold and came inside. "She's got talent, doesn't she?" he said. "The boys were never as interested in music, but she's delighted by it. The other day the babysitter found her bouncing around in her crib to music from some kids' program the boys were watching on TV." He jiggled Julie so she giggled, then snuggled her close. He looked up at Gloria, still grinning, "And I think we know who we can attribute that to, Madame Murray."

When Gloria enthused about Julie's talent to Robert, he warned her. "You let Frances and Daniel organize her education. I think it would be a great mistake all around if you tried to make a little genius out of her."

No, no, that wasn't what she wanted to do. She just wanted to share the joy that music had brought to her when she was little. Watching the child stirred her memory; she found herself thinking of a particular summer afternoon in the park when Mrs. Meade was babysitting her. It was hot and Gloria remembered that she'd been bored and had been spinning a story for herself in which she was a princess picking tiny clover flowers from the grass, then flinging them around, as if they were summer snowflakes. When she reached the end of the grass at the edge of the asphalt path that rimmed the pond in the centre of the park, she saw her shadow in the water. Light appeared to emanate from the shadow of her head, as in the pictures of Jesus Mrs. Meade had in her living room.

Gloria moved her head, and the halo moved with it. She shut her eyes and walked carefully around the edge of the pond, then looked again. The light was still there; even when one of the ducks moved slowly through the water near the shadow it remained, wavering.

Across from the park, the sound of someone playing the

piano poured out from wide-open windows. The music engulfed Gloria, the notes falling thickly around her, the high ones as cool and refreshing as the water in the pond, the lower ones rolling along underneath, rich and sweet.

"Hello, Princess," her mother said behind her. "I came to take you home."

"No, wait," Gloria said, reaching for her mother's hand. "Listen."

They stood for two minutes. Gloria's life changed.

"You like that?" her mother asked.

"Yes," she answered. "And look, do you see the light around my head?"

But the sun had gone behind a cloud and Gloria's shadow with its halo was gone. A door slammed across the street, tennis balls continued to plop, the tramway passed on Bernard.

"We'll have to see about lessons for you," her mother said. That must have been when she started the campaign for the piano that arrived two springs later, although Gloria had not linked the two events before. Her dear, loopy mother who, she had to admit, tried very hard to do right by her.

In the end Gloria had nothing to do with getting Julie's lessons, because the girl herself forced Frances and Daniel's hand. When she started kindergarten, she stole her brother's recorder and practised when he was at school. Carl was horrified — "She slobbered all over it!" — but when Daniel heard what she'd picked up on her own, he persuaded the teacher to allow her to come to school at lunchtime and play with the bigger kids before she went off to kindergarten. Julie's piano came two years later when Daniel convinced Frances she was being unfair to refuse the child even if what she wanted was a chance to make music like her grandmother.

"I told you she wouldn't stand in the way of the boys if they wanted to go to hockey camp, she sees that they get lots of extra ice time. She thinks soccer and swimming are important," he told Gloria when he dropped Julie off to spend an afternoon when the boys had back-to-back hockey games. "She's just being pigheaded about music for Julie. What did you do to her? Tie her to the piano bench so she'd practise?" He laughed to show he wasn't serious.

Gloria laughed too, even though what he said was dangerously near the truth. There had been one terrible afternoon when Frances, age about five, had refused to sit at the piano and play the little musical game Gloria had devised. Robert had come running when he heard Frances screaming. It was a memory that Gloria was profoundly ashamed of.

She let Daniel run with it when it came to Julie's musical education. Even after he and Frances separated, he was the one who saw that Julie got to her lessons on Tuesday afternoons and instructed Maria, their housekeeper, to keep track of how much she practised. Not that doing that was difficult; the child clearly enjoyed it.

During the first difficult summer after the breakup, Robert suggested they pay for camps for all three children, in addition to having them down to Bic for a couple of weeks. "This can't be an easy time for Frances. She didn't see it coming," he said. "I have no doubt she'll recover, but to have Daniel leave had to be a great shock."

Gloria agreed. Daniel's decision to quit engineering to set up shop as a surveyor in a small town was not part of what Frances had planned for herself. Rather quickly after her refusal to consider the move, he found another woman. Gloria tried to be sympathetic to Frances's sadness, but she also realized that this was the time to insist that a music camp might be just the thing for Julie. Frances was hardly in shape to fight her over the idea.

The camp Gloria had in mind was north of Montreal and offered many of the usual camp things: swimming, hiking, games. It had been set up by a priest who believed his mission was to bring classical music to small-town Quebec. The camp attracted kids who really loved music and a staff of excellent professional musicians who liked the chance to get out of the humid and polluted city for a few weeks.

Daniel was moving to the Eastern Townships that July with his new wife and her son; he was pleased not to have primary responsibility for his own kids. As for Frances, she was off to India to consult on the construction of a dam in the Western Ghats. "When I get back, I'll take everybody to Toronto and we'll go to the CN Tower and the Ontario Science Centre," she said.

Robert visited the boys at their camps, and Gloria and he went to see Julie on the Sunday of her second week. Gloria was delighted to find that her granddaughter had been picked to play a solo in the concert at the end of the week. It was a short polonaise by Bach, the one in G major: not terribly difficult but she played it with intensity and considerable joy.

After the recital was over — with the more difficult pieces performed by an older cellist and wind quintet, and the all-camp choir singing songs by Kodály — Gloria's instinct was to descend on Julie to sweep the child away with praise, but she forced herself to be calm.

"Very nice," she said when she and Robert had made their way to the front of the hall, which was ordinarily used for meals. The ventilating system had been off while the youngsters played; the temperature had soared. Gloria wanted to get away to some place cooler. Taking Julie to a nice restaurant in town for Sunday dinner where they could talk music sounded like a grand idea. "What led you to choose that particular piece?" she asked, putting her arm around Julie and beginning to lead her toward the doorway.

They were intercepted by the priest whose brainchild the camp was. "Dear Madame Murray, such a great pleasure to see you," he said, putting out his hand to greet her. Julie was surprised by the attention paid to her grandmother. The girl had never been to one of her concerts. Gloria made a mental note: it might be time for Julie to have more contact with her grandmother the musician.

By the time Gloria had freed herself, Julie was tugging at her hand, heading her toward a small group of adults who were, Gloria guessed, the camp's staff. "I want you to meet my teacher," Julie was saying. "It's because of her that I chose the piece, because she's Polish and it's a polonaise."

"Of course," Gloria said, thinking of her own Polish teacher, the friend of Lotte. There was a new wave of European musicians in Montreal, excellent graduates of the Soviet and Eastern European conservatories. They were arriving now in significant numbers, hoping for a better life, bringing with them enormous skill and great culture.

Alina, Julie's teacher, was obviously one of them. "Madame Murray," she said, shaking hands with a stiff formality. "It is an honour to meet you."

"And for me to meet you. My granddaughter admires you greatly."

Alina smiled as Julie edged closer to her; she put her hand lightly on the child's shoulder. "She loves music," she said.

"Indeed," Gloria said. "And do you teach young musicians in Montreal during the school year?" She watched Julie's eyes light up when Alina said she did. "Perhaps something can be arranged, then," Gloria said.

IT TOOK A while after they got back to town, but by mid-October Alina had become Julie's teacher.

For Christmas that year Robert had all three children make wish lists. "You can't be greedy," he said at a Papi's Saturday in mid-November. There was grumbling around the kitchen table where they were eating pizza, but Robert insisted. "You may have other presents. I have no control over what your parents might give you, but your grandmother and I need to know the one thing that you'd really like."

The boys spent a week coming up with their choices, which had to do with electronic games. Julie had hers by the next afternoon. "Alina is giving a concert," she told Gloria on the telephone. "I want to go hear her."

Gloria was charmed. No matter that the concert was on a school night, given as part of the winter program of the priest's musical series in the small town near his camp. Julie would have to miss at least one afternoon of school and possibly the following morning. Driving in February was chancy; winter storms were hard to predict. She managed, however, to convince Robert to argue with Frances, who eventually agreed. Daniel had waded in in favour too.

So Gloria took Julie to hear Alina Adamczyk play the harpsichord, which was a revelation to her granddaughter.

Until then the child had not seen one. They arrived early at the concert hall, after a quick meal in the dining room of the inn where they were staying. Julie danced out of the car, across the parking lot, and up the steps to the hall despite her heavy boots and snow pants. Under her snow jacket, she was wearing a party dress she wanted to show off. Once inside the hall, and settled in their seats, Julie gasped. "Oh, Grandmaman, where's the piano?"

Gloria looked at the stage. She laughed. "Well, now, that is a surprise." But, as she looked at the program notes, she saw that it had been there all along, she just hadn't noticed. Alina was going to play Bach, Scarlatti, and Mozart on a harpsichord copied from one in the court of Louis XV. Gloria had to explain that pianos like the ones she and Julie played weren't perfected until 150 years ago. Not only did early pianos have fewer keys — Mozart's had only five octaves instead of the seven or eight of today — but also the sound was very different. High quality steel strings and precision cast iron frames weren't available until the Industrial Revolution, she started to say, remembering a lecture Frances had once given her.

But Julie interrupted. "Shh," she said, "I think I see Alina on the edge of the stage."

And, indeed, there she was sweeping in from the wings, a small woman with elaborately curled, jet-back hair, dressed in chiffon that shaded from dark red to the orange of a bonfire. The woman was a good musician, and she brought forth from her instrument sounds that Gloria hadn't heard before. Cool and precise, the notes spilled out like bits of tumbling ice.

"Oh, Grandmaman, that's what I want to play," Julie whispered into her ear, halfway through the first piece. "It is so, so lovely."

Gloria laughed and kissed the top of the child's head. "We'll see," she said.

THERE WAS A certain irony, Gloria had to admit, that Julie's delight in music played on period instruments influenced the programming of the concert Gloria gave at Alice Tully Hall in New York's Lincoln Center for the Performing Arts two years later.

The invitation hadn't come on its own. Getting it took hard work on the part of her agent, as well as Robert's many contacts in the legal and diplomatic world. He said he wanted to hear her "triumph in the Big Apple before I lose my hearing completely." He got the cultural attachés of both Canada and Quebec involved.

She had played frequently in New York over the years, but Alice Tully was one hall where she hadn't performed, and to be invited to be part of the Center's Virtuoso series was an honour. Yet it wasn't her reputation as a concert pianist that interested the people planning the concert series, it was what she proposed to play: *The Road to Claude Vivier*. The tenth anniversary of his murder had just passed, and while the musical world outside Canada was becoming increasingly convinced of his contribution, little had been done officially to promote his accomplishment. Robert told Gloria that it probably would have been a lot harder to organize such a concert in Toronto than in New York. A prophet has no honour in his own land. Those who knew Vivier's work were unanimous: while he shared much with the masters like Stockhausen, with whom he'd studied, Vivier's work was original.

At the same time Gloria was considering Vivier, she also was watching Julie's exploration of the harpsicord. The girl was fascinated by the idea that when Bach wrote for the keyboard he had the organ, the harpsichord, or the clavichord in mind, but not the piano, except at the very end of his life.

As she began working on piano interpretations of Bach preludes, Gloria began to think about the way musical forms changed over time. By chance she heard a bit of Busoni's transcription for modern piano of Bach's "Toccata and Fugue in D Minor," a glorious piece of music written for the organ. Debussy also wrote a toccata, which she hadn't played in concert before. To play these two along with Schumann's toccata would be interesting, she thought. In the end she added Satie's "Trois Gnossiennes" and some Debussy, including "Estampes," for contrast and also because of the influence of Eastern music on their composition. "Shiraz," the pièce de résistance, would end the show. It would be the New York premiere of Vivier's piece and the high point of the concert.

"Love it," one of the organizers said enthusiastically. "A concept concert." The story of Vivier's murder added spice to the mixture; it attracted an audience who might not be interested in work by classical composers.

Julie protested that she didn't think Bach would be pleased to hear Gloria play the "Toccata and Fugue" on a modern piano. "No, Grandmaman, maybe I've got to play him on a piano now because I'm just a girl, but you don't have to. What you're doing is insulting Bach's intentions," she said.

"But you'll see," Gloria said, amused that such a child — she was just eleven — had such strong opinions. "It'll sound great. You can hear it on an organ later, but now how would you like to come with me and Papi and hear me play it in New York?"

Daniel was hard to persuade, but in the end he agreed. "Visiting New York with her grandfather and me will not be like the visits she's made with you and Frances," Gloria told him. "For one thing she won't be blown out of water by her brothers."

"They think she's terrific, and they don't mean anything by it, they're just enthusiastic," Daniel began.

Gloria waved away his protest. "I'm sure that's the case, but Julie gets lost in the traffic at times. Let us take her with us, and we'll make it up to the boys later."

Daniel's new wife was pregnant and he was having trouble organizing the care of his kids and her son. That Gloria and Robert were ready to look after Julie for a week in early December when the boys' hockey teams were very busy was a great plus, even if it meant taking her out of school. "Okay," he said. "Get Robert to talk to Frances. She'll listen to him more than to me."

That went without saying; and what Gloria might say would have no effect. Frances had avoided talking to Gloria since her divorce. Gloria suspected her daughter thought she was judging the failure of her marriage.

WHEN GLORIA WALKED into Marthe's workroom, she found Marthe brandishing a newspaper. On the front pages was a picture of Gloria being embraced by a former prime minister.

"So the old goat was putting some moves on you?" Marthe asked.

Gloria laughed and shook her head. "I'm too old for him. He has a two-year-old with a woman who's thirty years younger than me — nearly forty years younger than he is. He was just being gallant."

Marthe nodded and tossed the newspaper aside. Gloria was her last client for the day and she looked ready to relax a bit. "But there must have been others before. A woman like you ..."

"Someone dressed by a genius of a *courterière*?" Gloria grinned when her eyes met Marthe's in the mirror. "Being well-turned-out helps a lot."

Marthe laughed. "Virtue is its own reward, I'm told."

It was Gloria's turn to laugh; she didn't want to say more. Marthe knew more of her secrets than anyone, and they had stayed with her. That was part of Marthe's attraction: beautiful clothes, a sympathetic ear, and a tongue that didn't wag.

"I've seen those adoring eyes of men after your concerts," Martha said, tugging at the skirt of the dress she was fitting. "You're dealing with emotion when you play, you go direct to the heart without a detour through the head. All that passion directed at you."

"You've witnessed that?" Gloria asked, twitching her shoulders so that the red chiffon of the dress hung better. She looked down to see Marthe nodding her head. She looked at herself in the mirror.

The incidents were less frequent than they had been, and this she put down to age, rather than the vagaries of fame. But notes were still delivered to the stage door, and flowers now and again showed up in her hotel room.

One of her fans who lived in Toronto had become a joke between her and Robert. "Another Valentine from that old guy," Robert would say when he sorted the mail and found a letter with the telltale return address. "Doesn't he ever give up?" Gloria always answered: "He's getting senile and can't remember that I never respond."

Marthe straightened up for a moment. "Look, my dear friend," she began. "You know what your mother, rest her soul, said about you: 'that girl doesn't know her power, which is probably good for the people around her.'"

"And my mother was such a great judge of character," Gloria said. "Ended up dying alone in Florida when her intended cleared out." That was a regret. Gloria had been on tour and

Robert had a hard time making contact with her. By the time she cut things short and returned to Montreal, he had planned a funeral that her mother would have hated — lots of sad music, an elegy by a minister she didn't know — but Gloria didn't have the energy to change it.

"She knew men," Marthe said.

"Maybe," Gloria said. "Although, if she did, how to explain that loser she spent so much time with."

Marthe shot Gloria a look. "We all have our weaknesses."

"Indeed," Gloria replied. Remembering Pierre, who she'd never been able to banish entirely from her thoughts.

Marthe contined, "But you know what that rock and roll singer used to say, Janis Joplin? No man ever made her feel the way a crowd did."

"Yes," Gloria responded. And, after a pause, "Yes," she repeated.

"Your mother told me something else," Marthe said.

"What?"

"There was a mystery when you returned to Montreal, after your first year in Paris."

Gloria avoided looking at Marthe.

"She said you knew your father and music teacher were both dying but she hadn't expected you to leave your education to see them. She suspected something more."

"Did she say what?"

"No. But I have an idea."

Gloria's eyes met Marthe's in the mirror. Each registered the level of seriousness the conversation and their relationship had reached.

Marthe began, "Do you remember how I knew you were pregnant the first time you came to me, when you'd just married Robert?"

Gloria nodded, not taking her eyes off Marthe's reflection.

"At the time I guessed that this wasn't the first time."

"How?" Gloria felt the blood drain from her face.

"Because your belly wasn't as firm as I'd expect in a girl your age. The rest of you was thin, as I remember."

Yes, she had been, after that starvation year in Paris. "You didn't say anything to my mother, did you?"

Marthe laughed. "If she never said anything to you, you can be sure I didn't say anything to her."

Indeed, her mother would not have held on to such information quietly. But Gloria was shocked that Marthe had known. She reached out to brace herself on Marthe's shoulder. She wasn't sure she would be able to stand.

"Steady," Marthe said. "You don't need to worry. Keeping secrets is professional ethics." She laughed. "But, let's concentrate on what you came for." She patted Gloria's hand and stood up. "What do you say to shortening the sleeves a little and adding a small ruffle to finish them? I thought at first the usual plain edge would be best, but you know, there are not many women your age who have such lovely hands and forearms, and it would be nice to draw attention to them."

"Sleeves," Gloria said, sounding stunned. She forced herself to look at her arms. What was important was her freedom of movement and, after four decades, Marthe knew just how to give her that. At any other time the rest would be irrelevant. But this was not a time like the others. She shook her hands out and watched how the sleeves worked against her wrist. "No," she said. "That's not my style." She started to get down from the stool. She turned her back to Marthe so she could unzip the dress. "It looks very nice just the way it is. Perfect for New York in December."

Gloria saw Marthe smile in the mirror.

"Just what I hoped you'd think." She began to gather up her tools, the bits of material, the measuring tapes, the pins.

"But, you know, you're so right about so many things," Gloria paused. "And you have been for as long as I've known you."

Martha stopped what she was doing and waited. When Gloria did not say anything she hazarded, "So I wasn't wrong about a baby long ago?"

Gloria nodded. She turned and looked into Marthe's face. She had been as good a friend as she had. Tears began to stream down her face. She allowed Marthe to slip the dress over her head. Standing in her underwear, with her hands clutched tightly to her chest, like a child, she said in a small voice, "No one knows."

Marthe reached for a dressing gown that hung next to the door, then wrapped it around Gloria. "My dear friend," she said softly, holding Gloria for a moment. "How very, very sad. You gave the baby up? Or did it die?"

"No," Gloria said. "They took him from me to give to a good family. It was supposed to be best for everyone."

"And probably it was," Marthe said. "Probably it was." She took the dress Gloria had folded over a chair. "It is highly unlikely that things would 've turned out the way they have for you otherwise. And the child was probably somebody's darling."

"You don't have anything to drink, do you?" Gloria asked, knowing Marthe kept a bottle of Chivas in a cupboard.

"Of course," Marthe said, fetching the bottle and two teacups. She looked at her watch. "Sit a minute. We have the time."

Gloria told her the story, the entire story as she knew it, up to her discovery of Claude Vivier, his music, and his death.

When she finished, they sat holding their cups, Gloria wondering if she dare ask for a top-up. Long minutes passed.

"There's no way to know now, is there?" Marthe asked. "Can't the adoption records be opened? Aren't people doing that these days? "

"I don't know," Gloria said. "Wouldn't it be harder, since he's dead?" She reached for the Scotch and poured herself more. "But what does it matter now?"

"A lot," Marthe said, holding out her cup. "Have you seen pictures of him? Is there any clue there?"

"He looks like — he looked like — lots of people. Thin face, glasses, balding, apparently he laughed a lot. And he was gay."

"Bald? Gay? There might be something there. Doesn't baldness run in families?"

"As does music. Think of the Mozarts, the Bachs ..."

Marthe looked at Gloria, as if she were calculating.

"Baldness is transmitted through the mother. Was your father bald? Your uncles? Your son Alex is about the same age as this guy was when he died. Is Alex going bald?"

Gloria shook her head. "No. Alex is not going bald. Nor was my father. But I never met my mother's brothers, nor her father. Alex still might go bald. And not all children in a family are alike."

Marthe clapped her hands and laughed. "So, it's unlikely you're carrying the gene for baldness." She looked as if she were giving Gloria a gift.

Gloria shook her head. If the lonely child was not her child, she found the idea hardly a gift at all. After all those years of trying to forget, she had not realized how much she had come to like the idea of finding traces of that baby, of being connected to great talent.

She stood up and looked around for her clothes. "I've got to go," she said. She pulled off the dressing gown and picked up her skirt and sweater.

Marthe helped her dress. "Listen, my lovely. Don't rush off like this. Sit down again and let's finish off the Scotch."

Gloria shook her head. "Please call a cab, will you? I'll be outside." She knew she could not afford to think about Marthe's speculation. To entertain these thoughts meant a challenge to her certainty that she was the perfect person to premiere Vivier's music to New York. Gloria didn't return Marthe's call when the finished dress was delivered and the dressmaker phoned with good wishes.

ROBERT HAD A hundred details that needed attending to. Alex was dancing in Amsterdam, and sent his good wishes for a successful event. Frances wanted to make sure Julie's homework would be supervised and forgot to give hers. Claude Vivier's biographer wanted to talk to Gloria about what she, as a pianist, saw in his music. Did Gloria have any insights to him through her study of his work?

The day before the concert it snowed in New York. Robert fretted about how that might affect the attendance. He'd invited all their friends in the New York area and the cultural attachés had done their jobs; there was a gaggle of Canadian dignitaries, Mike and Mrs. Mike among them. He now was his law firm's senior man in the US and based in Washington. They came up for old times' sake. The majority of the audience were there either because they were Gloria's fans or because they loved contemporary music.

When she entered the stage, Gloria felt her heart lift at the warm applause that greeted her. Such a long way from the first concert she'd attended in New York City at Town Hall, when the arrogant young American student pianists had trashed their colleague's playing. She shuddered at the memory of just how ill-prepared she had been and how misguided were her dreams. But attending Juilliard would have led to a very different life.

Here she was, decades later, playing music of a difficulty she couldn't have imagined then. Physically, the program was a challenge. Toccatas are show-off pieces designed to test a pianist's abilities and limits. Schumann had thought his toccata the hardest piece of music ever written; the Debussy one required nearly as much skill and energy; and "Shiraz" was a percussive tour de force. In between there were more lyric pieces by Debussy, Bach, and Satie, which gave her a chance to regain her strength. But from start to finish she had to ride the river of music she had chosen; she had to tame the sound, she had to make sense of the path and connections she saw between the pieces.

There were four curtain calls, and when it seemed she really had to play an encore, she opted for her first success "The Girl with the Flaxen Hair." She saw Julie standing up right in front, next to Robert, clapping, so proud of her grandmother. She saw the sea of smiling faces. At the end of "The Girl with the Flaxen Hair" she held out her arms in a wide embrace, acknowledging everything — the audience, the city, the composers, and the music itself.

When it was over, they went back to the hotel for the reception Robert had organized in their suite. There were tartlets of duck and goat cheese, gravlax and caviar, bottles and bottles of champagne. The party went on until early morning, when Mike went out to buy the first edition of *The New York Times* because their music critic had been there. But, when he leafed through the arts section, he found nothing.

"Don't worry about the reviews," Mike said. "It was a triumph. I've never heard you play better."

Mrs. Mike nodded, and held out both her hands to grasp Gloria's. "I thought you played wonderfully when you were in Vancouver for the Expo concerts, but you've outdone yourself," she said. "We'll have to talk about what can be organized next. I'm working with a group in Washington ..."

But what she was saying was drowned out in the chatter of people coming to say their goodbyes, still excited by the evening.

When everyone had gone, and the room was empty, Robert led Gloria back to their suite. They made love and then Robert slept, on his back, his mouth open, his arms folded on his chest as if he were standing satisfied with his life, surveying the world. Gloria paced the carpeted floor in her bare feet, pausing once to curl up in a chair by the window and look out at the nighttime city while she wrapped her hands around her cold toes. She played the concert over in her head, as she often did, but for once she found only a couple of places that she would do differently. Would she perform the program again? It seemed to be so well received. Would she change the order? Start with the Bach transcription, then the Schumann, before the twentieth-century pieces. But she would end with "Shiraz." That was the whole reason for the concert. Despite Marthe's suggestion that Claude was not her son, she knew that she had a unique connection to this composer, whether he was her son or not.

Mrs. Meade would have said that flying so high only meant falling very far. Early on, Gloria had decided that attitude never got her anywhere. She was doomed to mediocrity if she followed it; and, if there was one thing Gloria was proud of, it was that she had refused to be afraid to fly. And she had flown — to heights she'd dreamed of. When Robert began to stir and the sky outside had changed to light blue, she climbed back into the bed and curled up next to him. Remember this, she told herself. It does not get better.

They'd told Julie she could come in any time after seven a.m., so she knocked at the door just as they had begun to move. Robert ordered up hot chocolate for Julie, coffee, and eggs Benedict. He placed a call to Montreal so Julie could tell her mother about the concert. They left a message for Daniel before they got Alex in Amsterdam. Call after call followed. Bouquets of flowers began to arrive, as did the flurry of invitations: cocktails with the Canadian consul and dinner with Mike and Mrs. Mike. It was good that they had Julie with them; she was their excuse, because there was too much to handle politely otherwise. It also helped that they had made arrangements to return to Montreal that afternoon; the flights were booked.

The one invitation they couldn't avoid was a meeting in late morning with Gloria's recording company. They sent Julie out shopping for souvenirs with Robert's secretary before they met Gloria's agent. "It's time to demand more in the way of promotion budgets for your next recordings," Robert said as he saw that their bags were loaded into the taxi. "You deserve a lot more than you've been getting."

Gloria patted Robert's hand. "I'm not sure record labels have promotion budgets anymore."

The taxi pulled up to the office building. Gloria stepped out and saw Pierre.

He was waiting for the light to turn, the collar on his topcoat turned up. His hair was white but still luxuriant, and from a distance he looked every bit as handsome as he had been in the last promotional photos she'd seen of him. As he waited, he reached for the hand of the younger woman standing next to him; together they crossed the street when the light changed. Gloria was not sure he saw her, but Robert saw him.

"Pierre," he called. "I didn't see you last night. Did you make it?"

Gloria hadn't known that Robert had invited him. She was glad she hadn't known. She couldn't help noticing that the young woman whose hand Pierre was still holding had the same curly chestnut hair that she had when she was about twenty.

Pierre stopped when he got to the curb, and dropped the girl's hand. "Robert, great to see you. Thanks for the invitation but, no, I couldn't make it, I had a rehearsal myself, a new project, you know," he said shaking Robert's hand. He looked for the first time at Gloria. "Alice Tully Hall. Congratulations, *ma belle*," he said, leaning forward to kiss her on both cheeks. When he smiled, she saw that despite his careful grooming he had neglected his teeth. One incisor was missing, and two lower teeth were stained badly. A terrible thing in a man who made his living with his mouth open.

"Thank you," she said, taking a step backwards. He was introducing the young woman, she worked with a booking agency; she was saying what a privilege it was to meet Gloria Murray. And then they were gone, rushing down the sidewalk to some meeting they said they were late for.

"Well," said Robert when he and Gloria were safely in the elevator going up to the twenty-fifth floor offices of the recording company. "He's had health problems, right? He lives in the States. Dental work may have been just too much after the other bills."

"Maybe," Gloria said. "But there were some things you simply shouldn't let pass, not when you're a public figure."

"He's not much of one anymore, not like he used to be," Robert said, holding the elevator door open for her.

She was thinking about that — about his still-thick hair, about how he would never know about that first child — when the elevator door opened. The company's offices were granite, steel, and glass, and their gloss and glamour grabbed Gloria's attention and jerked her into the present. When Gloria stepped forward, the heel of her boot slipped on the polished granite.

Robert tried to break her fall. He fell too. Gloria heard the bones in her right arm crack and felt an enormous wave of pain roll over her. "It's broken," she said, as they struggled to their feet with the help of the receptionist.

CODA

THE PIANO, WHEN JULIE CAME to visit her grandmother, sat in the centre of the large living room in Gloria's apartment. It was a Saturday afternoon in early April and the snow was just about gone. Gloria was scheduled to move out of the apartment in two weeks and into a residence where she'd have more care.

When Julie arrived, the apartment smelled like a greenhouse — the way she remembered the music room smelling in the Westmount house where her grandparents had lived so long. The jasmine which had grown for thirty years, next to the big windows, looking down from Mount Royal and beyond to the St. Lawrence, had been brought to this apartment and the perfume of its white starlike blooms filled the hot and humid air.

Gloria answered Julie's ring herself. The woman who spent most of the day with her had gone home. "There's no problem with that," she'd insisted to Frances. "I'm perfectly capable of feeding myself even if my hands don't work well enough to play the piano."

Julie saw immediately the deterioration that had prompted her mother and uncle to push for the move. Gloria was shorter than she remembered, although her hair was still the rich chestnut it had been always been. She wore a white pantsuit with a large red paisley scarf across her shoulders. Marthe had died of lung cancer years before, but, before she did, she'd handed Gloria off to a fashion consultant at Ogilvy's who helped her choose her clothes.

"I'm sorry it took me so long to answer the bell," Gloria said when opening the door. "Everything takes me longer these days. Come in, come in, my dear," she said. "You are so beautiful, it takes my breath away."

Julie hugged her grandmother very gently. Her brother Carl had broken one of her ribs two years ago. Gloria had not complained. "I know all about broken bones. You can't avoid them at my age," she'd said. That broken arm had been the beginning of the end of her career, after all.

"You look splendid yourself," Julie said now. *Splendid* was one of Gloria's words, and it still applied to her.

"Thank you, thank you," Gloria said, turning and starting back across the large room to the sofa and chair near the window. Carefully, she made her way around the coffee table. She lowered herself into a large black recliner. "You'll forgive me if I take this seat. I'm having trouble getting out of ordinary chairs."

Julie followed, settling herself as close to her grandmother as she could. Gloria's hearing wasn't as good as it was; talking loudly was essential.

"I hear you've made a record that's causing all kinds of scandal," Gloria said once comfortable. "There's a cover photo of you in all your loveliness playing music from the French court — harpsichord for the king's suppers." She wasn't smiling, but Julie sensed her grandmother's amusement. "And you're naked as the day you were born."

Julie felt her face flush. "It was the marketing department's idea," she said. "I'm not sure I like it."

Gloria laughed. "Your mother certainly doesn't. But show me, I'd like to make my own judgment."

Julie hadn't expected to be asked so quickly for the CD, but of course she'd brought it. She fished it out of her backpack and handed it to her grandmother.

"Lovely, truly lovely," Gloria said. The photograph was of Julie seated at the harpsichord, turned slightly toward the camera, with her long blond hair arranged artfully to obscure part of her breast. She looked very good.

"Lotte would be proud," Gloria said.

"Lotte?"

"Lotte. I've told you about her. My teacher. She knew that a little spice helps sell music. It's necessary for audience-building, pushing limits, getting support, all those things that we need to do." She paused and pointed to the tray on the coffee table; there were glasses, an ice bucket, a bottle of Glenmorangie, a crystal pitcher of water, and a bottle of red wine. "We'll talk about that in a minute. But first put on the CD and then get us a drink. My hands have trouble opening bottles."

Julie smiled. Her grandmother hadn't changed in that respect. When they were kids, before Papi died, before the house was sold, she remembered Saturday evenings when both her grandparents were completely gaga before their parents came to pick them up after a day of grandparently activities. "From Papi's cellar, right?" she said, looking at the wine bottle, a 1995 Pomerol. "He had very good taste."

"In nearly everything," Gloria said. "He didn't like contemporary music much, however."

"Papi had very good taste," Julie repeated, and the two of them laughed. It was a joke between them. He'd told Julie more than once how he was delighted that she took up the harpsichord because no one had composed music for it in the last 150 or 200 years. That wasn't true, of course — Julie's first teacher, Alina, was now specializing in athletic, modern harpsichord music — but his distaste for most new music was clear. Julie knew now how hard it must have been for him to be enthusiastic about the program for Gloria's final concert in New York. He'd done it for love for Gloria, and not love for the music that had been the centrepiece of what had become a legend.

Gloria nodded her head. "But he's no longer with us, and you are." She took a sip of her Scotch and water and smiled at Julie again. "You mix it exactly right," she said.

"He taught me," Julie grinned. She'd been so envious of her brothers when they had the privilege. Until she won the Concours de Bruges two years before she hadn't come across anything that made her prouder than being told by Robert when she was sixteen that she was old enough to mix a drink.

Gloria raised her glass. "We shall drink to his memory."

The wine was excellent. Julie sipped it while she watched her grandmother's face react to the CD. The music was by eighteenth-century French composers, well known among early music buffs, but she didn't expect Gloria to be familiar with them. Her career had emphasized twentieth-century composers; playing Ravel's *Le tombeau de Couperin* was as close as Gloria got to Julie's favourite period.

She had underestimated her grandmother.

"Beautifully played, my dear," Gloria said after the first track, Couperin's "Les lis naissans." "You bring such life to the music."

Julie was pleased, but surprised when Gloria asked her to stop the CD.

"Have you ever played it on a modern instrument?" she asked. "I know you might think it sacrilegious, but I'd love to hear how it would sound."

What could Julie say? Of course she would be glad to play the piece, even though she knew it would sound wrong. Its brightness, even its rhythm, was muddied by the piano's reverberation; no matter how hard she tried to keep her touch equal and measured the way Couperin would have liked it, the piano's different action added colours that no one in that period had ever heard.

Gloria was extremely pleased, however. "Lovely," she said. "I had hoped it would sound as good." She put her drink on the table next to her. "You know why I wanted you to come by today, don't you?"

Julie nodded, although she wasn't really sure. "To spend a little time with you before things are disrupted by your move?" she ventured.

Gloria nodded. "Partly. But I also wanted to offer you something."

Julie wasn't surprised, after all Gloria's new place was so much smaller, she was going to have to downsize again.

"Your mother and your uncle think I'm not aware of what they're doing," Gloria began. "They've been trying to keep the truth from me. But I've known for several years that those splendid assets your grandfather took such good care of have taken a beating. I don't have nearly as much as I might."

"The Nortel crash," Julie said, repeating what she'd heard her mother say.

"And others," Gloria added. "There's the big change in the recording industry too. This means that although I had hoped to be able to help you and your brothers quite handsomely, I'm not going to be able to. There will be some stocks for the boys, they'll get that after I die, but until then I'm going to need the income. But I thought what you would really like would be this piano."

Hopeful, she looked at Julie.

"You've heard the story, I know, how it was my teacher's and she left it to me but I couldn't afford to get it repaired so I had to sell it to pay for my studies in Europe. Years later your grandfather tracked it down and bought it for me. It cost a fortune to repair." Gloria beamed, her face flooded with emotions. "You played it when you were just tiny, I remember the first day you sat on my lap and played, you were that small. I was amazed at the gift you had."

She smiled at Julie and waited for her reaction. But the young woman hadn't anticipated the gift; she'd thought there might be some furniture, keepsakes, vintage dresses, some money. Money, yes: money would be very useful. Making ends meet was such a struggle; funding cutbacks meant there were fewer concerts, the recording industry was a disaster, and she was unlikely to make money from the CD no matter how sexy the cover photo. "Oh, Grandma, I don't know what to say," she began.

"There's something else for you," Gloria said. "The piano must find a good home before I can move from here, but the other thing doesn't take up much space and could wait until I'm dead." She lifted her bony hand with its gnarled joints and pointed at the cupboard where the sound system was stored. "Look in the drawer underneath the record player, and bring the box over to me."

"Don't be too impressed," she said, once she'd undone the clasp on the jewellery case. "It's fake, but a beautiful fake. And I'd love to see you wearing it and playing the piano. Now. While I'm alive to enjoy it."

Julie held up Lotte's necklace, then fastened it around her neck.

"You look absolutely splendid," Gloria said. "Lotte would be so pleased. Go take a look at yourself in the mirror in the bedroom."

It was not at all the kind of thing Julie wore, not on the stage or off. A black velvet ribbon with a cameo was her current favourite for concerts and offstage she wore simple stud earrings. She was rankled, because she'd been hoping that some of her grandmother's money would come to her. She wanted to buy her own instrument. What she didn't need was a piano; she needed a really good harpsichord at this stage in her career.

But she couldn't say that, could she?

She stayed in the bedroom for several minutes, staring at herself in the mirror, remembering how she'd loved to climb up on the dresser to examine the carving around the heavy mirror. Harp-playing cupids, garlands of flowers; it was beautiful — and apparently one that Gloria intended to keep.

"Julie, my dear, what do you think?" Gloria called.

Julie came out of the bedroom, wearing Lotte's necklace. "Are you pleased?" Her grandmother's face had an eagerness that she didn't remember seeing before.

"Oh Granny," she said. "I'm overwhelmed."

JULIE MODELLED THE necklace for her mother.

"Don't be snowed by what the old lady wants." Frances said. "When she gives you something, take it, thank her, and then do what you want with it. That's what I learned a long time ago. She's never been sentimental; she shouldn't expect us to be now. Now, the necklace might be worth keeping, if only for fun. It can't be worth more than a few hundred dollars. But remember that she sold that piano herself when it suited her, and if my father hadn't been so besotted with her, she never would have got it back."

"But she was almost pathetic the way she wanted me to carry on the flame ..."

Frances touched the necklace. "And ride the river of music to places she hadn't?" She sighed. "Oh, yes, she talks like that, the old dear. But you do what you want, just don't forget that to make a musical career you've got to be so tough that you'd sell your first born to get ahead. Selling a piano is nothing."

NOTES

Claude Vivier (14 April 1948–7 March 1983) is considered to be one of the most original composers of the late twentieth century. His contribution is better known outside Canada than in his home country. Adopted at age two, his biological parents are not known. He was murdered in Paris.

Gloria Murray (née Foster) is an invention.

JOHN M. CUELENAERE PUBLIC LIBRARY
33292900075080
River music : a novel